P9-BVG-922

TRAIL DUST

CLARENCE E. MULFORD

Trail Dust

HOPALONG CASSIDY AND THE BAR 20
WITH THE TRAIL HERD

AEONIAN PRESS, INC.
LEYDEN, MASS.

TRAIL DUST

FOREWORD

Red connors uncrossed his legs, picked his hat from the floor, and arose. He was grinning reminiscently, as well he might: to Red, any episode concerning the earlier life and activities of his friend Hopalong Cassidy was something set apart in value and sentiment from all other things; and Red knew more about Hopalong's earlier days than any other man on the ranch. He studied me for an instant, nodded cheerfully, and strode slowly toward the door. Then he stopped and turned.

"Well, that's th' story," he said, and the smile grew. He hitched up his belts instinctively, and his blue eyes twinkled in his freckled face. "They grew 'em tough, down in that country, in that day," he added and then swung through the doorway.

The story he had just told me was one that I do not wish to forget in any of its details, and to that end I shall here write it down. I had heard fragments of it before, and many allusions to it, and I had gathered the idea that whenever action happened it had happened swiftly. Now Red had welded it into its complete form and continuity. The time to do a thing is to do it now, and now it shall be done. Here's the story.

I

THEY had obtained the cattle from the ranches within a day's ride of the old Bar 20. Most of them were in their own brand, but to fill a herd of that size and specifications it had been necessary to call on their neighbors. They had Double Arrow, C 80, and O Bar O animals with their own. It was not a large herd as trail herds went, but in the old days of the Longhorn it is doubtful if any thousand animals, the equal of these, had trodden that trail. Buck Peters, who was foreman, had been critical to the point of arousing derisive profanity among his friends; but, being Buck Peters, he had not swerved an inch: and now the trail crew were drifting the finest and most uniform herd of four-year-olds that any of them had ever seen. They had an extra dozen for replacements, they had a good chuck wagon and cook, and they had a choice and hand-picked cavvy: eight horses to a man, and each remuda had trained night horses, a big-bellied animal for river work, and tough, swift mounts for the trail. Their road brand was Circle 4. The herd had passed the inspector, and they were well on their way.

The straw boss, riding on left point, saw a small dust cloud far up the trail. He turned in the saddle, waved his arm, and one of the flankers pushed up to his side. While he waited for his friend to join him, he looked back at the strung-out cattle, grazing as they moved. Perhaps he had let them graze too long; perhaps he should have pushed them until he learned about the next water. His gaze passed on and rested on the inconsequential drag, wreathed by dust. For a thousand-head herd, it was remarkably small. And then the flank rider joined him and stopped at his side.

"Take over th' point, Lanky," said Hopalong, a grin trying to displace the slight frown. He was feeling pretty good. His task was half over, for the last creek they had left behind them had been the halfway point. Up to now everything had gone well. "I'm goin' up to meet th' Kid."

Lanky Smith nodded, his eyes on the little dust cloud up the trail.

"I reckon there'll be plenty of water," he replied. "You want we should tighten 'em up an' make 'em step?"

"No," grunted the straw boss. "Be time enough for that if I signal."

Lanky watched his boss and friend ride away and nodded mechanically. It always was a good thing to be sure, especially when it had to do with a herd. It was a twenty-mile drive from the last water to the creek, and the weather was not too hot. It was a thirty-mile drive from the creek to the next water. If the creek was wet enough, the thirty-mile drive did not matter very much; but if the creek should be dry, it meant fifty miles without drinking the cattle. These were steers, hardy and full-grown; not cows, with calves. Nevertheless fifty miles without water was a good thing to know about in advance.

Hopalong pushed on at a lope, his eyes on the nearing dust cloud. What wind there was was keeping even with the rider, and the thick dust hid him. It would be a smother of dust when the cattle reached that place.

Johnny Nelson finally appeared in a rift, extended both arms out from his shoulders, and dropped them swiftly. Hopalong turned in the saddle and raised his big hat. Back with the herd, both point riders passed the signal along. The spread-out herd compacted into a line four to six animals wide and moved with faster stride. The dust suddenly doubled, climbing higher near the tail end and making the drag rider swear. Farther back a lazy cook tightened the reins and cracked his whip over the team. The chuck wagon lurched and rumbled, swinging wide on the windward side, and went past the herd at some distance from it. The cavvy, loafing along and grazing beyond the course of the chuck wagon, showed more activity. The day wrangler sent it ahead briskly. If there was any water at all in the creek, the horses must have it. Everything, should the cattle go thirsty, would depend upon horseflesh. They might have to cover several miles to the cattle's one.

Johnny pulled up. He was hardly out of his teens, but he had worked and was working with good cowmen. He was a good cowman himself.

"Little puddle in th' crick bed, about eighty rods south, around th' bend," he shouted. "It's dry every place else."

"Enough for th' cavvy?" yelled the trail boss.

"Yeah, if they don't puddle it," answered Johnny. He glanced at the distant horse herd. "Hadn't I better ride over an' tell Skinny?"

"Yes, an' stay with him. We'll see you at th' crick," answered the boss, his gaze on the chuck wagon. "Pass th' news on to th' cook, so he can get there first an' fill up his barrel. You tell him if he riles that water, I'll bust his neck!"

"I'll bust it for you, before you get there," replied Johnny, with a grin, and he was on his way to help Skinny Thompson with the cavvy.

Hopalong was not very much worried. A fifty-mile dry drive, with cattle like these, was hardly more than an incident in a trail driver's life. Why, he could remember the time when . . . Might be just as well not to start remembering things like that. And while he determined not to remember them, he was recalling every harrowing incident of that awful drive. He shook his head savagely. Should he go on to the little pool and mount guard over it, or should he stay with the cattle? That was a damn-fool idea. There was no reason to go on to the pool—it wouldn't evaporate, or blow up in the next few hours, and he could not stop it, anyhow. A trail boss should stay with the cattle. He sent his horse into a lope and rode back toward the herd. When he reached it, he chose the right side.

The first rider he met was Red Connors, rifleman par excellence, now riding right point.

"Enough water for th' cavvy?" asked Red anxiously.

"Yeah."

Red grinned. That was one of the reasons why Red was loved by his friends. He might lack initiative, but he did what he was told to do, to the very last word, and almost anything served him as an excuse for a grin.

"Shucks!" he snorted, the freckles threatening to run together. "What's fifty miles, to cattle like these?"

"Fifty pounds to th' head, mebby!" snapped Hopalong, thinking in terms of beef. The total was impressive.

"Shucks!" replied Red, the grin growing, as he glanced at the quickly moving herd. *"They* can lose fifty pounds a head an' not show it." He sobered swiftly. "Cook aimin' to fill his barrel before th' cavvy gits into it?"

Hopalong laughed. With a thousand head of cattle on their hands, and a fifty-mile dry drive before them, Red was worrying about the quality of the drinking water, about muddy coffee! Hopalong waved his hand and rode on, and with the same gesture replied to the flankers' questions. He swung in behind the drag, where Billy Williams was cursing footsore cattle, the dust, and the need for speed. When Billy had a reason to grouch he was as near happy as he ever could be.

"Why th' hell I allus git th' drag, every trip——"
began Billy, pugnaciously.

"Go up on th' left flank, an' swap places with Pete,"
ordered his boss. "We'll eat dust for you for a while.
An' you don't git th' drag every trip."

"Ah, I didn't mean nothin'!" growled Billy.

"I know it; but I do," said Hopalong. "We're comin' to some blame' fluffy soil. I don't want th' drag to
git too far behind. Send Pete back here an' git some
clean air in yore lungs. I'll eat some of yore dust."

"Be damned if I do!" retorted Billy. "Lookit that
fool O Bar O critter: he's blind in one eye an' allus
edgin' off."

Hopalong turned the animal back and grunted.

"So would you edge off, if horns was threatenin' you
on yore blind side. You git up there on th' flank an'
send Pete back here to me."

"Hell with Pete. I owe him three dollars, an' he's
allus bringin' it up, th' last couple of years." His mind
as well as his body seemed to be fogged with dust, for
only now did he give any thought to the condition of
the important creek ahead. "Did th' Kid find any
water?"

"Enough for th' cook an' th' cavvy," answered
Hopalong. "You go on up an' swap with Pete. Me an'
him'll take over th' drag for a little while, an' then
you an' him can handle it. I don't want it to get too
far behind."

"All right," replied Billy. Shortage of water had
changed his attitude He disappeared in the dust, and

soon thereafter Pete pushed through it. He nodded to his friend and boss and gave his attention to the footsore cattle on his own side. Hoofs thudded, horns clicked, the dust arose like a blanket, steadily growing thicker. The sun blazed down, and time intervals seemed twice as long. Then Hopalong dropped back, crossed the trail, and loped forward along the left flank. The cattle were moving rapidly, steadily, like veterans. Fifty miles would not be too dangerous if no time were wasted. When they finally got to water, he'd let them rest up for a day or two. They must be prime when they reached the shipping pens and were turned over to the new owners.

Billy nodded in reply to the gesture and stopped his horse, letting the stream of cattle flow past him. Hopalong took his place for a while and then, riding forward, took up his old place on left point and sent Lanky back to handle the flank position.

Little rises thrust up, drew near, and receded into the soaring dust blanket. Sage and brush rolled endlessly past. They reached and crossed the ridge which divided the watersheds of the two streams, and poured down the gentle slope. The cavvy should have watered by now. If he let the herd into what was left of the water it would be hard to get going again, sullen and stubborn with the taste of a few drops, without receiving any real benefit from the depleted puddle. Steady progress was the proper thing, with not a minute wasted. If the wind held as it was, there would be no water scent to make them ugly.

The twin lines of brush marking the stream bed came into sight. Hopalong could see the cavvy grazing on the farther slope, and the chuck wagon was below the horse herd and not moving. The trail boss swore under his breath: they all knew that there would be no stop at the dried-up creek! This was not like his outfit: something was wrong.

A group of riders pushed up into sight out of the dried watercourse. They rode steadily toward the oncoming cattle, and their rifles lay across their saddle horns. Hopalong turned, waved Lanky ahead to take over the point, and saw Red repeat the order on his own side of the herd.

Hopalong pushed on, Red crossing the herd and converging to join him. The flankers were riding as far forward as they dared. A distant rider streaked down the slope where the cavvy grazed, and then another as the cook left his wagon to play day wrangler and to stay with the horses. Why should Johnny and Skinny do a thing like that? Hopalong did not know, but it made him keenly alert. He knew his men.

The oncoming group of strangers slowed and spread out, and two of them faced around to watch the progress of the two wranglers. Hopalong stopped his horse, and Red did likewise. The two groups were perhaps fifty yards apart.

"Howdy," called the trail boss in even tones.

The leader of the strangers nodded shortly, curtly.

"Reckon we'll have to cut yore herd, pardner," he said, slowly.

"Got yore papers?" asked Hopalong evenly.

"Shore have. You want to see 'em?"

"No."

"No? All right. Might as well throw th' herd together here," said the stranger. He started to wave to his companions, but the trail boss stopped him.

"You better pull off to one side of th' trail, or you'll mebby get tromped flat," said Hopalong coldly. "This herd's in a hurry, an' it's not stoppin'."

"What?" asked the other in simulated surprise. "You resistin' us cuttin' this herd?"

"Any cuttin' will be done after we reach water!" snapped the trail boss. "We're plumb in th' middle of a fifty-mile dry drive, an' we ain't stoppin'. After we reach water I'll take a look at yore papers. We ain't wastin' time, with th' cattle gettin' thirstier every minute; an' we ain't chousin' 'em up while they're movin' sweet an' steady."

"Hell you ain't!" snapped the stranger, touching a paper which stuck out of a pocket.

"You show me that paper, an' I'll make you eat it," said Hopalong. "Up to right now I don't *know* that you've got any authority to stop an' cut a herd; an' I ain't goin' to find that out until after these cattle have watered. You can play that on yore gran'father's fiddle: it's mebby dance music."

"I've got th' legal right to cut this herd wherever I find it," retorted the stranger. "I'm cuttin' it here an' now."

"Judge Colt says that if you do any cuttin', it'll be yore fingernails!" growled the trail boss.

"I'm tellin' you to bunch that herd, so we can cut it!" The stranger's arm went up, and a rigid fore-finger indicated a steer on the edge of the herd. *"There's* a brand I got on my list. I claim that critter! If there's one, there'll be more. We cut this herd here an' now!"

"There's near a hundred C 80's in this herd," re-torted Hopalong. "You figger on takin' 'em all?"

"I'll take every critter you got that carries a brand that's on my list."

"Yo're a modest —— ——," said Hopalong grimly. "I told you it was mebby dance music."

"We got fiddles of our own!" retorted the stranger.

"An' you mebby got our road brand on yore list," said Hopalong, insultingly and ominously. "Then you can claim th' whole damn herd."

"You know I ain't!"

"Then cut yore drag," growled the trail boss. "Every C 80 here has got our road brand on its hide. *I* got a paper, too, It's signed by th' state cattle in-spector, an' *it's* got th' *road* brand, as well as th' other marks. Get outa th' way: yo're clutterin' up th' trail."

The cattle, well trail broke, poured along the faintly marked trail without guidance. All humans had de-serted it. Even the drag was on its own, for Pete and Billy had deserted their posts to swell the group be-hind their foreman, to stand shoulder to shoulder with their friends. Johnny and Skinny had not kept on riding. Their horses stood with empty saddles. The sage was thick over there and kept its secret well.

The leader of the strangers glared into the angry faces confronting him and then cocked an ear at something one of his own men whispered. His eyes glanced at the two riderless horses and then over the thick clumps of sage. He figured that the distance was under four hundred yards. The old service Sharps ate up such an interval with gusto. Fifty-caliber slugs were nothing to argue with. Two hidden riflemen, lying prone—huh!

"We're all gettin' too riled up," he said with a grim smile. "I know how you feel about wastin' time right now. We'll cut this herd on Bender's Crick, where there's plenty of water an' grass."

"You will," admitted Hopalong, "after I see yore papers; but papers or no papers, you don't cut out nothin' with our road brand on its hide."

"We'll cut out what our papers call for, an' don't you forget it!"

"I ain't likely to forget it!"

The stranger turned in the saddle and waved his companions back. The herd kept on pouring past, with the point men taking up their proper positions; but the flankers all seemed to prefer the trouble side. Be easy enough to shape up the cattle, if they needed it, a little farther on. Damn all trail cutters!

"Fine bunch," said the stranger conversationally; but his eyes glinted with avarice.

"Yeah," said Hopalong, also conversationally; but

he moved when the stranger moved, and did not miss a motion or a glance.

"Well," said the stranger, picking up the reins. "We'll see you on Bender's Crick. Come on, boys."

Hopalong rode slowly after them for a hundred yards or so and then smiled as Johnny and Skinny, once more in their saddles, raced forward through the sage, ready to leap into its shelter in an instant. They were not wasting time because their course would lead them to the cavvy, where the cook stood guard. The herd poured on, riders now on both points, both flanks, and back with the drag. Then Hopalong pushed into a lope and cut across to join his wranglers. The three of them rode at speed toward the distant cavvy, to the cook's vast relief. The dust soared, flattened, and hung; but the herd poured on.

II

THE cavvy, well watered all around, were now kept closely bunched. It was more than possible that mounts would be changed more often than usual: if the cattle became hard to handle this would be a certainty.

The long afternoon slowly faded into twilight, the plodding herd still indistinct in the ever-present dust. The stronger cattle, the leaders, had steadily maintained their position at the head of the column, and the size of the drag had increased. The distance from the front rank to the last was twice as long as it had been earlier in the day. Along with the soft thudding of the hoofs and the clicking of horses there now arose a new note, a disturbing one: the lowing of tired and thirsty cattle, its volume slowly but steadily growing.

Hopalong rode in to the cavvy. He was tired, thirsty, and covered with sweat and dust. He removed his saddle and threw it on a fresh horse, his hands moving by instinct alone.

"They got you worried," said Johnny, his gaze on the dust-streaked face.

"Unh!" grunted the trail boss. A half-hearted smile broke through the tense expression. "You keep yore thoughts on these hosses," he said. "Be ready to split

th' cavvy an' drive half of it on to Bender's Crick.
Then bring 'em back, an' send on th' other half."

"We've had drier an' longer drives than this," suggested Skinny, for the sake of adding a cheerful note.
"This ain't hardly nothin'."

"No?" inquired the trail boss, his blue eyes glinting
for an instant.

"Shore we have," said Johnny.

"Trouble with that is that them other drives are all
over, an' this one ain't," replied Hopalong wearily.

"Hell, there ain't nothin' to worry about," said
Skinny, lying like a loyal rider.

"With a bunch of fake trail cutters hornin' in to
make us trouble?" asked the trail boss. "I'm responsi-
ble for a thousan' head."

"You figger they're fakes?" quickly asked Johnny.
"If that's so, then we shoulda put 'em afoot, back
there, this noon."

"I'm figgerin' on gettin' water into th' bellies of
these cattle before I put anybody afoot," retorted
Hopalong. "An' if I have to put anybody afoot, he'll
never ride again." He swung into the saddle and
wheeled. "Well," he said, peering into the thickening
twilight, "they're movin' as steady as can be expected.
Be our job to keep 'em that way till we hit Bender's
Crick. You boys keep yore thoughts right on this
cavvy. Everythin' depends on it an' Bender's Crick."

"Th' crick'll be all right," said Skinny. "It's never
dry."

"Shore; but we got to get there with th' herd," retorted Hopalong; "an' it's a long ways off."

He rode off toward the streaming, heaving, lowing herd, the dust wrapping it like a shroud. The creak of leather, barely heard above the general noise, located the right point rider for him, and soon Red loomed up in the dim light, his head showing through a swirling opening in the dust. Red was tired, anxious, thirsty, and his throat felt like sandpaper; but he grinned.

"Be a good idear for you to change cayuses about now," said Hopalong, thinking of the coming darkness. "I'll take over th' point for you."

"You lettin' them fellers cut this herd, when they could see that every last animal in it has our road brand?" demanded Red with a trace of anger.

"If they cut it, they'll cut it while it moves," growled the trail boss, "an' only them animals that ain't got our road brand, an' tallies with th' brands on their list."

"But every last head *has* got a road brand!" protested Red quickly.

"You better get yoreself a fresh hoss," said Hopalong, moving farther into the dust.

In a surprisingly short time Red returned astride his best horse. He thought that he might need the best before time came to change again. Before he was quite certain just where the trail boss was, that person pushed out toward him.

"All right, Red. I'll drop back an' spell th' others while they shift saddles. A little wind would help."

"Help?" growled Red. "I got so much dust in my mouth that I spit clay buckshot!"

"Better hold 'em down to that size," jibed the trail

boss. "As long as you can spit a-tall, you ain't gettin no sympathy."

"Damn fool!" grunted Red and pushed into the thick of it.

Eventually Hopalong reached the left point, found Lanky by hearing his profanity, and bore in toward him.

"All we need now is some lightnin', or a wolf scent, to send 'em hell-to-lather an' gone," growled the point rider.

"I had allus reckoned Billy was th' grouch of this outfit," said the trail boss. "Better change cayuses, while you can see how to pick."

"If we'd get some wind to lift this dust . . ." growled Lanky and then shook his head and swore under his breath. "Hell, if we did, it'd shore come from th' other side."

"I'm takin' over th' point till you get back on a fresh cayuse," said Hopalong quietly.

"You reckon that bunch of trail cutters will be waitin' for us up on th' crick?" asked Lanky.

"Right now I'm thinkin' about water," retorted Hopalong.

"Who ain't?" growled Lanky, and the dust swirled in to fill the gap he made.

The night dragged its weary cycle, and dawn was not more than an hour away. Hard ground had killed the dust blanket, and the trail dipped and wound more and more as it led deeper into the rough, wild country on the Bender's Creek slope of the watershed. The creek was still miles away, but the chaparral, thickets, and squat scrub timber were promises in themselves and brought cheer to the tired, thirsty, and dust-covered riders who doggedly held the cattle into the semblance of a trail herd. The horns clicked more rapidly, and the lowing had become a continuous swell of sound; but the herd was forging ahead at the same brisk pace, here and there surging and calming down again, and the drag was four times what it had been when the dry creek had been passed. The coolness of the night had aided materially. Everything considered, the trail boss was well satisfied: things could be so much worse. All he had to worry about now was the break, and the stampede when those flaring red nostrils caught the faint but unmistakable scent of water. The run, of course, would stop at the creek, but numbers of injured animals might come from it.

Johnny had returned with the second section of watered saddle horses, and he and Skinny were holding the cavvy in a compact bunch not far from the trail. Again the men changed mounts, eager to have fresh, watered animals under them for the last few hours.

Hopalong was the last to ride up. He picked out a big roan and shifted gear, turning the tired bay into the cavvy.

"Kid," he said to Johnny, "Skinny can handle th' cavvy from now on. We'll be needin' you with th' herd. We're doublin' th' point riders an' lettin' th' drag get along by itself. No tellin' how soon they'll smell water. Th' wind's shifted an' comin' straight from th' crick."

"Just a few more hours, Hoppy, an' we'll be holdin' aces for our hole cards," replied Johnny, smiling. "After that it'll be sweet an' easy. No more drives without water after we reach th' crick."

"Yeah," responded Hopalong. "We'll let 'em lay over a couple of days on th' crick. After that things'll be as smooth as bull-butter. Give Lanky a hand, over on left point."

The wrangler watched his two friends melt into the darkness and smiled gently. Trouble usually looked worse than it really was. Two, three hours from now, and everything would be all right. If there was a place in Bender's Creek big enough to hold a man he would take a bath.

The thickets pressed in closer. One could see erratic lanes running back in the chaparral until the darkness blotted them out. To the clicking of horns was now added the clatter of hoofs on hard, stony ground. Here and there the rising wind made ghostly movements in the upper twigs of the brush. Here and there some wiser steer raised flaring nostrils to test the air currents. If they broke and stampeded in this thick chaparral section there would be scores injured and missing.

Single riders were on the points now, and their companions were back on the flanks. The constricting thickets drew apart again and fell away on both sides. Hopalong knew this place, knew it well: another mile and the country would be reasonably open, where a stampede would not be so bad. That mile was a hair-trigger affair. More and more animals were testing the wind and beset by a growing restlessness. Then it was past, and every man with the herd heaved a sigh of relief. All right: they were bound to break and run when the water scent struck their nostrils, but every passing minute now robbed the run of just that much danger.

The dark plain grew gray. The light increased swiftly. Mysterious blots of a moment before now stood revealed as clumps of brush and individual sage bushes. The leading cattle raised their heads again and broke into a run, a lumbering, ground-covering run. Open spaces grew in the herd, ever increasing. In a few minutes it was strung out four times its original length. In a few more minutes it was a series of bunches of cattle, running at their best speeds to trace down that scent of water. Even the foot-weary drag showed animation and the same strung-out formation, but on a much smaller scale. All that the riders had to do was —nothing. Let them go. Ten times their number could not change the direction of the cattle now, even if they wished to. Some of the riders, realizing the futility of their efforts, were dropping back to find and drive in any animals which might have become separated from the main herd in the brush. The limping drag plunged doggedly on.

The lead cattle awkwardly popped up over the last rise and poured down the slope to the wide, shallow creek. In a moment scores of hot, tired, and thirsty cattle were standing knee deep in the warm water, flicking it with their noses, plowing it with their tongues. The number steadily grew, and now the riders, leaving the main herd to look after itself, were scouting about over the plain and through the scanty brush, rounding up the stragglers and the footsore, and driving them on to the creek. Noon found the last of the cattle accounted for. The main part of the herd was strung out along the northern bank, placidly feeding; late stragglers and the belated drag still stood in the water, nosing it contentedly and gently bawling.

Hopalong had counted them as well as he could in their strung-out formation and was pretty thoroughly satisfied that he had lost none; to be certain of this he would have to point them as for trail driving and then push them through a narrow opening between two stationary riders. He was debating about doing this when the trail cutters of the day before appeared riding down the trail. He made up his mind at once: no count was necessary right now. He instinctively shook his holsters, glanced around behind him to see where his companions were, and then slowly rode up the trail to meet the newcomers, to meet them well beyond the herd. Leaving the creek and riding swiftly after him were Johnny, Skinny, Pete, Lanky, and Billy. Back at the chuck wagon, the cook and Red were on the far side of the vehicle, more valuable there than twice their number out in the open. The wagon box not only partly hid them, but also provided a solid rest for their rifles.

III

THE trail cutter pulled up and raised a hand, palm out. It was the old Indian greeting and meant peace. Hopalong stopped, his suspicious eyes on the group, but his attention was centered upon the leader.

"All accounted for?" asked the trail cutter pleasantly, his gaze flicking to the grazing cattle.

"Yeah," grunted Hopalong, hearing the nearing hoofbeats behind him. "Yeah, all accounted for," he said, but he was not thinking of cattle.

The trail cutter smiled meaningly.

"Well, they got their bellies full of runnin', an' full of water, too. They'll be easy to handle."

"We're doin' that," grunted the trail boss.

"Be a good time for us to cut 'em," said the stranger. He shrugged his shoulders a little, as if admitting that he knew he had a mean job.

"Mebby. Let's see yore papers," said Hopalong, riding slowly forward and extending his right arm.

"Shore! They're all right, all in order; an' they got one of yore brands on 'em. Better not have no trouble over a few head of cattle. You can't fight th' law, except, mebby, in yore own state. This is *my* state." He handed over the papers and quietly waited, and again his gaze flicked to the grazing cattle.

"Huh!" muttered the trail boss. "You've shore got C 80 on yore list." He looked up, his eyes blazing. "Last time we come up this trail, we met a cutter, an' *he* had a list. What happened to him?"

"He got into trouble an' left th' country," said the present cutter.

"Yeah? Well," continued Hopalong, "we had th' same brands then that we got now. He didn't claim a critter. He didn't have a single one of our brands on his papers. This C 80 outfit of yourn must be right new?"

"That's a right good way to explain it," replied the cutter. "It's on my list, an' I'm cuttin' out C 80 cows."

Hopalong's face hardened.

"You know an' I know that there's no C 80 in this part of th' country," he said slowly, "but, just lettin' that ride for a minute, every C 80 animal in this herd has our road brand on its skin. Our papers give th' number of animals in each brand. How you aimin' to get around them two facts?"

"*I'*m not th' one to make no explanations!" snapped the cutter. "But, just for th' sake of argument, seein' how much you like to argue, th' road brands coulda been run on right recent; an' th' papers mighta been forged."

"Shore," admitted Hopalong, holding down his temper as a trail boss should who had a thousand valuable animals to account for. "Except that th' road brands we can show all have had time to heal; an' that th' papers bear th' state seal."

"We might as well start cuttin' right now," replied

the trail cutter, sensing that his men were spreading out behind him. "I'm cuttin' out an' takin' all th' C 80 animals you got. You can't git away with local cattle that have joined up with yore herd."

"Hosses, too?" inquired Hopalong, his voice suddenly velvety. "We got some of them in th' C 80 mark; an' some fool puncher mighta scratched that brand on our chuck wagon som'ers. You reckon mebby *it* strayed into our herd?"

"This ain't no time to get funny!" snapped the trail cutter, his red face growing redder.

"Just what I'm thinkin' myself," retorted Hopalong, shoving the papers in a pocket. "If you can find any C 80 animal in this herd without our road brand, you take it along with you, an' then me an' some of th' boys will go along with you to take a look at this spang new C 80 ranch. It's yore move, either way, stranger."

The short line of men behind the trail cutter surged, hands dropping swiftly. Hopalong's left, and deadlier, hand dropped and came up again, smoke bursting from it. It was the draw which was to make him famous. The bearded rider facing him on his left sagged in the saddle and let the Colt fall to earth. The .44 had momentarily paralyzed him. The still smoking gun now looked squarely at the trail cutter's vest.

"Go back th' way you came," said the trail boss evenly.

The cutter's face was dark with rage, and his tight lips opened a little. The muzzle of the .44 did not waver.

"You know what you've just done?" he demanded ominously.

"Yeah—shot a skunk. Don't force me to make it two."

"You've shot an officer of th' law in th' performance of his duty!"

"Mebby," grunted Hopalong. "I'm gamblin' on him not bein' an officer. You played yore hand too hard. Clear outa here, an' do it pronto."

"I don't see that I can do anythin' else, with trail rowdies an' desperadoes. Gimme my papers."

"I'm keepin' 'em," said Hopalong, smiling a little. "I've took a great fancy to 'em. Clear out."

"You've shore got yoreself into a mess!" snapped the trail cutter.

"You'll be in a bigger one if you don't clear out. *Git!*"

The trail cutter glanced at the punchers backing up the trail boss, and then at the wagon, where two Sharps rifles were being held on a steady rest. He had not noticed the rifles before, and the sight was a little shock. It also was the determining factor, and he jerked at his horse, wheeling swiftly. The cutting-out operations could wait until a more favorable time. His companions copied his movements and swung in behind him on their way up the trail. Their language drifted back and made the trail boss smile again.

Lanky pushed up his hat and scratched under it, his grin slowly fading.

"We better git outa this country damn quick," he

said, glancing toward the west, where a state line lay not many miles away. "Any water over that way?"

"Don't know, an' don't care," replied the trail boss, reading his friend's thoughts. "We'll let th' herd feed an' rest up today an' tomorrow."

"Yeah?" asked Lanky wonderingly. His companions also were surprised: they were in a tight place; but they were Bar 20 men, and they turned slowly to ride back to the cattle. Nevertheless, interfering with a trail cutter in the discharge of his duties was a serious business.

Hopalong laughed, felt in a pocket, and pulled out the papers which authorized the trail cutter to protect the range brands along this cattle highway. The job was a necessary one, and while it was more or less of a nuisance to trail drivers, most of them were fair enough to aid a cutter in trimming a herd, thereby saving time and tempers. Not all the drivers were fair, and not all the cutters were honest. Hopalong glanced over the paper and then quietly handed it to Lanky.

Lanky slowly scrutinized it, his companions looking over his arms and shoulders.

"Great gosh!" he said, turning a serious face to his boss. "This looks mighty good to me. That seal ain't no forgery. We still got time to head west for th' state line."

"It shore looks all right," admitted Hopalong, wearing his poker face.

"This here paper was issued proper an' legal!" said

Lanky anxiously. To his way of thinking, it was not a good thing to run foul of the law in another man's state; not when a man had a thousand head of cattle on his hands.

"It shore was," acknowledged the trail boss, holding out his hand for it. "If you've looked it over, I'll take it ag'in. It might be right important, later on."

"*Might* be—later on?" muttered Lanky. "Great gosh, man! It *is*, an' right *now!* It's plumb legal, an' we're mebby monkeyin' with a buzz saw."

"You notice anythin' about it that didn't look just right?" asked Hopalong, glancing from face to face.

"You mean that spot of blood?" asked Lanky.

"Yeah. Anythin' else?"

"No-o. Can't say as I did," admitted Lanky slowly. "Was there somethin'?"

"Figger so, mebby," answered Hopalong. "Anyhow, I got an idear."

"Hell!" grunted Pete. "You usually have, not admittin' that they're worth a cuss. What is it *this* time?"

"Just for that remark you can find out for yourself," retorted the pride and joy of the Cassidy family, already showing most of the traits which were to make him famous throughout the wide cattle country and up and down a long and tough frontier. He shoved the paper back into a pocket, wheeled, and rode down the trail toward the herd, followed by his silent and thoughtful friends.

IV

HOPALONG sat up in the darkness, awake in an instant, with the sounds of shots in his ears—the sharp sounds of shots like faint punctuation marks in a steady roar of sound. The ground trembled under him, and he thought he could make out the clicking of horns on horns. As he rolled out of his blankets he sensed that his companions were stirring. Shadowy silhouettes were picked out by the cherry glow of the fire and turned into moving men. The roar was steadily becoming less, and from the sounds and the faint flashes of guns he knew that the herd had stampeded from the bed ground toward the trail; from right to left, from east to west; and he knew that it would break back the way it had come, the way it knew. Excited queries came from the darkness about him. Somebody threw wood on the dying fire and swung a big hat across it. All this had taken but an instant. The cattle were still tired, and heavy with water and grass: yet they had stampeded.

"To hell with that fire!" snapped Hopalong, running toward his picketed night horse.

Other figures ran after him. Leather squeaked, there came a vague and sudden bunching of horses,

ghostly movement, and then the swift pound of hoofs
toward the scene of disaster. At intervals Hopalong
fired into the air, the flash of his gun winking in the
dark. At last a distant flash answered him, and he led
the little group toward the sign. After a few moments
of steady riding he fired again, and the answering signal turned him toward the left. Soon a voice hailed
him. It sounded like Pete, and Pete it was.

"You hurt?" shouted Hopalong and slowed his
horse, the others slowing likewise.

"No!" answered the voice in a bellow and almost
tearful from rage. The darkness hid the speaker's
limp. The voice trailed off into meaningless profanity.

"What started 'em?" demanded the trail boss.

"Bunch of riders, shootin' as they came," growled
Pete, his huge hands clenching. "Shot my hoss. It fell
on me, but I histed him off." A casual statement, that;
but a true one; also, an amazing one, unless you knew
Pete. He was a squat giant. Once Pete lifted a man,
as heavy as himself, high up over his head and threw
him through a plank door. Pete had been in a hurry,
and the man had been the only tool at hand. The door
was ruined, and the man died. He would have died
anyhow in the next few seconds, and as it was, Johnny
was saved a cartridge which came in handy a little
later on.

"They shot my hoss an' dumped me plumb in front
of th' herd, damn 'em!" growled Pete, still swearing.
"Lucky I wasn't trompled flat; woulda been, too, if I
hadn't waited till th' last damn steer was past before

I histed th' dead hoss off'n me." Thus one might suspect that Pete used his head as well as his muscles. With the last word he started to limp toward the faint, winking light of the fire at the wagon, there to obtain a horse, and to go to work again.

As Pete faded into the night, the mounted group whirled and swung off toward the trail, to follow along in the rear of the stampeded herd, content to keep reasonably close to it and thus be on hand at the first crack of dawn. Unless urged, the herd would not run far, having fed and watered heavily; but as things were, it or part of it undoubtedly was being driven off. Dawn would be the signal for purposeful action.

"No questions," growled the trail boss. "Shoot first. Anybody found with our cattle has it comin' to 'em. Shoot 'em where you find 'em, an' let 'em lay where they fall. They'll mebby find out that trail cuttin' is damn risky business."

Growls responded. Every man was peering ahead into the night. At last one man spoke. It was Lanky:

"Wonder where Billy is."

"With th' cattle if he ain't been shot," said Hopalong. "Spread out: I'm goin' to signal."

His companions obeyed, guns in their hands. A signal might draw shots.

The heavy Colt roared and jumped. Ahead of them, to the south, came an answering flash and roar, and then two more, followed by another two. The group leaped forward behind its leader. That answering signal had started a gun fight. Billy was in trouble. There

was no caution now in the riding of the group. It tore
through the night to the aid of a friend. Three more
shots flared down the trail, and then there was silence.
The night wind whistled past their ears as they
streaked forward.

"Over here," groaned a voice, and the bunch
whirled like one man. One of the riders stopped and
leaped from the saddle, but the rest kept on, spreading out.

"They musta been waitin' for me to show 'em where
I was," said Billy. "Minute I answered you, they cut
loose. Got th' hoss first an' then me. Then they fanned
it outa here."

Hopalong's match flared, and he hastily examined
his friend.

"Nothin' to worry about a whole lot," he said, taking hold of the prostrate man under the armpits. "Get
hold of yoreself, Billy: I'm goin' to lift you into th'
saddle. All ready?"

"Shore," growled Billy and groaned. He was recov-
ering from the shock of the terrific impact of the heavy
bullet. In these days we hear a lot about small caliber
and high velocity, special thirty-eights, and thirty-
eight specials; but never was there a better cartridge
made for hand guns, a better necessary compromise
between speed and shock than the .44-40; and Hopalong knew it when he changed to the .45 in later years
because of the greater certainty of obtaining the latter cartridge. When a man was hit by the old forty-
four he was hit by a sledge.

Hoofbeats came down the trail, and Hopalong guessed that Pete was mounted and on his way toward trouble; but the trail boss left his burdened horse and ran a score of paces from it before he challenged, to save Billy from more trouble if the guess were wrong.

"Pete?" he called.

"Yeah. That you, Hoppy?"

"Yes. Ride over here. Billy's shot. Take him back to the wagon for th' cook to patch up."

"Got you, huh?" asked Pete of Billy as he rode up to the wounded horseman. He reached out his huge arms, and Billy was cradled as safely as a baby. The double-burdened horse turned to face the wagon, where the fire burned much brighter now. The cook knew that someone of the outfit might need that wagon, might need a beacon; but the cook was not foolish enough to be found in its circle of light. The cook was sprawled out in the wagon, a rifle in his capable hands. Pete said something to his horse and was on his way, riding straight for the campfire.

Hopalong climbed into the now empty saddle, wheeled, and loped in the direction taken by his friends. After a few moments a voice snapped a question, and the clicking of a hammer could just be heard. Hopalong quickly replied and bore off a little more to the left.

The eastern horizon had begun to glow, and it would not be long, now, before they could give their whole attention to rounding up the cattle. There would be a shortage: of that all were certain; but if it lay in their power to change this, it would be only a temporary shortage. Cattle leave tracks, and tracks can be followed. In this case there was more than a few head of stolen cattle to be paid for: and the debt was heavy enough to press for collection; but right now the round-up was the first consideration. The little group sat motionless, impatiently waiting for light, and light swiftly came. Eager eyes waited for what it would reveal.

V

THE bulk of the herd had stopped and was grazing as placidly as if nothing unusual had happened. No thanks to it, however: it doubtless had run until out of breath. As had been expected, they had followed the back trail, the way they had come up—the way they knew. This was but natural, and they received no credit for that. The group of horsemen cursed them as it rode on.

Hopalong waved his hand, and the group split up into its component units, each riding off to take up his place on the circle. It was not long before the greater number of steers was bunched up in a tight little herd, to serve as a magnet to others farther afield. Two men held this main bunch, and the others began to drive in the scattered animals. Apparently they had received no real injuries; and from the looks of them they would not be hard to handle; at least, not until later, when they got their gumption back. There was a thought in the foreman's mind that after this experience they might stampede more easily—get the habit, as it were. This, also, was a characteristic of cattle; but in this case they had been trail broken too long to easily become habitually hair-trigger. One stampede, thoroughly excusable, would hardly change them.

By mid-forenoon the plain had been dragged, the ravines and hollows combed. All the cattle within reasonable distance had been driven in. Stragglers, far afield, had been hunted down and brought back. Any now which might be missing had not kept on travelling of their own volition. How many would that be? Only a count would tell.

Hopalong and Lanky sat opposite each other, motionless in their saddles. South of them the herd began to move slowly, easily, and steadily. It grew wedge-shaped, with the point nearest them. Both waiting men held a handful of cartridges in their right hands. The tired animals began to stream past between them; and every tenth steer that passed caused the counters to drop a cartridge into a pocket. Their hands were emptied on the fiftieth tally; and after that, every tenth animal caused a cartridge to come out of the pocket and drop into another. The dust was still rising as the last steer passed through. Hopalong thought for a moment, looked at his companion, and spoke.

"Nine hundred fifty-two," he said, scowling.

"Nine fifty-three," said Lanky, with a sigh. If anybody should ask him, that was good counting. Sometimes the cattle passed in bunches, with following bunches head to flank.

"Countin' in th' extra dozen head, that's about sixty we're short," said Hopalong and unconsciously hitched up his gun belts. What assurance a man got out of the weight of a pair of .44's! And it would soon be time to use them. There was Billy, up in the wagon——

"Yeah," grunted Lanky, turning his head to look down the trail.

Hopalong looked in the same direction. Both men had noticed that cattle tracks led southward, superimposed upon those first made by the herd; and that they ran on beyond the tracks of the last, scattered steers that had been found.

"They shoulda got more than that," said Hopalong.

"Dark as pitch, it was," excused Lanky.

"Hell!" sneered the trail boss, with a vast contempt. "We've never tried our hands at it, but if we couldn't cut out an' run off three times that number, we all oughta be shot—like they're goin' to be."

"Well," said Lanky, smiling a little. "Let's go get some rations an' start after 'em." He sent his horse forward, toward the distant wagon. "Wonder how Billy is?"

"Oughta be all right, far's any danger is concerned," growled the trail boss. "You head in toward th' herd an' send Red on to th' wagon to get them rations."

"Ain't I goin' with you?" asked Lanky, hastily.

"I want th' longest an' coolest heads with th' herd," replied Hopalong, not mentioning that he wanted the best rifle shot with himself. "We've lost enough cattle as it is. Push 'em right along, Lanky. Get 'em out of this part of th' country soon as you can. I'll feel a lot

better after they're up at th' pens. Red an' me are
enough to handle this bunch of bunglers. An' here's
somethin' I want you to remember: take a good look
at every little thicket, every bunch of cover that you
pass on th' way, that's near th' trail. You'll likely see
his boots stickin' out, if you look close."

Lanky gazed steadily at his boss, his thoughts racing. After a few moments of intense cogitation he gave
up the puzzle and spoke:

"Whose boots?"

"Th' trail cutter's; th' real trail cutter," answered
Hopalong, grimly. "How else you figger they got his
papers?"

"Great mavericks!" muttered Lanky. "Then those
papers was real an' legal, after all!"

"Shore, except for th' one brand that was writ in
after they was issued. I'm headin' in for th' wagon.
Send Red after me."

Lanky scratched his head, swore under his breath,
and then glanced admiringly after his red-headed
friend. "Sixty head!" he snorted, with contempt.
"Shucks!"

The herd went on, tired and chastened by the
night's run. Off to one side dawdled the cavvy. Hopalong changed his mind about going to the wagon and
looked after it. It rumbled and rattled, its driver taking more care in its guiding than usual. Billy's profanity kept the cook's foot near the brake and the
whip in its socket. Billy was doing nicely, although
that was not well enough to suit him. They needed

every rider, and he swore that another day would find him in the saddle. He was lucky: the two-hundred-grain bullet had missed everything of importance, striking only flesh. When reminded of that fact, he claimed that if he had been lucky the damned bullet would have missed him altogether.

Red nodded to Lanky, listened for a moment, smiled broadly, and rode off after the chuck wagon. He told Billy what was in the wind, took a few lessons in profanity, a supply of food from the cook, and then headed back along the trail and joined his boss. He patted the Sharps in its saddle sheath: the old .50 caliber rifle was like an epidemic on the plains in its day. Its cartridges were obtainable everywhere, as the .45 Colts were later. Unlike most heavy rifles of its day, it was light and slender, its only ugliness being the thick, heavy breech.

Hopalong's eyes rested on the roll fastened behind his friend's saddle.

"Looks like you got grub enough to feed an outfit," he said.

"What you care: *I'm* totin' it, ain't I?" retorted Red.

"On th' prod already, huh!" jibed Hopalong.

For some reason there was no retort, and the two men rode in silence. Then Hopalong growled.

"We warned these fellers twice," he said. "That's enough. We know what they did an' how they did it. Shoot on sight."

Red nodded and sent his horse forward to keep even

with the roan. They had little to say. The tracks were plain. Their eyes were mostly concerned with picking up patches of brush, tufts of weeds, rain-washed gullies: possible ambush points. It seemed reasonable that the thieves would leave a rear guard. He would not be out in plain sight. He would have to be smoked out. After half an hour's riding they found the trail swinging into a wide circle, heading into the west along a shallow ravine. The two friends spread out now without verbal prompting, riding a dozen yards apart, hair-trigger with alertness.

"Headin' for th' new C 80," sneered Hopalong.

"They never heard of th' brand till they saw our cattle," said Red. "They had somebody out scoutin' th' trail."

A puff of smoke burst out against the top of a little hummock up the ravine, and the low-pitched whine of the heavy slug made Hopalong duck. He swore under his breath, and Red laughed. The horses leaped convulsively and streaked forward at an angle, in opposite directions. Red was heading for the shelter of a fringe of brush; his friend, for a deeper wash.

"Nervous, he was," grunted Hopalong to himself as he raced out of the wash and swung toward the distant marksman, riding erratically.

"He had his chance," growled Red, sending his horse from cover to cover in rushing zigzags. Red was making good speed and hoped to get behind the marksman. Neither he nor Hopalong had spoken of any course of action, and it had not been necessary to agree upon a plan: they had worked together many times, and their teamwork was well-nigh perfect. A little ravine ran off to Red's left, and he sent the horse into it, guiding with his knees. The Sharps lay breast high, balanced in both hands. He was an instinctive rifle shot, perfected by practice, and he used a rifle much as other men used a shotgun. Gripped between two fingers of his left hand was a second cartridge, dangling down below the slender wooden stock. He could flip out the empty and reload in almost one swift motion.

The gun lifted, steadied, roared: and the hat jerked and flopped from the distant rock. The smoke was still pouring from the barrel when the second cartridge snicked home and the breechblock slid up behind it. Red showed no chagrin at biting on an old trick: he had fired the shot to develop action and succeeded: for an instant the slanting sun flicked on metal, flashing its message, but before the hidden watcher could steady on his mark, Red's second shot struck the spot of light, knocked the gun from the hands that held it, and smashed the lock. Again the breechblock closed behind a cartridge, and Red sent his horse ahead at better speed. The Bar 20 was becoming known for its forthright action. Brush moved gently over there on the slope, but Red held his fire: he wanted a clean target for the next one. There was movement to the right of the first: a horse moved restlessly in a little thicket.

Red grinned and rode straight for it. If he could get between it and its rider there would be no warnings carried to make him trouble later on.

To the south, Hopalong pushed steadily on. The roar of the Sharps made him change his course a little. He heard the scream of the ricochet and then the second shot. He sent his horse into a run, and through a lane in the brush he caught sight of a running man, dodging from cover to cover. An instant later he saw Red reach the tethered horse and jerk at the cinch strap. He knew that Red would strip off the saddle and turn the animal loose, driving it off into the brush and away from its owner.

Hopalong pushed on, to head off the running man. Again he saw him as he leaped a rill. The man had no rifle, and this information changed the strategy: it would be six-shooter against six-shooter, now—and on these terms Hopalong dashed forward, his rifle again in its saddle sheath.

There was a little clearing in the brush on the side of the hill: a natural clearing, and into this the cattle thief stepped, tired from running. He stopped, gun in hand, and watched the trail boss approach. He still had a chance. If he could shoot the rider out of the saddle and get the horse, he would be all right. He slipped back into the brush, moving swiftly, the sounds of the hoofbeats steadily growing louder in his ears. They were heading around to the south of him, to cut him off. He expected this, and he smiled with satisfaction as he cautiously moved forward in that direction.

Just one clean shot was all he wanted. He gently moved the branches of a low bush and peered through it—and swore in sudden panic. A riderless horse had stopped to graze, not forty paces distant, and the invitation was too plain to be accepted; but where was the rider? He whirled quickly, gun in his upraised right hand, and saw a slowly moving puncher stepping out into the open. The upraised hand streaked downward, and then its fingers opened and stiffened as the gun fell from them. He saw the flame and smoke, but he never heard the shot.

Hopalong slid the heavy weapon back into its holster and walked swiftly forward. One glance was sufficient, and he kept on without checking his stride. A few moments later he was again in the saddle and swinging to the north to rejoin his friend.

Red was waiting for him, looking steadily from under the wide brim of his big hat.

"We all through here?" he asked, reaching for the reins.

"Yeah," answered Hopalong. "We'll cut that trail ag'in an' foller it. How come you shot twice?"

"Smoked him out for you. He was headin' yore way when he saw he couldn't make his hoss. You ever see him before?"

"Yeah; back on' th' cattle trail. He won't cut no more herds. Come on—let's get goin'."

VI

Noon found them following down the bed of a small, dried creek. They noticed that the sparse growth of trees and brush was thinning out. The tracks of the cattle were plain before them, and they still rode warily, losing time for the sake of safety; but, slowly as they rode, they were making better time than the cattle.

Night overtook them on a bend of the creek, which now had begun to show occasional pools of stagnant water. At one of these pools they stopped, looking curiously at it. It was clear and had not been disturbed. This told them nothing, for if it had been disturbed by cattle it would have had time in which to settle. Cattle tracks were all around it, but they lacked the appearance of freshness. A few yards ahead of them a little rill slipped along in its bed, feeding the main stream. It made an ideal place for a camp: too ideal.

"We'll drink th' horses an' make a dry camp," said Hopalong, his gaze on the rill. "Fill our canteens from that," he said, "farther up."

Red nodded, turned from the little stream, and pushed into the brush, Hopalong following at a distance. Thus they had a van guard and a rear guard:

little rills have been known to be treacherous. After scouting until satisfied that there was no ambush, they cautiously reapproached the stream. Filling their canteens and drinking the horses, they left the trickle and rode north, in the general direction whence they came. This was a subtlety characteristic of them. The natural move would have been to keep on riding to the south, continuing their journey and not losing mileage. Anyone finding their tracks and losing them in the darkness would be likely to cast around to the south in hopes of glimpsing their fire.

There would be no fire because there would be no coals. They came to a place where there was a deal of dead and dried brush, which crackled like miniature rifle shots. In it was a clearing with grass. Hopalong stopped, swung down, and stripped off his saddle. Red did the same. They staked their horses on the grass and went back to their saddles. These served for pillows. The noisy, crackly brush would play sentry for them, and there would be no need to take turns on guard. Eating sparingly of the cook's cold food in the gathering dusk, they waited for darkness, when they stretched out and were almost instantly asleep.

Dawn found Red stirring. He opened his eyes and looked at the horses, placidly feeding. He sat up and smiled at his clear-eyed companion.

"Take yore turn at th' wash bench, an' then grub pile," he chuckled.

Hopalong grinned and sat up. Wash benches were among the luxuries of civilization. He hitched himself from the ground and jerked the Stetson from beneath his hips, shaped it critically, and placed it on his head. Now that he was dressed he reached out for the bundle of cold food and placed it between them.

"Better pack in plenty of it, Red," he suggested, thinking that there might not be a chance for them to eat at noon.

While Red fastened up the remaining food, his companion saddled the horses. The hackamores went on, and the picket ropes were coiled in place. When they came to the rill they stopped, and found no signs but those made by themselves the night before. They stopped again when the trail came into sight and then, crossing it and the wet creek bed, rode up the slanting western bank and left it behind them on their left. At a suitable distance they followed a course parallel to it, long rifle shot from it.

"Reckon we'll catch up to 'em today," said Hopalong. Red grunted in affirmation.

The distant creek meandered into a shallow, basin-like valley. The sun was at the meridian, scorching and pitiless. A thin fog of dust drifted slowly across the far end of the valley, and both riders stopped.

"We ain't seen no signs of any watcher since that feller back near th' trail," said Hopalong. "Looks like they figger they've got clean away. If that's so, they'll mebby be restin' th' herd."

"Yeah," replied Red thoughtfully. "Mebby only a couple of riders with it. We better separate?" Red's gaze was on the distant dust sign.

"Uh-huh," answered Hopalong, searching the plain immediately in front of him. His gaze lifted. The face of a bluff could just be made out behind the thin dust. He motioned toward it, and Red nodded. They would meet near there if everything went all right.

A dry wash, fringed with dying brush, ran down the slope before them toward the creek. Hopalong moved toward it, Red nodding and swinging his horse to the right, going off at an angle. Little mounds, hummocks, and patches of dried brush offered him the screen he wanted. He placed his right hand over the hammer of the Sharps and was soon lost to sight.

Hopalong crossed the creek and chose a hollow at right angles to it. Ten minutes later he was on the far side of a little hill which masked him from the trail along the creek. There was no wind here, and perspiration trickled down from the sweatband of the thick Stetson, spread through the stubble on his face, and dripped from the point of his chin. His hands were sweaty and smelled of rawhide. They were too slippery, and he turned the horse in against the high bank of the hill and rubbed both palms with dirt and sand.

Had the cattle thieves left another guard? They might if they were resting the herd, or if this valley was its destination, for in either case they could spare a man. Hopalong pushed steadily on in the same direction, turning south again after several miles. If there was another sentry, Hopalong would push in between that interesting person and the cattle and take care of him if and when he showed up. Right now it was the cattle that counted. Sixty head, huh? Just like a slap in the face.

The hills grew smaller, and at last he came to the edge of the little valley, where it thrust farthest east. There was not much grass in it, and in this part of the country well-grassed valleys were the rule rather than the exception. This, then, could not be the destination of the stolen herd; and if this were so, then the cattle were still on the drive, and he doubted if there was a watcher behind him. A quick and cautious glance to the south end of the valley showed him that the dust cloud was dying out, and this told him that the stolen cattle were still being driven and had reached harder soil or grass. He pushed on again, bearing a little away from the edge of the valley, and made better speed.

Mid-afternoon found him passing the bluff that he had mentioned to Red, and it also found him much closer to the little herd, which once more was sending up dust clouds. Two of the cattle, footsore, were hanging back and spoiling the disposition of the drag man and his companion. The latter had ridden back to argue with the rear rider, and they were talking something over. Hopalong believed that he knew what the question was. One of them wanted to shoot the two animals and push the rest on more rapidly. The thought sent a little trickle of anger through him. If they shot two head, he could not recover the entire herd. He chose better cover and sent his horse on at a lope. Half an hour later he drew rein in the mouth of a dry wash and waited, gun in hand. The main herd was half a mile south of him; the two footsore animals were just coming up even with him, and the arguments of the following riders was now easily heard.

"Kill 'em or turn 'em loose," said Number One, with heat.

"They're too good to kill, but we might turn 'em loose," said his companion. "They'll be all right in a few days, an' we can pick 'em up ag'in any time. All right, Gawrge: let's ride."

"Just a minute," said Hopalong loudly, pushing out into sight. His thumbs were hooked to his slanting belts, just above the low-hung holsters.

Two pairs of staring eyes, over open mouths, were regarding him in stunned surprise. They believed what they saw, the mouths shut swiftly, and two right hands dropped like striking snakes; but as they dropped, Hopalong's hands were rising, a long-barreled gun in each of them. The double report was deafening. The two horses, suddenly freed of their burdens, surged, ran together, and stopped, their nostrils flaring at the scent of blood. Hopalong peered through the swirling black-powder smoke and grunted. He could rope both horses with one cast, but there was no need to try it: the sounds of the shots must have carried to the riders with the herd. He whirled his horse and raced back into the dry wash, leaped from the saddle onto a rock where the print of his heels would not show, and slapped the moving animal's rump to send it on. Steal his cattle, would they? Steal his cattle and shoot Billy, huh? He slipped behind the rock, crouching under its shelter, each hand holding a gun.

Down by the herd there was sudden shouting, gunshots, and more dust. The herd, suddenly left to itself, and frightened by the shooting, promptly stampeded. It would not run far, for it had been pushed hard, and it was tired. The two riders with the cattle wheeled about and galloped up the valley, rifles in their hands. From the west side of the valley there sounded the report of a Sharps, and the first rider rolled from his saddle, to sprawl in the dust. Red had gone into action again.

The second rider flashed a glance at his prostrate companion and then, panic-stricken, roweled his mount and headed straight for the nearest cover, desperately anxious to get out of range. Again came the report of the Sharps, and his horse went down under him. The rider cleared his stirrups, landed on his feet, and dashed into the brush as a third shot showered him with pebbles.

He kept on running, his high heels thudding on the hard ground. He bore to his left, following the lower ground between the little rises. He was not a runner, and neither was he in running condition, and his breath whistled in his open mouth. Then reason returned to him, and he stopped. He was now in good cover and could hole up and blow the daylights out of anyone who tracked him. With this thought in mind, he moved slowly around a bend and saw the very thing he needed. It was a big rock and nicely placed to cover both directions of approach. Once behind that bulwark, he would welcome pursuit. He dragged a sleeve across his streaming face and moved toward it; and then blinked at the sudden burst of red which appeared on the top of the rock. A calm, hard face appeared under the red bloom and he knew, then, that the red was hair. He reached for his gun, got it free from the holster, and then let it fall from his palsied hand. He fell across a stunted bush and remained there, prominently humped up in the middle.

Hopalong pushed out the smelly shell and shoved home a fresh cartridge, its grease soft, slippery, and greenish. He wiped his finger on his chaps, came out from behind the rock, and went after his horse. Perhaps ten minutes later he was again in the saddle.

The herd was milling, sending up so much dust that Hopalong could not make out the identity of the rider. It might be Red, or it might be someone else. He had to make certain before he blundered up to it, so he again forsook the valley and took to the brush. A faint yell reached him, and he grinned. That was Red, out there rounding up the cattle, and no doubt Red could use some help with the job. Hopalong wheeled his horse and rode at a lope toward the thickest of the dust.

Red's language was profane.

"You scared of eatin' a little dust?" he demanded.

"But I didn't know it was you!" retorted Hopalong, flaring suddenly. "I was ridin' off to slip up onto you!"

"Like hell you was!" snapped Red.

The ensuing argument was not interrupted in the least by the ensuing riding. It died out only as the cattle were bunched up and heading up the trail, back the way they had come. Hopalong rode off and returned with the two footsore animals, with two saddled horses before him.

"What you doin' with them hosses?" demanded Red, sharply.

"Might need 'em to spell our own," answered Hopalong. "Anyhow, those are two right good saddles."

"Might need 'em!" sneered Red. "An' get ourselves into trouble for hoss-stealin'. We ain't got their brands onto our list. Strip th' saddles off an' turn 'em loose, you damn fool."

"Sounds right funny, *you* callin' anybody a damn fool!"

"That so?"

"You know it is!"

Ten minutes of silence, and then Hopalong looked quickly at his grouchy friend.

"Hey, where's th' *boss* trail cutter? We've done lost him."

"*I* didn't lose him," rejoined Red. "I got th' cattle. That's all I want."

"*You* got 'em?"

"Said so, didn't I?"

"You say lots of things," grunted Hopalong, and then he nodded in sudden decision. "All right; we got th' cattle. To hell with him."

"Now yo're gettin' sensible," said Red. "You musta got a touch of th' sun."

Hopalong made no reply, but just jogged along in the dust of the recovered cattle. There was, he reflected, another fictitious trail cutter who had not been accounted for: the rider he had shot through the shoulder, out there on the main cattle trail. Oh, well: that was all right. They had the cattle.

Driving the herd shrewdly, and on the alert for vengeful humans, they went back the way they had come, and without any untoward incident. On the evening of the fifth day, both hungry from a two-day fast, they overtook the main herd, turned their little bunch into it, and loped in to the wagon. Half an hour later, their stomachs pleasantly filled with good food, they leaned back against a wagon wheel and rolled cigarettes.

"Well," said Hopalong, exhaling a lungful of smoke, "in about two weeks we'll turn these cattle into th' shippin' pens an' be shut of 'em. It'll be a good job well done."

"Yeah," said Red, his gaze on the cattle grazing on the bed ground. He was at peace with the world.

"Only one thing bothers me," growled his companion, stirring restlessly.

"Yeah?" asked Red, lazily regarding him.

"Yeah. That boss trail cutter," explained Hopalong. "I shore hate to lose him, an' I'd like to know how he got them papers."

"A damn fool would worry about things like that,"

said Red. "You know that he was a fake cutter because he stampeded th' herd. He didn't dare call for
a showdown of his authority. As for th' papers, he
might have stolen 'em. Anyhow, it ain't none of our
business."

"There is blood on 'em," growled Hopalong.

"Hell with it!" snapped Red. "We got th' cattle
back, didn't we?"

Hopalong nodded, tossed away the cigarette, and
rolled another. He arose and moved toward the fresh
horse which carried his saddle.

"Yeah," he grunted. "We did."

VII

THE placid herd plodded on, heads and haunches rising and falling in the thick dust like a huge blanket undulating in a ground mist. Horns occasionally clicked on horns, for on these cattle the spread of horn was prodigious.

The guardian riders loafed in their saddles, content to loaf for more reasons than the ordinary one: loafing along in the saddle meant peace, that all was going well—and in this interlude, all was going well. How long it would continue to go well, no man knew, but all were hopeful.

Today the herd had been allowed to feed well before being thrown on the trail, and was now marking off the miles at a slow but regular beat; in mid-afternoon it would again be thrown off the trail to feed well before bedding down for the night. The cattle were being driven easy, to hold the weight where it was; and as they drew nearer to the shipping pens the driving would not be driving at all, but a drifting forward as the cattle grazed.

The straw boss slouched in his saddle at left point, comfortably away from the blanket of dust rising slowly above the moving animals. To his left, at a considerable distance, moved the cavvy, half a hundred hand-picked horses. The chuck wagon had passed them already and was running gear down on the trail ahead. The boss was idly glancing at bushes and sage clumps along his side of the wide and dusty highway, in his mind the thought that he might see a pair of boots sticking out of some cover—a pair of boots with a dead man's feet in them. The thought was not fantastic.

Far up the trail there appeared a smudge of dust. Hopalong Cassidy sat a little more erect in his saddle, his gaze fixed steadily upon this telltale. Such a cloud of dust had ushered in all the recent troubles. A dark spot developed in the middle of the little cloud as it drew steadily nearer. He saw the approaching rider swing out to pass the chuck wagon; but he did not pass it: he swung in toward it and stopped. After a moment he came on again. One man, riding alone. Hopalong smiled: the stranger had gained nothing from his words with the cook. When the cook was sober he kept a tight mouth; when he was not sober, he——

Hopalong turned in the saddle, raised an arm twice, and pushed ahead of the herd as Lanky Smith moved up to take the vacated place at the point. The flankers behind Lanky spread out to cover his regular position. This trail crew worked with precision and dispatch. On the right side of the herd there was likewise a forward movement all along the line as Johnny Nelson pushed up to take over Red Connors's right point job in case Red should feel impelled to leave it.

"What you crowdin' me for, Kid?" asked Red, curiously. There was the suggestion of a smile around his lips.

"I ain't crowdin' you, Red," said the Kid. He felt for tobacco and papers. "You might want to ride on ahead."

The two riders were watching the nearing stranger and their trail boss loping along to meet him.

Red slowly shook his head.

"He's only one, an' Hoppy ain't needin' no man's help when th' odds are even—an' lots of times when they're right lopsided."

Johnny's eyes gleamed with appreciation, and he laughed in his throat. Then he looked accusingly at his companion.

"Yeah," he admitted; "but th' next time Hoppy takes any war party away from this outfit, *I'll* be with it. You ain't hoggin' everythin'."

"You got a razor?" asked Red, holding back his laughter.

"No. What's a razor got to do with it?" demanded Johnny with quick suspicion.

"Anybody that goes with Hoppy on one of his war parties should be growed up," explained Red and ducked barely in time.

Johnny laughed and then sobered as he watched the two riders well up the trail.

"Wonder who he is an' what he wants?"

"I figger he's Sittin Bull, an' he wants a drink of liquor."

"You go to hell," growled the Kid and stopped his horse to let his place with the cattle come up to him.

Up on the trail Hopalong slowed to a walk. He caught the glint of the sun on the stranger's nickel-plated star and smiled thinly. From what he had recently experienced it might now be a habit along this trail for men to steal other men's authority—even commit murder to steal it.

The stranger slowed and stopped, both of his hands in sight and on the pommel of the saddle.

"Howdy, friend," he said, nodding.

"Howdy," grunted the trail boss without warmth.

"Anybody cut yore herd yet?" asked the stranger.

"No," grunted the trail boss, his eyes glinting.

"Anybody try to cut it?" persisted the stranger, his interest unconcealed.

Hopalong regarded the questioner fixedly and coldly.

"Yes," he growled, his Irish ancestors urging war.

"Thought mebby they might," placidly admitted the stranger. "I've been busy sheriffin' up in th' north part of my county, an' just got back," he explained. "I'm lookin' for a trail cutter."

"Yeah?"

"Yeah."

"If you'd been with us, some days back, you'da seen him," said the trail boss, his gaze unwavering.

"You reckon you remember what he looks like?"

"Yeah; I'll know him when I see him again."

"An' th' fellers that was with him?" persisted the sheriff, in no way embarrassed by the direct gaze.

Hopalong ignored this question, and instead of answering it, asked one of his own:

"Where're yore deppeties?"

"Plumb tired out. I left 'em tryin' to make up on some lost sleep. Why?"

"Yore trail cutter had some friends with him," explained the trail boss.

"Reckon so," admitted the sheriff, smiling again. "I was kinda figgerin' on whittlin' 'em down to my own size."

A warm smile flashed across the face of the trail boss. This was the kind of talk he could appreciate. The sheriff looked like he might be able to do a good job of whittling—a mighty good job.

"You was goin' after that bunch alone?" he asked.

"I draw down my pay for sheriffin'," replied the officer, his smile growing. "An awful lot of my time is spent loafin'. That's fat; but sometimes there's some lean, an' lots of it—I got to take th' one with th' other. This is th' lean. So I'm goin' after 'em alone. I'll mebby change my mind after I see th' lay of th' land. Just th' same, I'll shore be obliged to you for whatever you can tell me about 'em."

Hopalong laughed, and then his face grew keen from speculation.

"Reckon I can tell you quite a lot," he said. "You know, I been watchin' th' side of th' trail, lookin' for a pair of boots. I wonder how close I guessed?"

The sheriff raised one side of his big hat, gentiy scratching under it, and his expression was one of admiring respect. He was beginning to like this red-haired gawk from the south. This trail boss had brains, and brains were so scarce as to be at a premium.

"Dirty Smith found th' boots," he said, his keen eyes on those of his companion. "Dirty is a nester, a little southwest of here, on Crooked Crick. He was drivin' in to Buffalo for a load of supplies. That's what *he* said. I figger he was drivin' in for a skinful of liquor. His hosses shied an' like to run away with him. Dirty got 'em in hand an' circled back to see what had scared 'em. He got one quick look at somethin' curious just as th' team bolted again. It looked like Hoke Redfield, our trail cutter. Dirty circled again, an' this time th' team behaved. It was Hoke. He was lyin' in th' brush with one boot out in plain sight. Th' back of his head was mostly missin'. There warn't no papers on him. Yore guess was right good."

Hopalong nodded.

"That was about th' way I figgered it," he said thoughtfully. "Is there any C 80 cattle outfit hereabouts, or back along?"

"Not none registered in our county brand book," answered the sheriff. He was still trying to read his companion's face. "Seems like, for such a good guess, you musta had somethin' purty damn right to figger by. I know how you fellers feel about trail cutters, an' I know they shore are a nuisance to a driver; but you got to admit th' right of it."

"I ain't got no bone to pick with a real an' decent cutter," replied Hopalong slowly. Blood surged into his face as anger flickered across it like heat lightning. "If it had been yore friend Hoke who had demanded a cut, I'd likely been saved a heap of trouble. Th' feller that killed him an' stole his papers shore raised hell with us. That was some days back. Yo're mebby headin' th' wrong way. Anyhow, you don't need no deppeties."

"That's a right consolin' thought," replied the sheriff, this time scratching under an armpit. "You lose many head?"

"Sixty, temporary. We got 'em all back ag'in. Every last one. You don't need no deppeties."

The sheriff pondered the last statement, a statement twice repeated. His eyes twinkled. Evidently homicide had been perpetrated in his jurisdiction; and, also evidently, it was justifiable homicide, and still evidently, it saved him the job of doing the same thing. These men were strangers, this trail boss and his crew, with a valuable herd on their hands. They would not want to be held up by any legal red tape. He decided not to press for certain details, and he scratched again, this time more vigorously.

"Take yore word for that," he said, with a faint chuckle. "I figger you most generally know what yo're talkin' about. You don't reckon you'd like to tell me about th' *other* things that happened, do you?"

Hopalong nodded and produced the papers of the defunct trail cutter. He handed them over without a word and waited patiently while the officer examined them.

The sheriff folded them carefully and slowly put them into a pocket, and then looked with interest at the silent trail boss.

"How come you got holt of 'em?"

Hopalong told him.

"I'll bet you two bits you got C 80 critters in yore herd," said the sheriff, grinning broadly.

"From what I've seen of you, I'd shore never figger that you'd bet with a total stranger on a shore thing," replied Hopalong, also grinning.

"An' that spot of blood," mused the sheriff. He looked up. "Young man, you got a right smart head on you. You wasn't guessin' about them boots, not by a damn sight. How many was in th' gang?"

Hopalong told him.

"How many are left?"

Again Hopalong told him.

"Hell!" swore the sheriff, glancing southward in indecision. His face brightened. "An' I reckon yo're shore right about me headin' th' wrong way; but——" he said, again changing his mind, and became silent.

"They mebby have their headquarters past where I turned back," said the trail boss. "All I wanted was th' cattle. Or mebby they was just circlin' through that country to lose us."

"Which you ain't told me nothin' about," reproved the sheriff. "You fellers will be usin' this trail ag'in, you an' yore friends. Th' safer it is, th' better it'll be

for you. An' Hoke was a likable feller. You figger
you'd like to tell me anythin'?"

Nodding, Hopalong told what there was to tell,
strictly from his own viewpoint, and described the
men who had been overtaken with the stolen cattle.
The sheriff listened attentively, nodding occasionally;
but when he heard the descriptions of the riders his
nods became more emphatic.

"Reckon I know about who they are," he observed
slowly. "Mebby I shoulda said *was*," he added, seemingly as an afterthought. He really was voicing an in-
quiry, which was made plain by his inflection.

"Don't reckon you need to bother with 'em," replied the trail boss. "I told you that you didn't need
no deppeties."

"Uh-huh," grunted the peace officer. "Which one
of 'em was th' boss?"

"None of 'em. Th' boss wasn't with 'em; neither he
nor th' feller I had to shoot, back on this trail."

"Then you ain't described them two yet?"

"I was holdin' 'em back while I made up my mind,"
replied the trail boss, smiling grimly.

"You figger to get 'em yoreself?" asked the peace
officer mildly.

"Reckon that was in my mind, but I dunno. I kinda
hoped I'd run acrost 'em; but I shore wasn't figgerin'
on wastin' no time in huntin' 'em up. I got a herd of
cattle on my hands."

While they talked, things kept on moving around
them. The chuck wagon had become lost to sight over

a rise. The front ranks of the herd drew steadily nearer, and the two men rode off the trail to let the animals pass. The sheriff was watching the plodding steers, and he nodded in sudden appreciation.

"Finest-lookin' critters I've seen in years, all in one bunch," he said, his gaze shifting from brand to brand, and then resting mildly on his companion's face. "You ain't said what th' boss trail cutter looked like," he suggested.

Hopalong described that interesting person, and the sheriff rubbed his chin thoughtfully.

"Common kinda coyote," he growled. "I know three, four men that that would describe. Two of 'em can be throwed out at th' start. That leaves Lou Mays an' Lon Hardy. H'm'm'm." He was silent for a moment and then nodded. "Well, that's a help, at that. I know where they hang out. Right in my own home town. There's a place over east, too, that might stand a combin'. Sorta hangout, it is."

Hopalong's expression did not change, but he knew about the hangout over east. He had good cause to remember it.

"Well," said the sheriff, "seein' I've rid so far, reckon I might as well go farther: that trail you follered, over southwest, might lead to their headquarters. I might find that wounded feller there. What you say he looks like?"

Hopalong laughed, but described the man he had shot a few days before.

"I figger he's a stranger to me," said the peace officer, with regret. "There's lots of strangers movin' around these days. Anybody that's got a right to throw yore herd up for a cut will shore have new papers, seein' we got th' old uns. I'm keepin' these, if you don't care. See you up at th' pens, mebby."

Hopalong glanced at the edge of the papers sticking out of an upper vest pocket, nodded, replied to the parting salute, and swung in behind the drag, his eyes critically studying the drag rider. Billy's wound apparently was getting along all right—at least the drag man was looking good. He said a few words to Billy and then passed the flankers on the left side of the herd and finally slowed at Lanky's side up on left point. Lanky concealed his curiosity and merely grunted a welcome.

"You don't have to worry no more about drivin' west so as to get on th' other side of th' state line," said the trail boss with a knowing smile. "We didn't commit no felonies when we turned back them trail cutters an' took their papers."

"Wrong man had th' papers, huh?" replied Lanky. "I figgered it that way."

"Like hell you did!" retorted the trail boss. "You was scared we'd all be put in jail."

They jogged along in silence for several hundred yards, the sound of the smoothly moving herd like music in their ears. Then Hopalong spoke again.

"I was just talkin' with th' sheriff," he said needlessly.

"Saw his badge," grunted Lanky and gently urged

an erring steer back where it belonged. As he returned to his chosen point position he looked sharply up the trail at another curling finger of dust. "Here comes Pete. He'll say th' crick's wet, like it *allus* is." He shot a sidewise glance at his companion and decided to rub it in. "Which any damn fool knows."

"I'd rather have *you* think me a damn fool than to be one," retorted the trail boss, pushing ahead toward the distant rider. Lanky grinned and thumbed his nose after his departing boss.

Pete reported that there was plenty of water in the creek, and rode on to relieve Billy from the distasteful job with the drag.

The herd pushed on, the rising and falling shoulders and hips of a thousand cattle, each set seemingly balanced on diagonals, giving a peculiar wavelike effect. The dust soared high, the sun blazed down. Mirage quivered above the heated plain and put ghostly pools and lakes in the hollows along the base of a far-distant ridge. Horns sometimes clicked on horns, and the *clack, shuffle, clack* of thousands of hoofs beat out an unending sound which was almost soporific. Through the mirage the distant chuck wagon, again climbing up a slope, swelled and shrank and took unto itself fantastic shapes and proportions. The herd pushed on.

VIII

THE cook spat into the fire and stirred, shifting his crossed legs. His huge shadow on the canvas cover of his precious wagon joggled and grew suddenly black as the fire fitfully flared.

"Damn th' gypsum water," he growled. "It shore gits my stomach an' bowels."

"We're near past it," said Hopalong, leaning back against his saddle.

"If a feller had three, four weeks of it," said Red thoughtfully, "it'd git him bad. I knowed a couple of fellers that near died from it."

Hopalong nodded, silently reviewing the subject from his own experience. He dug up a depleted tobacco sack, made a cigarette from the dust, and tossed the bag on the fire. He had been thinking about the hangout over east, which the sheriff had mentioned.

"You got any more tobacco, cook?" he asked.

"Not none to speak of," grunted the cook, leaning forward a little. "An' my flour's 'most gone. We got to tighten our belts an' chaw rawhide if this cow expedition goes on much longer." He frowned. "This is th' second time I told you."

"Uh-huh," grunted Hopalong. "Th' first time was

near two weeks ago, an' I reckon I was right when I
coppered it. You shore, this time?"

"Th' tin cup scraped bottom this mornin'," answered the cook. He looked worried, as well he might;
the nearest town, Buffalo, was many miles away.

Hopalong nodded, and a faint smile slipped across
his face.

"Me an' you'll get an early start in th' mornin', with
th' wagon, an' go get some," he said. "You better figger out just what you need. Start off with flour an'
tobacco."

"We're gettin' low on Arbuckle, too," said the cook,
whose love for coffee was almost proverbial, and
straightway lapsed into a near coma caused by intense
thought. Suddenly he looked up. "Th' wagon?" he
asked, in surprise. "Take a couple of weeks in th'
wagon. A pack hoss would be better."

Hopalong shook his head, and his smile grew.

"We won't be gone very long. We'll take th'
wagon."

The cook's expression bespoke a great curiosity.

"Whereat we goin' to git all this stuff?"

"Waggoner's store," answered the trail boss, glancing quickly at Red Connors.

Red stiffened and stared across the fire at his grinning friend.

"An' I never thought of it a-tall!" he exclaimed.
"By Gawd, that's right! We crossed Sulphur Crick
this mornin' an' Gypsum this afternoon: that's right!"
Blood surged into his lean, tanned face, and the fire-

light glinted redly from his high cheekbones. He turned and faced the cook. "Tomorrow mornin', cook, I'll show you where Pete thrun a growed man plumb through a two-inch plank door, an' where Johnny shot a feller right smack through a water barrel."

"Tomorrow mornin' you'll help Lanky bunch th' herd an' step it right along," said the trail boss shortly. He was thinking fast. He had turned a little so he could look out toward the bed ground, where the cattle were peacefully resting, and where he hoped they would continue to rest peacefully until dawn got them up. There were no bummers in the herd, and if they lay down again after their midnight stretch all would be well.

"Ain't I goin' in with you?" quickly demanded Red, with a show of spirit.

"You'll bunch th' herd an' step it right along," repeated Hopalong. "An' th' boys will all stay with 'em, only they'll ride well back in th' brush. All except Billy, behind th' drag. He'll be enough to keep 'em movin' rapid. There's a bunch of thick brush, in some mean, broken country, about two hours up th' trail. Before you get to that, you swing th' herd to th' left, out into th' open, an' you keep it in th' open till after you get past th' next crick. There ain't goin' to be no doors busted down *this* trip, not with a thousan' head on our hands. Besides, we've had one stampede already. One's enough. Time to relieve Johnny an' Pete?"

"We can let th' herd spread out near th' bed

ground," suggested Red, who owned a persistence annoying at times. This was one of those times. "They can look out for themselves for a little while. If you an' cook are goin' in to Waggoner's, then th' whole mess an' boilin' of us are goin' with you."

"I just told you who was goin' in there," retorted Hopalong. "You heard me, didn't you?"

"Shore, I heard you!" snapped Red. "An' you heard me!"

"I been hearin' you 'most all my life," retorted Hopalong. "She goes as I dealt it," he stated, blood surging into his dark face. "I'll git along all right."

"You? Hell, I ain't thinkin' about you! Th' whole Southwest is plumb cluttered up with trail bosses; but, lemme tell you, a good cook is kinda scarce. We can git along without a boss, but we got to have a cook an' chuck wagon!"

"Gettin' high-toned an' all swelled up, ain't you?" jeered Hopalong. "Many's th' time you've got along without no cook, an' with a pack hoss instead of a wagon. Me an' th' cook are goin' in by ourselves."

"You know damn well what kinda honkytonk Waggoner's is!" rejoined Red.

"Waggoner ain't so bad—it was th' crowd that used to gang up in there," retorted the trail boss. "Since we had that ruckus that time, I'll bet you Waggoner's a whole lot sweeter."

"Just th' same, he'll be layin' for you!"

Hopalong smiled, the flickering firelight playing over his face.

"Well, then we'll be even up on *that*," he said. "Push th' cattle right along, Red. We've got 'em this far, an' they've got to go through."

"All right," grunted Red, with reluctance; "but if you two hoss thieves ain't back in camp by dark, *Mister* Waggoner shore is goin' to look like that water barrel of his'n, come mornin'." Despite himself, his frown shifted into a grin as he remembered that water barrel, with a dead man behind it, and two little streams of rainwater squirting gently to the ground.

"We'll be in camp in time for cook to get supper for you all," promised the trail boss, himself grinning. "Time for you to relieve Johnny an' Pete, ain't it? You know how much you have to say when yore relief is late."

Again Red glanced at the alarm clock hanging on the side of the wagon, grunted something, and slowly uncrossed his legs. As he stood up, Lanky also got to his feet. The latter had remained silent, along with the others, preferring to enjoy the little squabble without taking part in it. Skinny and Billy, already rolled up in their blankets, now drifted off to sleep. Everybody knew what would happen over at Waggoner's if the trail boss and cook failed to show up before dark. Red and Lanky tightened their belts, glanced up at the star-riddled sky, and moved slowly toward the picketed night horses over beyond the tongue of the wagon. Leather suddenly squeaked, hoofs sounded loudly and swiftly died out.

The cook, watching the indistinct movements beyond the wagon tongue until the two riders were swallowed up in the night, turned a curious face toward his boss.

"What happened at Waggoner's?" he hopefully asked. He had heard of Waggoner's trail station, but this was the first time he ever had been near it.

Hopalong stirred, came back to the present, tossed a weed stem on the glowing coals and watched it flare up and shrivel.

"Tell you that some time when I don't need my sleep," he grunted, reaching out a hand for the little roll of blankets behind him. He took off his hat, pulled off his boots, unbuckled his crossed belts, and then flipped the blanket roll. Another flip opened them up into a trailer's bed, minus such fancy fixings as a mattress, and in another moment Hopalong was in and between them. He sighed, shifted a little, and relaxed. By the time Johnny and Pete, still grumbling over the lateness of their relief, rode in from the bedded herd and picketed their horses, the trail boss was gently sleeping.

The two men stopped at the water barrel, both making faces as the gypsum made itself known. They each rolled a good-night cigarette and lit it. The cook glanced up from arranging his own blankets and nodded. He pampered himself with a hay-stuffed mattress. In a few minutes shadowy, blanket-swathed figures, feet to the warm glow of the fire, radiated like spokes of a wheel, and the silence of the night was disturbed only by the loud ticking of the noisy nickel alarm clock, pounding away with a generous sounding board behind it. Out in the blackness of the night time dragged slowly past, and then the herd, getting to its feet for a stretch and to change position, blew, grunted, and slowly lay down again. The two guardian riders let their singing drop almost to a hum and kept on with their slow circling.

IX

TOM WAGGONER was a relic of the buffalo-hunting days, days not so far in the past. His part had not been hunting, or even skinning; but he had made a modest stake. His equipment had been a two-horse team, a strong, light wagon, a barrel of trade whisky, and an assortment of tin cups. He would leave town with a full barrel and head out over the prairie for the buffalo hunters' camps and rendezvous, peddling whisky. There was danger in his business, for whisky starts fights; and fights in buffalo hunters' camps were not parlor affairs. There also had been the steadily growing hostility of the Indian tribes as their food supply was slaughtered off and the remainder driven ever southward and out of their territory. Tom Waggoner had survived because he was as hard, as tough, and as vicious as the men among whom he moved.

The buffalo-hunting business did not last long, but another activity grew up as the buffalo were killed off. The growth of the latter depended upon the death of the former: driving cattle over country covered with buffalo was just not done. The first longhorn herds through this section of the country followed, by choice, a difficult trail, but one reasonably devoid of buffalo; the incidental hardships of the poor trail were to be preferred to a better trail through roving buffalo herds.

Waggoner was a whisky peddler, but soon the peddling was done. He adapted himself to the changing conditions without giving up the whisky business, and he did it by digging and building a sod hut within a mile of the cattle trail and west of it. The building had one room, which served as bar, kitchen, and bedroom. There was a small stock of trail necessities, but he placed his chief dependence on his old line of goods.

His was the only shelter, the only habitation for miles around. It was located on the top of the north bank of a small ravine, in the bottom of which was a small but unfailing spring of fairly good water. Farther down the ravine he had thrown up a small dam and thereby made himself a pond, which he surrounded by a rough but strong fence. Trail herd cattle could drink here at one cent a head; and there were periods of varying duration each summer when the pond was a distinct asset.

Naturally enough, Waggoner's became the gathering place for all kinds of men, many of whom had no visible means of support, no visible trade; but who usually had money in their pockets. Cattle were steadily on the move from spring well into the fall, keeping the dust stirred up like a yellow fog. Waggoner's business thrived, and he steadily built up a reserve, which he banked far from his place of business.

The last of the buffalo were killed off or driven onto the Staked Plains or into the wild, rough country

around them. A better cattle trail was discovered farther west, one with better and more plentiful water,
and with better grazing and less thickets. The course
of the herds changed, and followed the new way; but
Waggoner, apparently rooted to the bank of the little
ravine, did not follow. The new trail was west of him,
and a considerable distance away. Earning a living was
not so vital a question for him now: he had earned it
and laid it away; but the trade he was in had become
a part of him, and he kept it going for want of something better to do.

He was a person of some importance. His stand was
a rallying, a gathering point for the men who had become his friends and cronies. The little dam had long
since crumbled away, the fence had been used for firewood; but Tom Waggoner's stand of buildings had
grown. There was now a ramshackle stable, built
against the threat of the swift and punishing assault
of occasional northers; there was a frame building
with a long walnut bar, a cannon stove, round tables,
a score of heavy chairs, and a provision counter with
shelves behind it. A flyspecked chromo of Robert E.
Lee hung askew behind one end of the bar; one of Jeb
Stuart, behind the other end. A long tie rail ran past
the front and along one side of the building. The sod
hut was now a bedroom exclusively, stocked like an
arsenal, its low walls strengthened by a thickness of
adobe. On that great expanse Waggoner's was but a
speck; but it was not unknown up and down the long
frontier. And wherever it was known, it was spoken of

as being as tough a hangout as any of its kind. Its habitués were ex-buffalo hunters and skinners, army deserters, horse and cattle thieves, and others "wanted" in various parts of the country.

The cook drove the wagon, but his boss preferred a horse and rode even with the wagon seat. They passed over the top of a gentle swell and at once the trail was lost to sight. They headed directly into the rising sun, its rays slanting in under the brims of their big hats. Being so early in the morning, it was still cool —even chilly—and the mirage was not yet in evidence. In the dry, clear air, vision seemed to be almost telescopic. The tar bucket, filled with axle lubricant swinging underneath the running gear, jerked at its chain at the end of each swing. The wheels slid back and forth on their thimbles, making a sharp, clacking noise; and occasionally the kingbolt clicked as the strain abruptly changed on a downward slope. The nigh horse clamped his tail over the reins and made the driver swear.

The cook's curiosity was simmering. He was riding straight toward a tough joint where his companions of the trail had fought a battle with its habitués. His foot lifted to the brake handle and eased the wagon down a steep pitch, and as the tugs tightened with the pull up the other slope he glanced at his silent boss. In his mind he was picturing a crashing plank door and seeing little twin jets of rainwater gently squirting from the opposite sides of a water barrel, one of them to spread a crimson stain over the ground. The trail boss was placid, but submerged in thought. The cook cleared his throat inquiringly, but the sound was ignored. After a moment he spoke, loudly.

"What started th' fight at Waggoner's, that time?" he asked, his eyes on the horseman. The reins sagged, and the nigh horse promptly clamped them down.

"Water-hole charges for drinkin' our cattle," growled Hopalong and went back to the business of thinking. Matters of strategy were in his mind. It was always well to think out the lay of the land before-hand. He was searching his memory for details.

"Water-hole fees are regular," asserted the cook, frowning because of deep thought.

"Cent a head: yeah," grunted Hopalong and again submerged.

The cook scratched his head and cogitated. That was right and customary. Again he glanced at his silent and preoccupied companion in the saddle.

"Nobody had no cause to fight about that," he stated dogmatically.

"No," grunted the trail boss.

Silence ensued.

The cook squirmed and tried again. There was some mystery here; he had always found his companion to be fair-minded.

"How come there was a fight, then?"

"Water fees: ten cents a head," growled the trail boss, somewhat irritably, and resumed his thinking.

"Great —— ——!" said the cook, his mouth open-ing. "*Ten* cents a head!"

This marvel occupied him for perhaps a minute as he turned it over and over in his mind. Color surged into his face. Ten cents a head: just like holding a man up and taking his money. It was worse than that, even. Why, even an idiot knew that a cent a head was the regular price. Phew! Again he glanced at his companion and then at the rear end of the nigh horse. A sudden jerk freed the reins from the tail which held them clamped down, and caused both horses to turn swiftly to the left. He got them straightened out and said unkind things to the nigh horse.

"Did you pay 'em?" asked the driver, holding the reins high, out of the reach of that damned, persistent tail.

"Yeah: with lead," grunted the trail boss. "Yo're as per-sistent as a fly before a rain!" he growled, glaring at the cook, and forthwith sank back into the depths of his thinking. The picture was clear now.

Hopalong was getting the buildings arranged in his mind as they had been at the time of his last visit. The stables joined onto the wagon shed, and the wagon shed joined onto the main building at the rear, and on the south side. Joined to the wagon shed were the stables, and against them on the south was a closed shed for holding firewood, harness, and junk. This also butted against the rear, north corner of the sod dugout, whose door opened against it. The wagon shed was open to the east. A man could pass through the whole range of buildings without being visible to anyone on the trail side, the front. He could leave the store and saloon and gain the shelter of the dugout fort without showing himself to anyone who might ride up from the direction of the new cattle trail. From the east he could be seen, perhaps, passing through the open wagon shed. Hopalong unconsciously nodded: it was a right good layout and well worth the thought which had been bestowed upon its construction. Then a new thought struck him obliquely: why hadn't Waggoner moved when the trail shifted, so as to be handy to it for the selling of supplies and drink to the trail outfits?

"How come Pete thrun that feller through a plank door?" asked the cook, glancing quickly at his boss.

"Pete was in a hurry, in a damn tough place, an' th' door was closed," explained the trail boss an: again mentally submerged.

Again the cook savagely jerked the reins from under the nigh horse's tail and damned the animal in no uncertain language; but he was careless a moment later and let the reins sag; and again the nigh horse clamped down on them, and again was heartily damned.

The air close against the earth now began to simmer and dance. A blur outlined distant objects, and they quivered and became distorted. The hatbrims now adequately served their destined purpose against the direct rays of the sun, and the heat steadily increased. The tar bucket jerked against its chain, the nigh horse again caught the driver unawares, and the wheels slid back and forth on the thimbles. Behind them lay a faint line of dust, but the stirring wind kept it there. A flint-covered flat was covered, another long slope mastered, and then the wagon stopped for a breather which was not needed. A line of indistinct warts sat perched on the edge of a ravine, bleached silvery gray by many suns. Tom Waggoner's trail station was now in sight. The two men regarded it thoughtfully.

Down on Red River it was Doan's; up here, Waggoner's. They were similar only in the fact that they both served travelers. Doan's was law-abiding, a mail point, and gave no invitations to outlaws. Doan's was reputable and a godsend to trail outfits.

Hopalong sat quietly in the saddle, considering a point which had been well debated. Should he ride in with the wagon, from the front, and perhaps put himself at the mercy of some hidden watcher; or should he turn aside, ride in a circle, and come up from the rear, toward the open side of the wagon shed? Time had passed since his last visit, and time blurred a man's memory; but it was to be doubted if Waggoner ever would forget anything connected with that fight.

He looked at the cook.

"Head straight for th' door," he said. "They've never seen you before. Jog along an' take it easy. Comin' from th' trail like you are, in a chuck wagon, they'll know what you want as soon as they see you. There ain't nothin' to make 'em suspicious. I'm driftin' south, keepin' off ridge tops. I'll get there just about th' time you do. If everythin' goes sweet they won't know that I'm around, mebby. Let th' liquor alone, don't waste no time, an' pull out for th' trail as soon as you can."

The cook gathered up the reins, swore deeply at the

nigh horse, and watched his companion ride off down the hollow behind the ridge. He started the team and jogged along toward the distant warts, which steadily came nearer. Several horses could now be seen, and then the tie rails to which they were fastened. Then he could see a dusty flour barrel through the grimy window near the left-hand wall. The wagon stopped, and the cook climbed stiffly down. He stretched his cramped muscles and lazily moved around to the head of the team, to tie it to the rail. He heard a door open and glanced up to see a bearded man standing on the threshold.

The cook grinned, pushed the Stetson back on his head, and reached for the tobacco tag hanging out of an upper vest pocket.

"Mornin'," he said cheerfully.

"Mornin'," grunted Waggoner, his gaze on the brand of one of cook's horses. He appeared to be a little puzzled and uneasy. Neither of the brands was Bar 20; but cook could see the man's memory scratching in the litter of the past.

"Got a empty flour barrel," said the cook. "Near out of tobacco, too. Could use a little more bacon and sow belly with our beans. How you fixed?"

"Got all you need," answered Waggoner. "Where you from?" he asked carelessly. His eyelids drew a little closer together.

"Down south," answered the cook, which anybody would have known without being told.

"Trailin'?" asked the proprietor needlessly. His eyes were on the chuck wagon, taking in its details.

"Yeah," answered the cook and then yielded to an inspiration to lie: "Old man bought a beef herd down south an' sent us down to bring it home."

"What's yore road brand?" asked the proprietor, stepping back into the room so that the cook could enter.

The cook thought swiftly. Any statement regarding road brands could be checked up. This man might even know the brand right now. He voted himself a medal and told the truth:

"Circle 4. I better lay in another jug of sorghum, too, while I got th' chance. Strikes me yo're considerable off th' trail, for a trader."

"That's so," admitted Waggoner, turning toward the supply side of the big room. "They shifted th' trail. Too much trouble to move an' build again. How come you knew about me an' where to find me?"

Cook could now see the other end of the room, where five men had temporarily suspended a card game to interest themselves in Waggoner and the customer. One of them stood up to look through the front window at the chuck wagon. Strata of blue tobacco smoke wavered in the sunlight near a side window, climbing or dipping with the slow and lazy air currents.

"Met a feller goin' down th' trail an' started pow-wowin'," answered the cook. He threw a heavy sack of flour on a shoulder, bracing his arm by a hand on a hip, and turned toward the door. As he did so the proprietor slid a molasses jug across the counter, and the cook hooked a finger of his free hand through the handle. In a few moments he was back again, to point out the rest of his needs, and then he looked idly around the room as the proprietor tossed the rest of the order into a big wooden cracker box, laboriously added up the little column of figures, and announced the total. Cook dug deep down into a pocket and brought up a handful of hard money, paid the bill in silver dollars, and pocketed the change.

"Have a drink," invited the proprietor. It was not a question.

"Shore will," said the cook, ignoring the good advice of his boss. One little drink would not hurt a man; do him good, instead. The trouble with that is that there is no such formula, not under the vicious American customs regarding drinking.

Waggoner put a glass and bottle on the bar, shoving them both toward the customer. Cook had one, a good one; and then, of course, Waggoner had to have one with him. This stuff was powerful and had no gypsum flavor. He grinned, carefully adjusted his hat, and looked at the waiting card players. He waved a hand at them and chuckled. He was beginning to feel warm and friendly.

"You hombres ain't afeared of a little hard liquor, are you?" he asked.

An unshaven horse thief slowly pushed back his chair and stood up.

"Naw," he grunted, moving toward the bar ahead

of his friends. "Naw," he repeated. "I kin lay down right alongside a jug of it ary time." He laughed while he considered the amount of supplies he had just seen bought. He could use those supplies, he and his friends. "If I had a mind ter, I could show you who's afeard of good liquor," he boasted. "There ain't no man outa Texas who can drink even with me, glass fer glass."

"Hell there ain't!" retorted the cook, motioning for the proprietor to slide out more glasses. He was not out of Texas, but that was a detail of no moment. He was out of the South, and Texas was in the south. It became a sectional matter. This bartender had the right idea: one bottle for one end of the line-up, and another bottle for the other end. Saved reaching and pushing. Saved time, too. After these thoughts had registered he paid no more attention to the bottles, and therefore found no significance in the fact that he alone drank from the bottle nearest him. Had he tasted of the second bottle he might have detected the flavor of gypsum water.

Time passed, the level of the liquor in the bottles steadily lowered, and the level of the cook's common sense kept equal pace with it. Finally:

"Tha's right," boasted the cook. "Bar 20. You fellers look funnier ev' minute. Jes one li'l drink before I go. Shore: it was Pete—he thrun that coyote right plumb through a plank door. Yeah. I heard about that, too: shot him through a water barrel. . . ."

X

THE trail boss stopped his circling, rode slowly up the slope of the gentle rise until he could just see over it, and scrutinized the distant trail station. He was south of it, and the building nearest to him was the original sod hut. It had no windows on that side, and the door of the shed next to it was closed. By riding on a little farther he could get the shed between him and the two windows of the main building.

The only sign of life was the chuck wagon and the saddle horses at the tie rail. He backed down the slope and rode on again. It should not take long now for the cook to load up and get started; and, consequently, there was as yet no reason for Hopalong to get closer to the buildings. He stopped again, waiting patiently in the saddle. From where he was he would be able to see the chuck wagon a few minutes after it left the store. From the time which already had passed, it should not be long before the cook left. As soon as Hopalong saw the wagon moving across the flat he would retrace his own trail and join the cook at about where he had left him. There was no reason to be apprehensive: the cook was in no real danger if he followed instructions. Hopalong had accompanied him just to be on the safe side.

The sun climbed higher, and the shadows crept closer to the weeds which cast them. There was no sign of the chuck wagon; also there still was no sign of life around the buildings. Could the cook have driven from the store at such an angle that he had been screened by it? He must have left by now. Suddenly Hopalong wanted to have a look at the tie rail —and as quickly as he could. To ride back as he had come would take up too much time and put him too far from the station in case he should be needed. There was one thing to do, and only one. He pressed his knees against the horse and pushed up the slope, over the crest and into the open.

When he approached the shed he was a little in the rear of the line of buildings, screened by them from the sight of anyone in the store; but for effect he hid his desire for speed and rode nonchalantly, innocently. Reaching the buildings, he swung from the saddle and stood motionless for a moment, listening and thinking. Then he slipped into the closed shed, peered through a crack between the boards, and saw the tailboard of the chuck wagon. It made him swear. The wagon was right where the cook had left it, the team tied to the rail. He knew the answer to that: a few drinks—and what that meant: too much talking. He slipped outside, stared at the horse for a moment, and quickly made up his mind. So far his presence was not suspected, but it would be if they saw the horse.

He led the animal into the shed he had just quitted and closed the door upon it. Then he stepped around

into the open wagon shed and paused as the murmur
of voices came to him. A covered freight wagon shared
his quarters with him. It had been backed in, and its
tongue lay on the ground under it. Waggoner took
good care of it. Its canvas cover was closed at the rear
end, leaving only a small oval opening the size of a
man's head in the exact center, just above where the
pucker rope crossed itself.

Hopalong peered through this opening, and then,
moving swiftly along the side of the vehicle, climbed
the front wheel, and was almost instantly swallowed
up.

The murmuring voices persisted. He would wait a
few more minutes and then take the bull by the horns.
Damn a man who had to drink in spite of hell and high
water; and doubly damn a man who could not stop in
time. Then he heard angry shouts and a screamed
curse, the latter bit off in the middle.

He was climbing down the far front wheel when the
store door opened and a man jumped through it, ran
through the wagon shed, and darted around the corner of the stables, in too much of a hurry to open the
doors which stood in his way. He was in such a hurry
that he did not see the puncher crouched down against
the wheel of the big wagon.

Hopalong froze for a moment longer and heard the
man hammering on the door of the dugout, calling
eagerly to someone within. The trail boss slipped
around the front of the wagon and leaped for the open
door of the store. He slipped into the big room as

three men were carrying the limp form of another through the front door, which was being held open by Waggoner. The fourth man had picked up the cook's hat and was slowly following his companions. If they heard the trail boss they took it for granted that it was their friend returning. The man holding the hat was speaking.

"Take out th' supplies first an' then dump him in an' turn th' wagon loose." The speaker laughed. "If anybody rides up to ask questions, Tom can tell 'em that this coyote bought liquor exclusive. He'll mebby have to tell 'em somethin' because they can track th' wagon here."

"If it wasn't for that I'd fill him full of lead—may do it, anyhow!" growled one of the trio carrying the cook.

"I'd do it now, only he's a new man an' wasn't with 'em that time," said Waggoner.

Hopalong had stepped back so as to have the side door well in front of him.

"Better drop him where you are," he said, grimly and evenly, over a pair of Colts.

Five heads jerked around, five pairs of eyes regarded him with amazement. The five expressions changed from strained incredulity to even more strained belief. The man carrying the hat closed his mouth, and the three carriers let loose of their burden. The jar of the fall momentarily brought the cook back to consciousness, which he proved by kicking one man in the pit of the stomach and another on a shin.

The first doubled up in agony and the second man's eyes filled with tears as he grabbed at the shin with both hands.

Waggoner's hands went up slowly, grudgingly. He was too experienced a hand to become foolish in such a situation. There might be a break in the luck. The hat bearer and the man nearest the door followed his lead, swearing under their breath. There came the sound of running feet out in the wagon shed. Waggoner opened his mouth to shout, but the slight shift of a gun muzzle made him change his mind. The lucky break had not yet come. The bewhiskered bully who could drink down any man out of Texas leaped into the room, stiffened as he slid across the floor, and raised his hands with a jerk.

"You get up there with th' rest of 'em!" growled the trail boss in a low voice. "Not a sound out of you. I'm waitin' for yore friend of th' dugout. I'm Bar 20: Waggoner can tell you what *that* means. Get!"

Other steps hurried across the wagon shed, and the occupant of the dugout popped in through the door. It was the boss trail cutter of only a few days before. He caught sight of the newcomer as he crossed the threshold, and leaped back, reaching for a gun as he jumped. The crash of Hopalong's .44 filled the room and shook the bottles on the back bar. Heads seemed to swell with the concussion. The man who had leaped backward struck the ground outside flat on his back, one booted foot caught by a spur and held grotesquely upward on the second board of the steps.

Hopalong shuffled forward, his two guns waist

high. One quick glance at the quiet cook told him how
utterly useless that worthy was. His eyes rested on
Waggoner, and he smiled faintly. That smile sent a
shiver up Waggoner's back.

"I told you once that I'd shoot you on sight," said
the trail boss, evenly. " 'Tain't necessary. Unbuckle
yore belt an' drop it at yore feet. . . . Good. Now
step back, ag'in th' bar."

Hopalong watched him for a moment and then
glanced swiftly at one of the others.

"You with th' hat! Do th' same thing, pronto!"
The trail boss nodded as the man lined up with the
proprietor, and gave the same orders to the others.
When they were all in line, he spoke again:

"Turn around slow, all of you."

They slowly turned around.

"Waggoner, you back over here to me. I'm prayin'
somebody makes a motion!"

Motions were out of order.

One by one they were searched from behind and
then grouped again. Hopalong walked to the prostrate cook, unbuckled his gun belt, jerked it from under
him, buckled it again, and slung it over his own shoulder. He holstered one gun, shoved the other forward
suggestively, and scooped up the rest of the gun belts
with his free hand. They slid over his forearm and
made quite a weight.

"Pick up that drunken damn fool, all of you, an'
put him in th' wagon," ordered the trail boss crisply.

He followed the slowly moving procession, and
after the cook was placed in the wagon with unjustified

tenderness, he lined them all up again, this time against the front of the store. Jerking at the tie rope of the nearest saddle horse, he freed it and climbed into the saddle.

"All right," he said with a flourish of the gun. "Get started, an' head west."

"What you aimin' to do?" demanded Waggoner with sullen rage.

"Shoot th' next man that opens his mouth!"

"Hell you say!" growled the erstwhile hat bearer and grabbed his own hat as the black-powder smoke rolled toward him. He sucked in his breath and froze in his tracks.

"Get started!" snapped the trail boss, waving the gun westward.

One mile. Two miles. Then the horseman left them to their own society and returned to the buildings at a gallop. He collected the remaining horses and tied them, with the one he had ridden, to the rear end of the wagon box. This done, he ran into the store, grabbed all the rifles in sight, and smashed them against the big cannon stove. The rifles were ruined and so was the stove. The last gun was a Sharps special buffalo rifle, with the ten-pound barrel. The total weight was seventeen pounds. When that gun struck the cast-iron side of the stove, Waggoner was out just what it cost him.

Hurrying through the side door, Hopalong gave one quick glance at the fictitious trail cutter, and without pausing went on to the closed shed. In a moment he was out again, leading his horse. In another moment he was around in front, tying it with the others. Distant figures were running toward him, waving arms.

He freed the team from the tie rail, climbed into the seat, and departed in a generous cloud of dust. Tied to the framework beside him was the cook's rifle. Behind the wagon every horse carried its owner's rifle in the saddle scabbard. He laughed at the idea of pursuit, now or later.

Perhaps an hour had passed when he stopped the team near an upthrust ridge of rock, climbed down, and went back to the captured saddle horses. He took the rifles out of the scabbards, unsaddled the animals, and turned them loose, leaving the saddles where they had fallen. One by one he whirled the rifles high over his head and brought them down against the rock ridge. In every case one swing was enough. Climbing back into the wagon, he sent the team forward again, and for the next half-hour amused himself with the captured hand guns. He took them one at a time, removed the cylinder and then threw the frame off in one direction and the cylinder in the other. He took plenty of time between each throw, and he had disposed of the last part when the cook moaned, stirred, and tried in vain to rise on one elbow.

"Whas masser?" mumbled the culinary artist in slobbery tones.

"You—go—to—hell!" grated the driver. He looked for the roughest ground he could find and sent the team on at a gallop. Once or twice the cook's head struck resoundingly against the hard floor of the wagon box, and he passed out again.

XI

THE chuck wagon wandered a little, but it held fairly well to the proper course, the team knowing its job and doing it with small aid from the driver. The driver was the cook, and a mighty sick cook, at that: for him it was the morning after the day before, and all the well-known symptoms were present, with various bruises added.

The herd shuffled along in the dust, sending the yellow fog streaming into the air, minute after minute, mile after mile. Lanky Smith now rode at left point, for the trail boss had given himself another job. The corresponding place on right point was proudly handled by Johnny Nelson, youngest of the riders. Occasionally he yielded to a certain restrained eagerness and turned in his saddle to look behind him on his right. He was looking for signs of war, but all he saw was grim preparedness: two distant riders moving parallel with the plodding herd and a little behind it. He thoughtfully rubbed his chin, and the motion reminded him of Red Connors's uncalled-for criticism of two days before. He flushed and faced around again: just because he didn't have a beard was no sign that he wasn't a man. In this he was right, for a great deal of the history of the West was written by beardless youths. During his abstraction two steers had pushed out from the herd and started for a distant bunch of grass, which was exactly no better than the bunches in front of them. Others pushed out to follow them, and Johnny was busy for a moment.

Behind him Johnny heard a voice raised in song, telling Susannah not to cry. He wondered why anyone should feel like singing in all the dust and heat, and then he grinned as the question answered itself: Billy Williams was glad to get away from the smother of dust which he had so long endured as drag rider. Misery, too, is comparative.

Again Johnny turned around in the saddle, this time all the way around, and rested one hand on the back of his horse. He tried to pierce the thick dust cloud for a glimpse of the drag, which was now getting along on its own, and then gave it up. The dust was like a curtain. However, he did see a vague figure rising and falling in the fog, and he replied to the cheery wave. Billy's song continued uninterrupted, and the herd pushed on, heads bobbing, hips and shoulders rising and falling, and the imponderable dust blanketing everything. Thirty dollars a month and found; constant discomfort, potential dangers ever present, double and treble tricks with the herd instead of sleeping the short nights through when stormy weather threatened. But it got into a man's blood, crept among the fibers of his being. Johnny himself began to sing Billy's air; but the words he chose cannot be put into the record.

Over east of the slowly moving herd the trail boss, a mere youth himself, jogged silently along beside his silent companion, who was another youth. Now and again one of the two would pivot at the waist and look searchingly behind them over the shimmering plain.

"I don't reckon they'll be botherin' us today," said the trail boss, grinning widely. "I busted their guns, an' they got nothin' to ride."

"Then why you lookin' behind you?" jibed Red Connors.

Hopalong sighed.

"Because I got this damn herd on my hands," he answered. The weight of responsibility rested squarely on his shoulders. "I wish Buck would meet us at Bulltown an' handle th' money part of it hisself."

Red nodded and absent-mindedly stroked the lean stock of the Sharps rifle bobbing before his knee. The money part consisted of taking care of a draft and being certain that it was in proper order; or the handling and carrying of money. A possibility for future trouble popped up in Red's mind, and he chuckled. A thousand dollars in silver would weigh sixty-two and one half pounds,* which any southern cowman knew. This herd, delivered into the shipping pens, would mean in the neighborhood of twenty thousand dollars. He gave up the mental arithmetic and chuckled again.

"Suppose they pay you in hard money?" he brightly asked, his grin threatening the safety of his ears.

---

*Note by author: This was the customary computation in use on the southern ranges at the time of this story.

"Suppose you go to hell!" growled his companior indignantly. "Ain't I got trouble enough now, without you pilin' it on?"

"Boy, wouldn't that old wagon jingle goin' home?" pursued Red with relish.

Hopalong turned in the saddle and looked backward and then eased around again. Red looked at him and laughed.

"Takin' care of th' money already, huh?" he prodded. "Thought you said you busted all their guns an' turned loose their cayuses?"

"Shut up!" snapped Hopalong. "That feller Job had his boils, but, by Gawd, he didn't have you!"

Mile after weary mile jolted along behind them, and then Red saw the chuck wagon pop into sight as it rolled over the crest of a distant rise.

"I've been on a couple of hellbenders, myself," he admitted; "but cook shore wins th' prize. When he put his hat on this mornin' he held it a foot above his head an' then lowered it plumb slow an' gentle." His sudden burst of laughter startled the horses.

Hopalong swore under his breath.

"Th' damn jughead!" he snapped. "Lemme tell you that I figger to bear down hard on any man in this outfit that takes a drink of hard liquor before we get home ag'in!" His growl drifted into silence.

"There you go!" snorted Red indignantly. "All dressed up in yore eagle feathers an' wampum! You shoulda brought yore Sunday school along to trail these steers!" He glared and continued almost without taking breath: "You can start bearin' down on me any time you want, for I shore aim to drink some hard liquor right pronto after we turn these animals loose at Bulltown!"

"Oh, is that so?"

"Yes, that's so!"

"I can wait till you start!" snapped the trail boss.

"Suit yoreself!" retorted Red.

"You sound more like yoreself now!" sneered the trail boss.

"An' you'll mebby find that I'll *act* more like myself when you start bearin' down onto me!"

"Yeah?"

"Yeah!" snapped Red.

Hopalong snorted and then stood up in his stirrups, the better to see. He looked straight ahead, long and searchingly.

"There's a branch trail comes in, up yonder," he said. "So far we've had lots of room an' ain't been crowded."

Red nodded his agreement to both statements. Their herd had seemed to be the only one on the trail, but he knew that this was just the luck of the spacing. Cattle stretched ahead of them almost to the Canadian line and behind them to the Gulf Coast, all moving, all sending the dust aloft.

"We'll be comin' into dust that ain't our own," he said, also peering ahead.

"Yeah," agreed his companion.

Again a period of silence. They dipped down into

the little depression between the two rises and then rode slowly up the farther slope. At the crest they drew rein.

"If it wasn't for th' heat waves, I'd figger that was dust," said the trail boss; "an' there ain't no wind," he added significantly.

"No wind a-tall," grunted Red. "If it's dust, it's being stirred up by hoofs," he said and rode forward at the side of his friend.

They gradually edged over toward the herd, which moved over the hot plain like some huge, varicolored worm. Then Hopalong said something out of the side of his mouth and pushed ahead at a lope. Red looked up the trail and forthwith spurred to overtake his friend. A solitary rider was coming down it, an animated blob in a little cloud of dust.

They passed the herd and kept on riding, and the stranger pulled up at the side of the trail to wait for them. He was smiling, but they were not. He raised a hand in salute, but they ignored it. Then Red saw a paper sticking out of a pocket in the stranger's vest and swore.

"Trail cutter! Great Gawd, ain't they got nothin' else in this part of th' country?"

Hopalong ignored the outburst, nodded to the solitary horseman and stopped at his side. The trail cutter's gaze had flicked to the brands on the punchers' horses and away again.

"Howdy," he said, with a smile.

"Howdy," answered Hopalong without friendliness.

"What's yore road brand?" asked the stranger carelessly.

"Circle 4," grunted Red shortly.

The cutter nodded, offered his tobacco sack and papers to his two companions, and in turn rolled a cigarette. The three men sat smoking in silence, their eyes on the slowly approaching herd. Hopalong made a slow gesture, and in answer to it the riders with the cattle opened up the herd. The animals plodded past, spread out so that the brands on most of them could be seen. The road brands were uniformly just back of the left shoulder; the range brands, according to the marks. There wasn't a vent brand on the lot, which meant that they had never been sold or traded. The herd went by, the curling dust rolling over it, and slowly closed up again. The cutter glanced at the inconsequential drag and nodded approvingly.

"Nice bunch," he grunted, once more looking at his companions. They nodded, but said nothing.

"Might be a right good idear not to make too much time along here," continued the cutter. "There's eleven herds ahead of you in th' next thirty miles."

"Great mavericks!" grunted Red.

Hopalong's expression also bespoke surprise, and he looked inquiringly at the cutter.

The trail cutter smiled and explained the situation.

"They found th' Squaw roarin' over its banks," he said. "It's a mean river. After it went down they had to wait for th' bottom to pack an' settle. There's a sight of quicksand in it. Th' first herd that reached it simply had to wait, an' th' others caught up with it. They lost so much time waitin' that they crossed over as soon as they could, all of 'em, an' moved right along, without worryin' very much about spacin'. It was poor feedin' country, an' they wanted to get shut of it. They took a chance, for if any of th' leadin' herds had stampeded, there would have been a mess from there back that woulda taken so much untanglin' that it wouldn'ta been good news for nobody."

Hopalong nodded, but he was not thinking of what might have happened on that trail. He was thinking that what was left of the grazing along the main trail, after eleven closely spaced herds had passed over it, also would not be good news for the Circle 4.

"How far ahead is th' last bunch?" he asked.

"Plenty. Near ten miles."

"Th' feed won't be none too good for us," growled Hopalong.

"You can get by with it," said the cutter. "Th' grass was extry good this year. Th' first three, four herds are keepin' right on th' trail, close-bunched, an' steppin' right along, figgerin' to open up longer gaps an' get outa th' way. They're all range stockers, an' losin' a little weight won't make no difference to 'em."

"Hope they keep on steppin'," growled Red.

"Many beef herds?" asked the trail boss, thinking of the possibility of a glutted market and falling prices, although this contingency did not affect him or his herd.

"Two. Th' others are headed for the open ranges,

north an' west. One of 'em is bound for Dakota, another for Montana, an' one of 'em is goin' clean through to Canada." His eyes glistened, for while he was a cutter now, he had been over the trail with the herds; and once that virus gets into the system, the patient is usually ruined for life—that is, any other kind of life. "*That's* a drive I'd like to be on; but they had a full crew." For a moment he was silent, looking after the placidly moving herd, and then he glanced back along the trail it had followed. "Anythin' behind you?"

"Not that we know about," answered Hopalong. "We ain't had no visitors from th' rear, an' we ain't seen no dust sign behind us."

The trail cutter nodded and regarded the two riders rather closely.

"See anythin' of th' sheriff?" he asked.

"Shore," grunted Hopalong, grinning. "His tail was up, an' he was pawin' th' ground; when he left us he had quit pawin', but his tail was still up. If you should run into him, you better tell him that I got th' fake trail cutter he was gunnin' for. Got him over in Waggoner's trail station."

"You *did?*" quickly asked the cutter. "By Gawd, mister, I'm right glad of that. Did he try to run a cut on you?"

Hopalong explained recent history as briefly as possible, and the three men rode slowly after the herd, talking things over. They passed the feeding branch trail, now deep with dust and littered with broken bushes. Far ahead there was a faint, yellowish tint in the lower sky, where the dust, freshly churned by thousands of hoofs, was still soaring. The trail boss shook his head.

"When we bed down, from now on, it'll shore be well off th' trail," he said.

"Yeah," said Red, nodding. "There's shore a mess of cattle up th' line, an' if anythin' busts loose we want to be well out of th' way."

Hopalong glanced at the trail cutter, a grim smile on his face.

"When you figgerin' to throw us for a cut?" he asked.

"Not yet," answered the guardian of the surrounding range. "I looked 'em over while they walked." He glanced from Hopalong to Red and back again, a grin wreathing his thin lips. "I'll mebby ask for a cut before you get outa my territory, but not before. I don't aim to be no more bother than I have to be. I been up th' trail myself. A cut, down here, with all th' rest of th' range to cross, wouldn't mean anythin'." The grin grew. "I'd only have to cut you ag'in, an' that's plumb foolish."

"Friend," said Hopalong, slowly, "yo're shore one of them fellers we hear about but don't often meet up with. Any time you want to cut us for range cattle you say so. Once, or more'n once. We'll pitch in an' help you trim out th' range strays so fast it'll open yore eyes. An' any time yo're near our wagon, drop in an' sample th' cook's cookin'. You have any trouble cuttin' them herds up ahead?"

"Not yet," chuckled the trail cutter. "I don't figger to cut none of 'em till they're about ready to clear out of my country. That means I got nothin' to do to-day; an' that means I'm droppin' my war bag at yore wagon tonight." He shoved his hat back on his head and sighed. "I'll be plenty busy tomorrow, with three or four herds to cut. Those first few range stockers are steppin' right along."

The herd was watered shortly after noon, and it moved slowly forward again until about four o'clock by the sun, when the riders turned it aside and drove it more than a mile off the beaten track. The distance was none too far, considering how the trail was cluttered up ahead of them. Here it was loosely herded and allowed to spread out and feed unmolested on good range grass, which assured full bellies, which in turn promised a placid night. The weather was clear, with no threat of a storm.

Hopalong rode back to the busy wagon and found the trail cutter lending a helping hand to the sullen cook. He glanced at the culinary artist, but said nothing: the cook was paying for his recent mistakes. Hopalong tossed the reins over the horse's head and for a moment sat quietly in the saddle, looking steadily northward. As he finally swung to the ground the trail cutter, glancing from the clear, dustless air under the northern sky to the trail boss, nodded slowly and spoke.

"Th' feed wasn't so good along th' branch trail from th' Squaw," he said thoughtfully. "Them fellers pushed their cattle purty rapid, to get over it an' onto th' main trail. Th' last two herds I passed, comin' down here today, was spread out an' feedin', which was killin' three birds with one stone. It fed th' cattle up, let 'em rest, an' gave time for th' gaps to open up between th' herds. I figger yo're far enough off th' trail not to worry none about them fellers. Yo're located about right."

Hopalong nodded gravely, and a smile crept over his face. It was a little strained, but it was still a smile.

"Shore, I know that," he replied, "but I figger to keep movin' ahead a little every day. I got a delivery date to think about. I don't want to step on them fellers' heels, an' I don't want to speed up th' pace an' go around 'em. That ain't hardly polite. I've got somethin' in my mind that's been botherin' me all day. Oh, well, what th' hell! Just whereabouts in th' line-up are them two beef herds that you spoke about?"

The trail cutter was regarding him curiously.

"They're th' last two," he answered with a smile. He couldn't understand why his companion should be worrying about anything.

"Well," growled Hopalong, "there are times when I'd ruther see dust in th' sky than not see it. This here is one of them times. I hope to see plenty of it in th' mornin'."

"Somethin's got you worried," said the trail cutter curiously.

"Reckon that's because I'm allus puttin' myself in th' other feller's place," replied the trail boss.

The cutter grinned, said something to the cook, and added a few sticks to the fire.

The shadows lengthened with increasing swiftness, and the heat grew suddenly less. The herd was still grazing, without unified forward movement, its guardian riders purposely keeping well away from it. Men rode in to the wagon, laughing and joking, eagerly waiting for the cook's call. The cavvy fed industriously and paid no particular attention to the departure of the night horses. The wrangler knew what horses would be wanted and had cut them out to save time. Hopalong and the cutter stretched the flimsy rope corral from the front wheel of the wagon and closed the gap after the night horses were inside it. The smell of cooking food followed the air currents to tickle appreciative nostrils, and the eyes of the busy cook turned more often toward the coffee pot nesting on the incandescent coals. Cook held strong prejudices against letting it boil over.

The shadows died out, absorbed by the greater shadow of a ridge which had traveled eastward like a bullet. The cook took three quick steps, grabbed the coffee pot as its contents began to swell, and placed in on the ground near the outer fringe of the fire. He lazily moved a hand and yelled loudly, whereupon action became instant and general. A brief burst of action, of men moving past the tailboard of the wagon, of men seating themselves expertly on the earth with

both hands full, was followed by a silence broken only
by the scraping of steel knives on tin plates, or the
grateful exhalation of some feeding human.

The twilight deepened, and then came darkness
under a suddenly star-stabbed sky. The faint glow of
the fire lighted the faces surrounding it and picked out
the more prominent features, turning some of them
into gargoyles. The trail boss sat as silent and rigid as
a statue, a grave, troubled expression on his face. He
was frozen into the immobility of deep thought; and
from surface indications his thoughts were not pleasant. Responsibility wears heavy spurs.

". . . he climbed right straight up in th' air an'
went over backwards," Johnny was saying.

Hopalong arose and motioned to the speaker and to
Red.

"Take a little ride with me," he ordered and strode
toward his saddled and picketed night horse, closely
followed by his obedient but curious friends. In silence
they mounted and swung into the night, straight
toward the place where the cavvy should be found.
After a short interval of riding a voice hailed them,
and they replied to it and soon joined Pete Wilson.
The horses were still grazing. On Pete's face was a
look of curiosity, masked by the darkness.

"What's th' matter?" he asked, a little sharply.

"Not nothin' *yet;* but we come out to help you shift
th' cavvy," replied Hopalong. "We'll drive it back
acrost th' trail an' hold it there. Red'll stay with you.
You'll have to spell each other."

Grunts of surprise sounded in the darkness.

"What fool idear you got now?" demanded Red, with some asperity.

"One that I've had all day, off an' on," retorted the trail boss. "Come on; let's get busy an' shift this cavvy."

"This may be yore idear of a good time, but it shore ain't mine," growled Red.

"Yo're so damn grouchy you wouldn't know a good time if you saw one," retorted the trail boss. "Come on: quit grouchin' an' let's start!"

They drove the horse herd slowly northward and then on an arc of a circle until it reached a point as far east of the trail as it had been west of it. There the trail boss stopped the driving and quietly watched the cavvy until thoroughly satisfied by its actions that it would settle down.

"Pete, you an' Red can figger out yore shifts to suit yoreselves," said Hopalong, wheeling his mount to face the trail. "Drive 'em back ag'in at daylight."

Red raised an indignant voice in the darkness.

"Wait a minute, Hoppy!" he called, his words clipped. "What you figger yo're doin'? Don't you reckon I need my sleep?"

"I know what I'm doin', an' you'll get yore sleep, some of it, if you ain't bothered; an' I don't reckon you'll be bothered over here," replied the trail boss. "You ain't takin' yore shift with th' cattle, are you?" He continued without giving Red a chance to reply: "While you an' Pete are takin' things easy over here, me an' th' rest of th' boys will be ridin' guard on th' cattle, over west, till sun-up. Them fellers back at Waggoner's have had time to get hosses an' guns. How could they get square? How could they pay us back an' hurt us plenty? By stampedin' an' drivin' off our cavvy. We've already had one sample of a night raid. They could run cayuses a long ways before mornin'. If they did that, then everythin' would purty near go to hell. I've been smellin' trouble 'most all day. They won't be able to find th' cavvy now, unless you go loco an' light a fire for 'em. *We'*ll be in th' spot they'll head for. You an' Pete will mebby have it easy, compared with us." He kneed his horse and spoke to Johnny: "Come on, Kid, let's be ridin'."

"Hey! Listen, Hoppy!" yelled Red frantically, fearing that he was missing a fight. "You'll be needin' me an' my Sharps! Hey! *Listen!*"

Over the sudden drumming of the departing hoof beats came a derisive voice as the trail boss made reply:

"You an' yore Sharps! It'll be too damn dark to see rifle sights. You stay there with Pete!"

Johnny's voice chimed in, jeeringly, eagerly. It was his opportunity to return Red's insult of a few days before, and in Red's own words.

"You got a razor, Red?" he asked, and the Kid's laughter died out swiftly.

Red pushed up his hat with an angry gesture and swore loudly; but that was all the good it did him.

He remained with Pete, whose voice now intruded on his thoughts.

"What shift you want to take?" asked the night wrangler, placidly.

"Any damn shift a-tall!" snapped Red.

Whereupon Pete calmly chose the first shift, which would let him enjoy the comfort of his blanket roll from midnight until dawn.

XII

Hopalong pulled up at the fire, while Johnny rode out to join the two riders with the cattle.

"Between now an' mornin'," said the trail boss calmly, and with a faint smile, "this fire will mebby be right unhealthy." He looked at Billy, who was unrolling his blankets preparatory to turning in. "Fork yore cayuse, Billy, an' foller me."

Billy looked up with some surprise, his hands holding to the blankets. His trick with Red was some hours off.

"Where's Red, an' what's up, Hoppy?" he asked curiously.

"Red's with Pete, an' nothin's up *yet*," answered the trail boss. "Roll up them blankets an' come along with me." The speaker turned, as Billy obeyed, and looked down at the cook and the trail cutter.

"I don't know where to send you fellers," he slowly said; "but I figger almost any place will be healthier than this. Th' darker it is, an' th' quieter you keep, th' better off you'll mebby be. Waggoner's gang ain't likely to forget th' blazer I run on 'em. Me an' th' boys will be out with th' herd. Th' cavvy's been shifted. It'll take some time to find it in th' dark, if they can find it; an' if they do find it, Red an' Pete will be waitin' for 'em. We prodded Red before we left, an' he'll be pizen mad till daylight. If you boys want to risk it you can stay right here; but I'd shore copper that if I was you. We'll see you in th' mornin'.''

"Wait a minute!" snapped the trail cutter, remembering that this trail boss had killed the man who had murdered another trail cutter. He was holding that man's job, right now. "I'm a right pore sleeper, an' I crave excitement. Hoke Redfield was a friend of mine. I'm teamin' up with you boys."

"You needn't put on no airs!" snorted the cook, reaching for his boots. "I'm doin' th' same thing. I owe *that* gang a plenty." While he talked he was kicking dirt over the fire. Somehow his head began to feel much better, but he still had a healthy grouch and a Winchester. He fairly yearned for slaughter. He had no horse, but the trail cutter proved to be a friend in need, and the horse did not seriously object to carrying double. In another moment the dead fire stank beside the deserted wagon.

The sleeping cattle lay on the little prairie swell, caressed by a gentle wind. Here or there some animal blew contentedly or chewed its cud in bovine placidity. The two shift riders drifted endlessly on a wide circle around the bedded herd, softly singing and paying no attention to a certain point on the prairie just southeast of them, where reinforcements were hidden by the night. Midnight came and passed, and then there came the sounds of many movements as the cattle got to their feet for a sort of midnight stretch, stood quietly for a few moments and then again lay down, changing sides. Sometimes this was a critical moment, but all was peace and tranquillity on this night.

From the southeast there came a low singing, steadily growing nearer, and the slow, steady beats of walking horses could be heard. The night herder on the side nearer the trail stopped his horse and waited. Two figures pushed into sight and then into a silhouetted definition. They still were singing, and they did their talking in song.

"Well, th' night's half gone an' nothin's happened yet," chanted one of them cheerfully.

"Shore suits me," grunted the shift rider, pressing knees against his horse. "They've just got up an' lay down ag'in. See you at breakfast." He drifted off into the darkness, his relief moving off on the circle.

The second relief man sat quietly in his saddle, waiting for the owner of the barely heard voice to come around to him. A blot in the night grew slowly and became a mounted man. The low chant continued, but its words were now different.

"Any trouble?" he asked, well knowing that if there had been he would have heard it when it started. After two hours of being by himself it was a relief to talk to a human.

"Not none a-tall," softly answered his relief. The speaker yawned prodigiously and grinned in the dark. "Seems like I just got to sleep when Hoppy shook me. Everythin' all right out here?" he needlessly asked.

"Shore," grunted the relieved shift rider, facing in the direction of the dark and silent camp. "They're all yourn now: take 'em. I can use some sleep." He rode away in the night, his place taken by his friend, and the low chanting continued, but in another voice.

The first relieved night rider on his way to camp heard the metallic clicks before he could see anything. He pulled up abruptly.

"All right, Hoppy," he softly called.

"All right: come ahead," said a low voice from the dark ground somewhere to his right.

The rider grinned. This was businesslike. A man lying flat on the ground could see at night for a surprising distance. Anything moving against the faint light of the sky would be visible long before the prone watcher could be seen. The blotting out of the light of a star was all that was needed.

The rider went on again at a walk. When he stopped he could make out the shapeless blots on the ground which were sleeping men. He took care of his horse and returned on foot. In a few moments his blankets were spread, his boots off. In another moment he was asleep.

The second returning rider also heard the sharp clicks. They were on his left. He, too, pulled up abruptly.

"Don't you shoot me," he chuckled. "I reckon nothin's goin' to happen."

"Mebby not," grunted the prone sentry. "Hope not, anyhow."

"Yeah," replied the rider.

"Cattle quiet?" asked the sentry.

"Yeah. They just lay down ag'in."

"You boys ridin' wide of 'em, like I said?"

"Yeah."

"All right. Get yore sleep."

"Reckon Red an' Pete're makin' out all right," said the rider.

"Reckon so. Get yore sleep."

"Buenas noches."

"Good-night," replied the sentry as he turned around to face in the other direction. There was a ridge a little to the south which was silhouetted against the faint light of the sky, and Hopalong watched it closely. His eyes played him tricks, but he knew all about that.

Two hours later was another shift, and still another two hours after that. Dawn paled the eastern sky and stretched its pearly sheet swiftly westward. That strange thing on the ridge which had puzzled the trail boss all night now became two clumps of grass, peculiarly arranged in relation to each other. He grinned at them and stretched.

The sleeping figures in camp stirred restlessly but did not waken. After a moment the cook moved an arm, pushed the blanket from him, and gravely observed a new day, crisp and bright. He sat up, looked around him with an expression of wonderment on his sleepy countenance. Where in hell was —— Then he nodded, turned at the waist, and saw the wagon just where they had left it the night before. He yawned, stretched, and reached for his boots. Shortly thereafter he was on his way to the wagon, there to light his fire and get breakfast started. The riders out with the herd were watching him with a keen interest. They were hungry.

Some distance from the little camp in the other direction Johnny Nelson moved under the hand on his shoulder.

"Yes, Hoppy!" He was wide awake.

"Time to get up, Kid. Cook's headed for th' wagon a'ready."

Johnny nodded and drew on his boots. Then he looked at his friend accusingly.

"You let me sleep right through!"

"Yeah," replied Hopalong. "Somehow I wasn't a mite sleepy." He ignored his companion's protests and looked at the distant herd, now on its feet and already spreading out to feed. Then he glanced at the little temporary camp, and from it on to the wagon. The cook was bending over his economical fire, and the first faint streamer of smoke was climbing skyward, straight as the flight of an arrow.

Things seemed to move even smoother after breakfast. Sleepiness went out of all faces, smiles began to appear. Here and there a snatch of song could be heard. A little good-natured chaffing rewarded the trail boss for his needless precautions of the night before; but the trail boss, enjoying his first cigarette since last night's supper, was placidly looking at the feeding herd, and the pleasantries glanced off his hide like hail from a roof. He saw the cavvy appear, and it brought a grin to his face.

Two men rode off to relieve the riders with the cattle, so the latter could enjoy their breakfasts. Saddle girths were being tested. The fresh mounts had been selected, the night horses turned into cavvy, and the cavvy driven off again, to graze and move forward under the watchful eyes of the day wrangler. For some reason Red had nothing to say, and that meant that everything was serene.

The trail cutter, ready to ride on about his day's business, stopped at the side of the boss.

"Well, they didn't bother you last night," he said with a smile.

"No, they didn't," imperturbably replied Hopalong. "Which was just as well; but that makes it a little more certain for tonight."

"Uh-huh," said the trail cutter for the sake of saying something. He pulled his hat down a little more firmly on his head. "Well, I got me some work to do. I figger to start with th' herds farthest up th' trail an' work back this way. In case I'm anywhere near you tonight I'll join up with you, in case I'm needed."

"Good. Be glad to have you," said the trail boss with a grin. "I shore figger to be waitin' for 'em ag'in tonight. They're mebby due."

"Uh-huh," grunted the trail cutter. "Well, so-long. So-long, cook."

"So-long," said the cook, smiling for the first time in thirty-six hours. His head had resumed its natural proportions, his mouth was sweet again, and so was his disposition. As he poured the boiling water on the eating utensils in the wreck pan, he burst into song.

The trail boss regarded him for a moment, glanced at the work horses harnessed and hitched to the wagon, flipped a hand carelessly and rode slowly off in the direction of the drifting cattle. The slight frown on his face disappeared: there was no use worrying any more about Waggoner and his crowd until night fell.

XIII

IT WAS mid-forenoon before the Circle 4 really started up the trail. Hopalong had been content to let the cattle drift lazily along, from one bit of grazing on to the next, satisfied under the circumstances to let them feed rather than to gain mileage, but he was conscious of the fact that he was supposed to have them at the pens in Bulltown on a specified date.

On the trail north of him were the herds which had come in over the branch trail from the Squaw, and, according to the trail cutter, the last two of these were beef herds bound for the open range near Bulltown and the shipping pens. These two, in turn held up by the closely spaced range herds ahead of them, were marking time and letting the cattle feed well while the gaps between the whole eleven herds opened up into more reasonable distances.

Hopalong, riding up around the left side of the scattered cattle, at last reached Lanky Smith and stopped for a moment to speak to him.

"Reckon I'll go up th' line an' see what things look like up there," he said.

"You figger on passin' some of 'em, if you get th' chance?" asked Lanky.

"Reckon so. We're beginnin' to lose some of th' time we saved back along," replied the trail boss. "We got a delivery date to think about. If I find them two beef herds well off th' trail I'll begin to think about passin' 'em. I don't mind gettin' behind th' range stockers, because they'll be movin' faster than we will. It's them two beef herds we got to think about."

"Might make trouble," said Lanky, not speaking from fear but rather from the angle of fact. "Some trail outfits are right touchy about bein' passed."

"There's a right side to 'most everythin'," replied his companion. "An' nobody's got th' right to block a drive trail. I'll know more about it when I get back."

"Then we'll keep 'em as they are," said Lanky.

"Yeah. See you later."

Hopalong rode on, his questing gaze on the northern sky. There were no dust signs, no indications of moving cattle. Mile after mile went behind him, and then he saw what he had ridden up to find. Two miles to the east of the patchy trail was a grazing herd, well spread out. Its position, in regard to his problem, was plain enough: it had given up its place as a trail herd and could be passed by any herd behind it. Of course, there was no law against a forced passing, but custom was rather strong against it. It was not polite.

The trail boss turned toward the distant wagon and replied to the gestured greetings of a rider with the cattle; and as he changed the course of his riding, he saw a rider leave the farthest fringes of the herd and also head in for the wagon. The two men reached that point at the same time. It was nice timing on the stranger's part.

Hopalong nodded to the loafing cook and raised a hand in salute to the slowing horseman.

"Howdy," he said. "I got a bunch of Circle 4's a few miles down th' trail, an' figgered I'd come up an' see what the chances are for us to make up a little lost time. You fellers figgerin' to throw back onto th' trail right soon?"

"Yore herd beef for th' market?"

"Beef for th' pens," answered Hopalong.

"Well," said the stranger slowly, "we pushed 'em purty hard from th' ford of th' Squaw. If we found that we had plenty of time, we was aimin' to let 'em put some flesh on their bones. Yo're headin' for Bulltown?"

"Yeah," answered Hopalong.

His companion was regarding him closely.

"You said for th' pens. Then you ain't lookin' for a buyer?"

"No," answered Hopalong. "We're sold on delivery."

"Yeah. That's right good," replied the other trail boss. He now did not need fear that the Circle 4's would lower cattle prices at the pens in case general conditions were unfavorable. They were not in the market, but were sold already. "Reason I asked," he said, with a grin, "was because we'll be lookin' for a buyer, an' already there's one beef herd ahead of us."

"You hadn't oughta have no trouble findin' a buyer this early in th' season," said Hopalong, also grinning. "We're purty well ahead of th' peak of th' beef outfits this year. Th' trail cutter told me that nine herds ahead of me are range stockers. That leaves you, an' that other outfit ahead, a purty clear field. That also means that if I get in behind th' trail stockers they'll be movin' further out of my way every day we travel."

"Yeah," grunted the other trail boss.

"How big is th' gap between you an' th' next herd?" asked Hopalong.

"Not so much north an' south; but plenty when you figger it east an' west. I understand they're not goin' to throw back onto th' trail for two, three more days. They're over on th' other side of th' trail. Turn to th' left at th' next crick an' you'll find 'em without no trouble."

"Reckon I will," said Hopalong. "What's their road brand?"

"T Dot Circle."

"Well, reckon I'll drift," said Hopalong, wheeling. "See you up in Bulltown, I reckon."

"Reckon so. So-long."

Hopalong rode back to the trail and followed it north. In due time he came to the creek, a trickle of water meandering eastward. He turned and followed along it.

The T Dot Circle cattle were well spread out, the guardian riders at reasonable distances from them and loafing in their saddles. Then Hopalong saw the thin finger of smoke which indicated the position of the chuck wagon, and not long thereafter breasted a sharp little rise and found the camp in the hollow on the other side. He drew rein on the crest, waited for a moment, and then pushed down the slope at a walk.

The three men at the wagon stopped their conversation and watched the newcomer in silence. They replied to his raised hand, and one of them slowly stood up.

"Howdy," said Hopalong.

"Howdy. Light down," invited the T Dot Circle man.

"Hardly stayin' long enough," replied Hopalong, with a smile. "I been ridin' up th' trail to kinda look things over. I got a bunch of cattle back aways. I don't want to be crowded, or crowd nobody else; but I got a delivery date to figger about. So I just dropped in to learn how you boys are located. I see yo're off th' trail an' feedin'."

"You got a delivery date, huh?" asked the T Dot Circle boss. "You headin' up for Bulltown?"

"Yeah, for th' pens."

"For th' pens, huh?"

"Yeah. Our herd's sold to Phillips Brothers, of Kansas City, when we get it into th' pens," said Hopalong.

"Huh!" muttered the T Dot Circle boss thoughtfully. He turned something over in his mind and eyed the horseman speculatively. "We been waitin' for th' range stockers to open up an' get outa our way.

They've been doin' that right along, an' I was figger-in' to throw back onto th' trail tomorrow or th' day after. How far you behind us?"

"Near a dozen miles, I figger."

"Then yo're crowdin' th' 3 TL outfit purty close."

"No. Anyhow, they crowded in ahead of us," said Hopalong, still smiling. "That's th' trouble with a branch trail. We was on th' main trail, comin' up. Th' 3 TL, you fellers, an' nine range herds cut in ahead of us from th' Squaw. Of course, nobody's to blame for that. Th' question is, have I got to stand still, let you two outfits graze yore cattle, an' nine more move along as they feel like? My herd is sold, an' I got a delivery date to worry about. You say yo're goin' back on th' trail tomorrow or th' day after. Why not make it th' day after? Th' 3 TL are still grazin' an' won't be crowdin' you. I just talked with their boss. By day after tomorrow I can go past both you fellers, an' be outa yore way."

"Then that'll put us between you an' th' 3 TL," growled the T Dot Circle boss. "How much of a gap will you open up between you an' us?"

"As big a gap as you want," answered Hopalong, turning his horse.

"Well, all I want is plenty."

"All right: I'll see that you get plenty. We'll push right along an' get outa yore way. Much obliged," said Hopalong and rode up the little slope and over the crest.

The T Dot Circle boss stood quietly looking in the

direction of the departed visitor. His seated companions had nothing to say, and one of them reached
out and broke off a weed stem, idly twirling it between
thumb and finger. The seconds slipped past. The weed
stem broke with a sharp little snap, and the cook
looked up curiously.

"Phillips Brothers, huh?" he muttered, glancing at
his boss. "You reckon his herd's shore sold?"

The boss shifted his gaze from the crest of the little
rise and looked thoughtfully at his seated companions.
From the questions he had asked the trail cutter he
believed that he would get good prices for his herd at
Bulltown; but that, of course, depended on other
things. He knew that, so long as he was off the trail,
the trail was open to any following herd; if he was on
it, trail ethics urged that he be not passed without his
permission.

"Don't know," he growled. "That feller had a lot
to say. Too much, mebby."

The man with the broken weed stem tossed the
halves away.

"Me," he said, slowly, "I'd figger that th' gaps are
wide enough ahead of us. An' they wouldn't have to
be very wide, at that, to suit me. He's been drivin'
along, havin' things all to hisself. Suddenly he finds
himself plumb behind eleven trail outfits. Count 'em—
eleven! That put th' lather on him."

"Yeah," grunted the trail boss. "Them gaps are
shore long enough," he said with sudden decision. He
swung toward his horse. "I'll send in yore work hosses,

cook. You put 'em to th' wagon, an' light out. Come on, Jim: we're throwin' back onto th' trail, an' we're doin' it now." He laughed derisively. "Sold on delivery, huh? Hell, I wasn't weaned yesterday!"

Jim hesitated and then, dismissing his scruples with a laugh, still gave them utterance.

"This good weather's due to break," he said. "If we throw back onto th' trail now, it'll put that hombre purty close behind us. We all know that trail cattle allus stampede th' way they came. He'll be right close ahead of that 3 TL herd, an' we'll be out in th' clear if anythin' busts."

"Shore, but I wasn't thinkin' so much about that as about prices in Bulltown," replied the trail boss. "To hell with him, an' th' 3 TL, too!"

XIV

Hopalong rode straight toward his herd, parallel
with the trail. When he reached it, he gave orders to
step the cattle right along. He had promised the T
Dot Circle boss a reasonably safe trail interval, and he
would make good that promise, even if it meant to
drive for half the night. He did not especially care for
night driving, but the situation might require it. The
herd had been drifting lazily along, moving as they
grazed, with no thought for the gaining of much mileage; but now they were pushed into a brisk trail gait,
which made the dust climb into the sky. Hour after
hour went past, and at last they reached the little
creek beyond the 3 TL, where the T Dot Circle were
holding. Not far beyond the creek, heavy cattle tracks
cut into the trail from the west, and Hopalong regarded them with surprise. His own herd, well
watered at the creek, was moving at the same brisk
gait again. He let the animals pass him and then
crossed over behind the drag. It was not long before
he overtook the right point rider.

"Red," he said, "foller up that creek we just crossed
for about two miles. You oughta find th' T Dot Circle
outfit close to it. I want to know if they're still there.
Get a move on."

He turned in his saddle, swung his hat, and Johnny Nelson left his swing position and rode ahead to join him.

"Take th' point, Kid, till Red gets back ag'in," ordered the trail boss. "Somethin's wrong, an' I'm goin' on ahead for a look. I passed th' words to th' swing riders to keep 'em steppin' right along. I'll be back soon."

It was mid-afternoon when he returned, and he was scowling. He made a gesture to the left point rider which meant to keep the cattle moving as they were, and Lanky acknowledged it with a like gesture. Hopalong then joined Red at right point.

"Yo're loco," greeted Red pleasantly. "There warn't no herd, wagon, or nothin' else up that crick. Nothin' but signs."

"I know it, now," growled the trail boss, his eyes glinting. "That T Dot Circle outfit has deliberately run a blazer on us. They told me to come right along an' get outa their way, an' then they threw back onto th' trail an' put us between them an' that 3 TL crew. There ain't no harm in that, but I'm damned if I like to be made a fool of." His lean jaws tightened. "All right. They gave me th' right of way, an' by Gawd I'm takin' it! I'm takin' it if it means to drive all night!"

"Yeah!" grunted Red. "All night, all day, an' all night ag'in, if we have to! What you figger he's got in his mind?"

"Brand worms, mebby!" snapped the boss. "Red, you go up th' trail far enough to see their dust, but not so far that they can see you. As soon as they throw off for th' night, you streak it back here an' let me know which side they take." He quickly placed a hand on the arm of his eager friend. "Wait a second. Cook's up ahead with th' wagon. I didn't stop to speak to him. Tell him to keep a mile behind you till you ride back, an' then to move right along till somebody tells him to stop."

Red grinned, pulled his hat firmly down on his head, and left a trail of dust behind him. The boss rode off to speak to the day wrangler with the cavvy and not long thereafter returned to Red's place at right point, where Johnny was doing the honors.

"All right, Kid," he said. "Pass th' word back to keep these animals movin' as they are, an' then take yore reg'lar place."

The afternoon went slowly past, and it was twilight before Red returned from his scouting expedition up the trail. He joined Hopalong and rode with him leg to leg.

"They just left th' trail an' threw off it to th' west," he reported. "Cook's goin' right along as soon's it's dark enough to hide him."

'How far ahead are they?" demanded the trail boss.

"Three hours good drivin'."

"All right," growled Hopalong. "I don't like night drivin' any more than th' next man, but we're goin' on for more'n three hours. Th' whole damn thing is, they thought I was lyin' when I told 'em I was sold on delivery." He laughed grimly. "They told us to pass 'em, an' pass 'em we will!"

Through the twilight and the growing dusk stepped

the herd, steadily marking off the miles. The point riders laughed, the swing riders grinned, and the drag rider swore, but the herd kept to its steady pace. It was dark when Red, who had been closely watching the landmarks along the trail, waved a hand and spoke.

"Here's where they turned off," he said.

"Two hours more, then," growled his companion. "I'll take over this job while you find th' cook an' tell him when to stop. As soon as he stops, tell him to get supper, an' right quick. Then he's to kill his fire. We'll throw off a mile west of th' trail. When he's located, you come back to th' trail an' wait for us, to show us th' way to camp. You savvy?"

"Shore," replied Red and again rode northward, wondering why his friend and boss was laughing. Red could see no reason for mirth in a forced night drive: but he lacked the imagination of his friend.

The herd marched on, six to eight cattle wide, and moving like the trail-broken animals they were. In the early days of the drive they had moved twenty to thirty miles a day to keep them too tired to "raise hell" at night; since then, however, they had been allowed to take things easy with an average daily progress of less than ten miles. And since then, in turn, they had averaged less. *Clack, shuffle, clack; clack, shuffle, clack.* A figure suddenly appeared out of the night and spoke to the right point rider.

"Hoppy?"

"Yeah, Red. This th' place?"

"Yeah. Head 'em off an' over. Cook's got a little fire goin', down in a hollow. It's just a bed of coals, an' it's all right: you can't see it over th' rise."

Swiftly the word passed down the flanks. Lanky drew rein and let the leaders swing past in front of him. *Clack, shuffle, clack.* Hopalong glowed with pride over the regimentation of the cattle in this herd. They moved, with hardly a break in their formation, from the well-beaten trail and plodded westward. Some of their good behavior was doubtless due to fatigue. In less than half an hour they were checked, stopped, and allowed to spread out over the bed ground, where expert knowledge of cattle psychology in letting them spread out enough but not too much, of not riding too close to them, and in letting them feel the least possible restraint, had its reward. They were full of water, they had been well fed, and they were tired. After a little while they slowly, one here, a bunch there, lay down for a well-merited rest. The riders hurriedly ate a still warm supper, and the two men with the cattle rode in shortly after the first-trick riders had departed. These fed themselves and flipped their blanket rolls, but as the rolls unfolded they remembered the watch of the night before and looked inquiringly at the boss.

Hopalong stood up and motioned to Red.

"Well, boys," he said, "we hit th' trail at noon."

"An' give them T Dot Circle coyotes a good six hours to get on th' trail an' put us behind 'em again?" asked Lanky pugnaciously.

"They won't hit th' trail at daylight, or at noon, or even by dark tomorrow," replied Hopalong, grinning. "They're goin' to have troubles of their own, come mornin'. It will all come from tryin' to run a blazer on th' Bar 20."

"Yeah?" asked Red, with total lack of whatever reverence a trail boss is supposed to receive.

"Yeah," grunted Hopalong and then laughed outright.

"We goin' to fool around all night, waitin' for Waggoner an' his gang, like we did last night?" demanded Skinny.

"No, not tonight, or any night," answered Hopalong and laughed again. "All you boys have to do is to roll up, get yore sleep, an' take over yore reg'lar tricks with th' herd. That T Dot Circle boss is laughin' in his sleeve, right now; but there won't be no laugh left in him when mornin' comes. Red, you come along with me. I'll mebby show you what happens to smart Aleck trail bosses. Th' rest of you boys turn in an' get yore sleep."

"Where you goin'?" asked Red, who thought that he, too, could use a little sleep.

"I told you to come along with me," rejoined his friend and boss.

"Oh, I heard you," growled Red, but he followed his friend from camp without further grouching.

Cook, obeying the orders given a few minutes before, grudgingly poured water over the incandescent coals of the fire; and not long thereafter the little camp was wrapped in sleep.

Hopalong reached out and touched his companion's arm when the faint glow of the distant fire became visible.

"We stop here," he said and laughed again.

"What th' hell's so damn funny?" asked Red politely.

"What herd was th' last up th' trail this afternoon an' just before dark?" asked his boss, chuckling.

"We was, of course," growled Red.

"Right," grunted Hopalong. "An' what would a trail herd outfit do with a beef herd, if they had common sense, when it got to be near dark?"

"Why, they'd throw off th' trail an' bed down," answered Red.

"They shore would," agreed Hopalong. "An' bein' last on th' trail at dark, they'd nat'rally be th' first herd that would show itself to anybody ridin' *up* that trail, except th' 3 TL outfit, which ain't moved, an' which we passed miles back."

"Yeah," said Red after due thought. "An' then what? An' what'n hell are we settin' out here for instead of gettin' some sleep?"

"I'll show you that before mornin'," answered his cheerful companion, his eyes on the flush in the night which marked the location of the T Dot Circle fire. He laughed in his throat. "There she burns, for everybody to see."

"An' why shouldn't it?" snapped Red, buttoning his coat against the coolness of the night air.

"Shore: why shouldn't it?" chuckled Hopalong. "Well, Red, I'll take th' first watch. Get some of that sleep you been bellyachin' about."

Red took him at his word.

Time moved slowly. Midnight came and passed. Another hour, and then one more. Suddenly Hopalong shook his sleeping companion, and Red came to instant wakefulness. There were faint flashes to the south of them, but so far away they barely could hear the roar of the heavy black-powder loads. They imagined they could feel a slight tremor of the earth, and a faint roaring sound came to them like a ghost out of the night.

"Stampede, by Gawd!" muttered Red.

"Yeah, stampede," said his companion, with satisfaction. "It's their cavvy, an' mebby some of their cattle. Waggoner's gang has run it off, thinkin' that it's ourn. It's where ourn ought to be, ain't it? I told you they'd be too damn busy tomorrow to throw back on th' trail. That's what they get for bein' smart Alecks. Well, come on. Let's get back to camp an' catch up on some sleep. You an' I'll sleep late. Th' herd will graze till noon an' then amble peacefully on its way."

"Well," said Red. "You long-headed ol' coyote! I'll be teetotally damned!"

"There ain't no question about *that* a-tall, Red," laughed his boss and led the way to camp.

XV

They had held the herd on the creek after a night drive for the gaining of miles, to give the cattle a well-merited rest. They knew that a herd is hard to start from water, that the animals would be sullen and reluctant to begin the day's journey; but in this case it did not matter. They would leave so late in the morning that their slow grazing would take them away from the stream before the day's drive was begun, and they would be on their way before they realized it.

Skinny Thompson drove the cavvy from the wagon, to start it on its lazy way northward, parallel with the trail but a considerable distance from it. He was chuckling and slowly shaking his head in admiration for the brains of his boss, which even at that early day were noticeable.

The herd had spread out in its unmolested grazing, not realizing that it was being drifted slowly and gently up the slope and over the crest of the long rise north of the creek. Most of the cattle were already over the crest and out of sight of the camp. The two riders with it loafed in their saddles and exchanged long-distance grins as they recalled the incidents of the previous night. The contented animals grazed ever forward, rested and full of water and grass. Everything was lovely and the goose honked high.

At the chuck wagon the grinning cook was preparing his important vehicle for the day's journey. The two work horses, harnessed and ready to go, chafed their bits and impatiently switched their tails. There was a time when there were no flies on this great, elevated plateau; but the white man with his animals had brought them with him. Johnny Nelson, his face still red from laughter, pulled the cinch strap up to a plainly marked hole and made it fast. The hour was late for a trail herd to get under way, scandalously so; but the herd had clicked off double distance the day before and well merited this additional rest. Johnny pulled the kerchief around in front of his chest and swung up into the saddle.

Red Connors hung the tin cup back on the water pail, drew a sleeve across his lips, and chuckled. He had missed most of his sleep the night before, but his temper was sweeter than usual.

"Our friend, th' trail cutter, will shore be sorry he missed this wagon last night," he said. He turned and looked southward and laughed outright. "So them fellers figgered we was holdin' th' sack, huh?" he said, turning to face his friend and boss. "After tellin' you to step th' herd right along an' get past 'em, an' outa their way, they up an' threw back onto th' trail, so we'd be jammed in between them an' that 3 TL outfit. Well, they got what was comin' to 'em, an' they got it good!"

Hopalong Cassidy nodded and slowly got to his feet.

"When that bunch of cattle thieves an' bums from Waggoner's store didn't raid us that first night," he slowly said, "I figgered that it made it a dead shore thing for th' second night, because we was gettin' farther away all th' time. We was th' last herd on th' trail, an' we was due to stay that way. When we passed them T Dot Circle coyotes in th' dark last night, that made them th' last herd on th' trail. Waggoner's crowd just nat'rally raided th' wrong cattle. It was too dark for 'em to tell th' difference. Well," he said, slowly looking around, "I reckon it's time to get started. We're now ahead of both beef herds, with only fast-steppin' range stockers ahead of us. Th' cattle have had a good rest, they've been drifted gentle from th' creek, an' now we'll step 'em right along."

He turned to the cook.

"Th' next creek is Elkhorn, an' th' second is Blacktail. You make camp a couple of miles north of th' second creek an' about a mile to th' east. There ain't much chance of stampedin' cattle runnin' back down th' trail an' pickin' up ourn, not th' way them mixed herds are movin'; but usually there's better feed well off th' trail. Get goin' when you feel like it."

He swung toward his saddled horse and glanced at his grouped friends.

"All right. Let's hook onto th' herd, shape it up, an' get it movin'."

Johnny Nelson let out another notch of his grin,

this time from hopeful anticipation. Youth craves excitement, and he was the youngest member of the outfit.

"You figger that T Dot Circle outfit will mebby try
to take it outa us?" he asked, his eyes glinting.

"Mebby," grunted Hopalong; "but not today.
They'll be too damn' busy to take anythin' outa anybody. It looked to me an' Red that they lost their
cavvy as well as their herd. There was plenty of shootin' around their wagon, so they mebby lost their night
hosses, too."

"Then that puts 'em afoot!" said Johnny eagerly.
"Great mavericks!"

"All but th' two riders with th' herd," replied
Hopalong. "Come on: let's get goin'."

Pete and Billy had the herd strung out, and already
it was swinging along at a fair pace when their friends
joined them and took up their accustomed places with
the cattle. Billy, grumbling a little, thereupon dropped
back to take charge of the drag, which already had
found its place at the rear of the herd. The dust was
heavy, so he let the drag open up a bigger gap between
it and the main herd and settled back in his saddle to
face the passing of the miles and hours.

The sun was at the meridian, blazing down through
a cloudless sky; the heated air quivered and danced
close to the ground, and mirage ponds began to hold
out false hopes to the foolish. The shuffling, dust-
kicking hoofs of a thousand steers filled the air with
a yellow-white fog, and the miles dragged past reluc-

tantly. Mid-afternoon found the first creek in sight—
Elkhorn. The cattle watered, soaked themselves, and
milled around. It took a little time and effort to get
them going again, notwithstanding the fact that they
had been well watered only a few hours before; but
go on again they did, and as they passed over the top
of the gentle slope the trail boss rode up to Johnny's
side.

"I'll take yore place, Kid," he said. "Go up th' trail
an' see how close to us that last mixed herd is. If you
don't sight 'em in two, three hours, come back ag'in.
Watch both sides of th' trail in case they've throwed
off to graze an' rest. I don't want to get too close to
anythin' ahead of us."

Johnny nodded, swung away from the herd, and
then pushed ahead. He rode in close to Red, who was
riding at right point, stuck a thumb in an armhole of
his vest, and threw out his chest.

"I've been given a special job," he said importantly.

"That so?" asked Red, not visibly impressed.

"Yeah," replied Johnny expectantly.

"You figger you can do it?" asked Red, yawning
slightly.

"Shore!"

"All right, Kid. Better get about it, then."

"I'm goin' up to locate th' next herd ahead," said
Johnny, with a trace of importance.

"Well, I reckon you can do that, all right, unless
——" said Red, and broke off to yawn again, and this
time not slightly.

"Unless what?" demanded Johnny, somewhat bel-
ligerently.

"Unless you fall off yore cayuse," said Red.

"Some day," retorted Johnny, his face redder under
its tan, "I'm goin' to take you apart just to see what
makes you tick!"

"That's been tried two, three times already," replied Red. "You know, Kid, that herd's shore gettin'
farther away every minute you hang around here."
He looked at the indignant set of the Kid's back,
growing smaller up the trail, and then threw back his
head and laughed.

The dust climbed, flattened, and slowly spread out
on all sides of the herd, but the animals kept on moving, *clack, shuffle, clack,* all that hot and wearisome
afternoon. The weary drag, grown but little larger,
lay behind it like the dot of an exclamation point.
Then, as the fierceness of the sun's heat began to lessen,
twin lines of greenery came into view far ahead.

The cattle approached the creek with more restraint
than they had shown over any water so far on the
long journey. The creeks were closer together along
this section of the trail. They hardly quickened their
stride, but they went into the water and stood in it
while they nosed it contentedly. They showed less reluctance, too, to get going again, and soon were plodding up the sharp slope on the farther side. Not long
thereafter the cook's chuck wagon could be made out,
a dark spot on another gray-green slope. Half a mile
farther east grazed the cavvy. Hopalong sighed un-

consciously and sat up a little more erect in the saddle. The long and tiresome trail journey had been cut down by one more day. The herd was checked and allowed to spread out, and twilight found the animals grazing along the upper slope of the rise, gradually working toward the bed ground on its crest.

Hopalong rode in to the wagon, got out his war bag, and took from it his spare shirt.

"Where's th' dance?" asked the cook, grinning.

"Up th' creek," answered Hopalong, smiling like a boy, "if I can find a hole deep enough to get into all over."

"Well, you could wet one side, an' then th' other," said the cook, and suddenly had a thought. "Hey! You want to look out for cottonmouths!" he warned, his experience with reptiles based on territory much farther south.

"There ain't no moccasins up in this country," replied the trail boss. For a moment he reflected upon the cook's manifest ignorance. "You better keep *yore* eyes skinned for prairie rattlers. They ain't very big, but they're damn mean."

"How big are they?" asked the cook, his gaze slowly passing over the ground in his immediate vicinity. He missed the twinkle in his companion's blue eyes.

"I ain't never seen none more'n fifteen feet long," confessed the trail boss with a straight and sober face. "Most usually they come smaller—say mebbe a dozen feet; but they shore make up for that by travelin' in threes."

"Great —— ——!" said the startled cook, his eyes wide as saucers. "Rattlers a dozen feet long, an' three to th' pair! Great land of cows!"

"Three to a pair," muttered Hopalong, experimentally. Somehow it didn't sound right. "Huh. All you got to do is sleep with a hair rope around you," he stated, closing the war bag and pushing it from him and farther up in the wagon.

"Hey! You shore want to copper that hair-rope idear!" said the cook hastily and with great earnestness. "One time I went to sleep with a hair rope round me, an' I woke up with a rattler layin' right smack ag'in my side!"

"Mebby these here prairie snakes have got better taste," said the trail boss, swinging into the saddle.

"That so?" snorted the cook with a trace of belligerence. "I hope yore swimmin' hole's full of quicksand!"

"See you later," called the trail boss, making dust.

"That's *my* hard luck," growled the cook, turning to feed his fire. He had placed the coffee pot handy to the fire and was blowing the dust from the tin plates when Red Connors rode up and stopped. He glanced from the cook toward the departing horseman.

"Where's Hoppy goin'?" asked Red. "Up to meet th' Kid?"

"He's figgerin' to dance with that redhead at Traynor's honkatonk!" snapped the cook.

"Oh, that so?" snapped Red, strange glints in his eyes. "Where's Hoppy goin'? Up to meet th' Kid?"

The cook raised his head, saw the glints and changed his mind.

"Naw. Huntin' up a swimmin' hole with a change of clothes," he growled.

"Never saw one like that before," replied Red, urging the horse against the wagon. He stuck his head under the cover and reached out a long arm, dragging his own war bag toward him.

"Never saw one like what?" asked the cook, his red face growing redder.

"Where'n hell is my other shirt?" demanded Red, glaring at the cook.

"I never knowed you had two shirts!" retorted the cook, with a gleam in his eye. "Mebby it's under that one you got on," he jibed.

"That so?" growled the owner of two shirts, one of which was missing. "Hey! What kinda shirt did Hoppy take?"

The cook searched his memory hastily, and his memory came through in the pinch.

"Red-an'-white check," he answered hopefully. "I remember it because I thought that nobody but a halfbreed or an Injun would wear a shirt like that. It reminded me of a nightmare I once had."

His hopes were justified by the way Red's horse got into motion. And then the cook's grin slowly faded while he scratched his head in deep cogitation of serious matters. He made up his mind quickly and ran to the wagon. He dragged out his war bag and, taking a clean and vivid red-and-white checked shirt from it, hastily crammed it into the bag nearest his hand. He felt that he might have started something which would take a deal of stopping. Having done this good deed, he sighed with resignation. He thought the bag belonged to Pete, and Pete was big enough to handle any man in the crowd, unless he should run up against that double-barrel left-and-right of the trail boss. There was no need for him to bathe now, since he had no change of shirt, which might have been an attitude of mind peculiar to trail cooks. He looked up at the sound of hoofs and saw Pete Wilson and Lanky Smith nearing the wagon, and his expression became bland and innocent.

The two riders pulled up and looked quickly and curiously around. It was getting on to meal time, and the camp was deserted.

"Didn't Hoppy an' Red ride in here?" asked Lanky in some surprise.

"They shore didn't walk in," growled the cook, watching Pete out of the corner of his eye.

"Smart Aleck, huh?" grunted Pete, wiping the dust paste from his grimy forehead.

"Where'd they go?" persisted Lanky with quick suspicion. He was looking down the trail, in the general direction whence trouble would appear if it came at all.

"Swimmin'," growled the cook, fussing at the tailboard.

"Swimmin'!" barked Lanky eagerly. "Where at?"

"Up th' crick," answered the cook grouchily. "You

want to look out for these damn prairie rattlers," he warned. "Sixteen feet long an' they gang up in threes!"

Lanky's mouth was still open when Pete, after studying the cook's face for an instant, gravely made reply. Pete shoved his head and shoulders in under the wagon cover as he spoke, and his voice sounded a little muffled.

"That's right, they—— *What th' hell!*" he grunted in surprise as Red's pet shirt confronted him. He carelessly shoved it into the nearest bag and pulled out his own blue-and-white, a shirt approaching a tent in size.

"What you mean, 'what th' hell'?" barked the cook.

"I never knowed you'd seen any of them snakes," said Lanky, talking to the cook, but crowding Pete. "You musta been drunk as all hell."

"Drunk nothin'!" retorted the cook, flushing at this bald and careless mention of a very touchy subject. Couldn't a man ever live anything down? "I ain't seen one, yet," he confessed; "but Hoppy was tellin' me about 'em."

"Oh," said Lanky, still crowding.

Pete, tying the arm of the clean shirt around his thick neck, got out of Lanky's elbowing way.

"He was, huh?" asked Pete, speculatively. "Did he tell you how they bulldog growed cattle? No? Didn't have time to, mebby; or th' presence of mind. Why, th' number one snake just throws a runnin' loop over th' cow's head an' flops it quick as a wink. Th' number two snake turns a hitch around one front laig, pullin' it back; an' th' number three rep-tile rolls a loop around th' other front laig, pullin' it frontwards. That's why they travel in threes. Let me tell you that these snakes are smart; an' they're dangerous, but most dangerous at night. Reckon I'll be sleepin' in th' wagon tonight."

"Yeah?" snapped the cook. "I'm boss of th' wagon, an' you know it'll only sleep one!" His voice was rising. "Why don't you lay a hair rope round you? You'll be plenty safe that way."

"I don't take much stock in hair ropes," growled Pete.

Lanky backed from the wagon, looked curiously at the excited cook, and then, holding a change of clothes high over his head, yelled shrilly and led Pete by a length as they passed the fire.

The cook watched them go, studied his fire for a moment, and decided to let it die down a little. Supper would be late tonight, thanks to the swimming mania. He looked at the distant herd, where Skinny and Billy were on duty, and he grinned: those two would have plenty to say about the tardiness of their relief. Suddenly he thought about Pete's war bag and the red-and-white checkered shirt. Pete certainly had found it, and he would be quite certain to pass it on. The cook sauntered to the wagon, found his own bag, and examined its contents. The shirt was not in it. As he turned from the wagon he saw a little cloud of dust roll over the crest of the rise and head straight for camp. Something about the rider made him grunt and nod his head. It was Johnny, back from his trip up the trail, and Johnny was singing:

"I'm through trailin' cattle," said Big Foot Sam.
"I won't trail cattle for no damn man.

"When I draw my pay I'll strap my roll,
  An' pull my freight, dod gast my soul.

"I won't nurse th' cavvy, an' I won't flank th' herd,
  For I aim to be free as any damn bird.

"I'm plumb sick of beans, an' sow-belly, too;
  An' I'm tired of th' boss an' th' whole damn crew.

"I've swum th' last river an' rode my last trick,
  An' I'm goin' back to Texas, an' goin' back quick.

"I've rid all night long in a pourin' rain,
  An' I'll shore be damned if I do it again."

  Then th' boss come a-ridin': "Hi-yuh, Sam!
  We're drivin' these steers to th' Promised Lan';

"We're goin' past Dodge, an' goin' 'crost the Platte—
  Fust thing we know we won't know where we're at!

"We're goin' down th' Powder, an' 'crost th' Yaller-
    stone,
  Headin' for them Canucks like a dog with a bone!"

"I've never been to Canady," said Big Foot Sam:
"I've never seen th' Powder, nor airy Promise' Lan';

"But if they're goin' to Canady, then I'm a-goin' too:
Me an' my roll with th' whole damn' crew!"

In a few minutes the rider pulled up at the wagon, his eyes sweeping the camp and the plain.

"Where's Hoppy? Where're all th' boys?" he asked, curiously.

"Off swimmin'!" snapped the cook, who had begun to acknowledge the wish to feel water sliding over his hot and sticky skin.

"Where?" quickly demanded the Kid.

"Up th' crick. They're gettin' into clean clothes. What you find, up th' trail?"

"Gettin' into clean clothes, huh? They won't have nothin' on me!" chuckled the Kid, crowding the wagon and reaching inside of it. His energetic pawing was followed by a muttered exclamation and then more pawing. It looked like Red's shirt, but whomever it belonged to, he did not want it. He jammed it into the first bag at hand.

"What you find up th' trail?" persisted the cook.

"No cattle in sight, far's I went," answered the Kid. "Them range stockers won't never bother us."

"Pete was tellin' me how these here big prairie rattlers bulldog cattle—growed cattle," said the cook tentatively.

"Yeah? They're mean critters," said Johnny, waiting for a better cue. Coming from the south, he viewed the prairie rattlesnakes with a fair amount of contempt. He hauled a fresh blue shirt into sight and dove back under the cover.

"Hoppy says they grow up to fifteen feet an' travel three to th' pair," continued the cook, again scrutinizing the ground around the camp.

"Shucks. I'd say that was a couple feet too long; but they're damn dangerous, 'specially at night," said Johnny's muffled voice. "Bein' so long, they stretch out over considerable ground. Their head will be on one side of you, an' their tail on th' other. That's what makes 'em so dangerous at night, an' why you never want to shoot toward th' rattle. When you hear *that,* you want to watch th' other way, where th' business end is. An' you want to watch damn close. See you later!"

In one point, at least, Johnny had corroborated Pete: they were most dangerous at night. The cook scratched his head thoughtfully. This was a hell of a country for a white man. He knew who would sleep in the wagon from now on; and it wouldn't be Pete.

XVI

THE swimmers returned in a bunch, Red still wrangling about his missing shirt, and when they dismounted at the wagon Red climbed into it and began to shift its contents like a hen scratching gravel. Bag after bag was examined, and then, holding the last container in his hand, he leaped to the ground, strode to the cook, and thrust the bag under that pious person's nose. Red had a chip on each shoulder.

"This yourn?" he demanded ominously, shaking the bag.

"Yeah: it shore is," admitted the cook, having perfect faith in the contents of that bag.

Red opened the bag, pulled out the missing red-and-white shirt and jammed it against the cook's face.

"Then how'd that shirt get into yore bag?" he demanded, his words clipped.

The cook's surprise was so apparent, so natural and unforced that it was very convincing, and the owner of the shirt let his gaze drift from face to face.

"I'd like to know th' answer to that, myself!" shouted the cook, in no way embarrassed or awed. The last time he had seen the damned shirt it had been in Pete's bag; and, after Pete had rummaged around and left the wagon, the cook had again looked into his own bag, just in case Pete had put it in there. He turned accusing eyes on Johnny, the last man who had meddled with the war bags. "What *you* know about it, Kid?" he growled.

"Me? *Me?*" inquired Johnny innocently; and then his face hardened. "Why, I'll tell you what I know about it, cook: if you ain't got th' guts to stand up for yore own shirt-stealin', don't you try to saddle it onto me! *That's* what I know about it!"

"That so?" snapped the cook. "Th' last time *I* saw that shirt a piece of it was stickin' outa Pete's bag!"

Pete slowly turned to look at the disputants. He very ostentatiously sized up Red and then glanced with satisfaction down at his own huge chest girth. Then he waved a hamlike hand. It was almost a regal gesture.

"Any time I steal a shirt it'll shore be one that I can squeeze into," he said. "I found it in my bag, though; an' not none of it was stickin' out. That means that nobody would know it was in there, 'less they looked, or put it there themself. How come *you* knowed it was in there, cook?"

Cook sidestepped the direct question and then went on the offensive.

"Then what made you put it into my bag?" he demanded. "You want to get me into trouble?"

"I didn't put it into yore bag that I know of," placidly replied Pete. "But I'd just as soon get you into trouble as not, if you don't put yore mind on yore job an' get us somethin' to eat right smart."

The cook growled something about shirts, swimming, and the lateness of the hour and turned back to his job.

Red looked slowly from face to face, muttered something about damn-fool jokers, and strode back to the wagon, shirt in one hand and bag in the other. As he emerged from the canvas and stepped down from the doubletree he chanced to look off toward the trail.

"Here comes th' trail cutter," he said and grinned. It was the first trail cutter he had ever taken a fancy to. "He shore missed somethin' by not comin' back last night."

Welcoming smiles greeted the newcomer as he stopped not far from the wagon, and the cook tried to drag a frown over his wide smile and failed; but if he could not frown he could be verbally abusive.

"My ——!" he snorted. "Now we'll be et outa house an' home!"

"You oughta be glad that any human bein' would eat yore damn grub," retorted the trail cutter, punching the cook playfully in the ribs as he passed the wagon. The cook kicked him gently in the seat of the pants and wiped his butcher knife on his own pants. The trail cutter looked the crowd over and addressed the boss.

"Couldn't get back here last night," he said. "Hope I didn't miss no ruckus."

Conversation became general, and during the course of it the trail cutter learned just what he had missed. His slight frown of disappointment slowly changed into an expression of mild eagerness.

"Mebby they'll make a play tonight, to get square," he suggested. He showed his teeth in a smile. "You mebby got two gangs on yore tail now."

Hopalong pulled out a sack of tobacco and some papers.

"Yeah," he grunted thoughtfully, "but I don't look for no trouble tonight. There was a gun fight down there last night. They rode right up past th' wagon, judgin' from th' flashes. Somebody got hurt. If th' raid went through all right, then Waggoner's crowd will still be drivin' th' stolen animals. Th' T Dot Circle outfit will be mighty busy. If they got any cayuses left, they'll be usin' 'em to round up their animals. If they ain't got hosses they can't bother us—— *Hey!*" he exclaimed, suddenly. "By ——, *we* got hosses! If they've lost theirs they got to get others." He looked shrewdly up at the trail cutter. "Mebby you did get back in time, at that."

The trail cutter laughed suddenly. It sounded like a bark. He dropped to his haunches beside the trail boss and dug up tobacco and papers. The cook grabbed the lid-lifting coffee pot, swore under his breath, and then waved both hands. The grub line formed magically and filed past the tailboard of the wagon. The trail boss, seated on the ground with his tin plate and tin cup, looked speculatively toward the bed ground. It would have been better to push the herd a mile or two farther on, away from the stream: it would begin the next day's drive easier, with sweeter tempers, from a dry area. To do that now, besides disturbing the cattle, he would have to break camp, get the work horses from the cavvy—it wasn't worth the trouble, so long as he wasn't trying to gain even average mileage. He would meet trouble when it arose; but after tonight they would not bed down the herd so close to water. He glanced at Johnny, busily eating, and unconsciously nodded over the report that the Kid had brought to him at the swimming hole. Johnny had seen no cattle on his ride up the trail. There was nothing ahead to worry about, nothing to threaten them with a stampede. Ahead of them things were sweet and normal; behind them, hell might be popping. Huh!

There was only one rider with the herd now, and Hopalong glanced from him to the cavvy and smiled as he saw it in motion and halfway to the wagon. Skinny drifted it up and held it while man after man, hastily getting to his feet, dropped his culinary utensils in the wreck pan and went about getting his night horse from the bunch. Lanky, well fed and cheerful, took Skinny's place with the cavvy and drove it off again, while the day wrangler charged the tailboard and filled his plate generously. Two riders went off toward the herd to take it over on the first night shift and to send Billy in for his supper. Billy made a race of it to camp and dropped down beside the wrangler, balancing a well-filled plate.

"I didn't see nobody relieve me when they shoulda," he grunted between bites.

"They all went swimmin'," said the cook, volunteer-

ing the information with malicious pleasure and waiting for the fireworks.

"Hell they did!" growled Billy and fell to eating
again.

The cook sighed with disappointment.

Twilight developed swiftly, and the fire took on a
depth of color which it had lacked but a few moments
before. Billy and Skinny, a good job well done, rolled
cigarettes and contemplated the economical blaze. The
night was clear and without wind. Conversation was
jerky. The two men who had the next shift knew that
it would be foolish to turn in so early, and preferred
to sit up until time for them to go out to the herd. The
others were already beginning to think of their blankets. Riding, open air, and full stomachs conspire
toward drowsiness. The cook's fire was an Indian fire:
its sticks radiated like the spokes of a wheel, and now
someone pushed a few sticks farther in toward the
center, and the little blaze slowly grew, lighting up
the lean, tanned faces about it. On the range and on
the trail, this was the precious moment.

Hopalong suddenly cocked his head and arose. He
moved toward the wagon until it stood between him
and the revealing fire, giving him the tremendous advantage of invisibility, turning him into the poten-
tiality of a masked battery. The hoofbeats were plainer
now, and two more of the seated outfit raised their
heads to listen. Then even the cook heard them and
took his mind from sixteen-foot rattlesnakes. A slight
frown formed on his face.

"Why'n hell don't they come in at meal time, before everythin's put away?" he grumbled, his mind on the troubles of his trade.

Johnny carelessly moved his right arm behind him, leaning back on it and using it as a prop. His gun belt lay on the ground back there, and his hand was touching walnut. Johnny was young, and he had imagination. Red glanced at him curiously, smiled gently, and let his gaze flick toward the wagon, somewhere back of which a very capable trail boss was standing alert in the darkness. Red tossed his cigarette butt into the fire and began to roll a new smoke. Johnny caught the meaning, flushed a little, but did not shift his position.

Red lighted the cigarette and chuckled.

"Hell, Kid: that feller's got you covered right now," he said.

The trail cutter smiled with the others and waited with them for the oncoming rider to materialize. A bright gleam jiggled in the darkness, where the fitful firelight played for an instant upon a shining belt buckle or some other bit of bright metal. Then the light played upon gleaming chestnut as a horse pushed into sight and stopped. The rider sat quietly in the saddle, looking down upon the seated group.

"Howdy," he said. "This th' Circle 4?"

"Yeah," lazily answered Red. "Light down an' set."

The stranger's eyes slowly passed from face to face, and he looked inquiringly at Red.

"I don't see th' feller I'm lookin' for," he said

mildly. "Yore boss," he amended. "He was at my wagon a couple of days ago."

Red's eyes glinted in the firelight, but he frowned at Johnny's alert eagerness.

"You from th' T Dot Circle?" he asked coldly, his gaze coming to rest on the horseman.

"No," answered the horseman, slowly dismounting. He dropped the reins over the horse's head and stopped at Red's side. "I'm boss of th' 3 TL," he said, dropping down to squat on his toes.

There was movement in the darkness on the far side of the campfire, and Hopalong slowly emerged into the faint, outer circle of light.

"Here's th' boss now," said Red.

"Howdy," said Hopalong, moving lazily forward.

"Howdy," replied the newcomer, looking up. He stood erect. "I reckoned I'd pay back yore visit to my wagon. My name's Gibson."

"Mine's Cassidy. Meet my boys."

Gibson nodded to each in turn and then sat down at Red's side and crossed his legs.

"Hell busted loose last night down our way," he said, looking up at the Circle 4 trail boss.

"That so?" asked Hopalong with interest.

"Yeah," replied Gibson. "Bunch of cattle thieves raided th' T Dot Circle."

"I reckon this is a kinda mean part of th' trail," said Hopalong.

"Reckon mebby it is," agreed Gibson, pulling idly at a dead weed stem. "Seems like they wanted hosses.

They only stampeded th' cattle for a blind. They got all but two head of hosses. That put th' outfit afoot, except for th' two riders that was out with th' herd."

Red nodded wisely.

"They figgered by drivin' off th' cavvy they could pick up th' cattle 'most any time. Losin' their cavvy shore puts a drive outfit in a right mean hole."

Gibson nodded and looked around the circle. It was plain to be seen that he was worried.

"I lent th' T Dot Circle some of my hosses," he said. "My boys jumped in, rounded up their herd, an' two of 'em stayed with it. I began to figger about throwin' back onto th' trail, an' that's what I've done. Th' sooner I get outa this part of th' country, th' better I'll like it. I pushed my herd, after a late start, till it got too dark for anybody to locate it. We stepped 'em right along, let me tell you."

Hopalong nodded his understanding.

"You've done th' best you can accordin' to what you know," he said. "But you didn't have to drive tonight. Waggoner's crowd are too busy takin' care of what they run off; besides, they won't bother you: it's us they're after. If I didn't have so many head on my hands, I'd shore help them coyotes find us!"

"It's *you* they're after!" exclaimed Gibson in surprise. "Last night it shore looked like they was after th' T Dot Circle!"

Hopalong shook his head and explained the situation as briefly as he could. At the conclusion he smiled at his wondering visitor.

"That's th' way she lays," he said. "They reckoned that they was raidin' us. You keep right on a-comin', though. We're a considerable distance ahead of you now an' figger to keep outa yore way."

Gibson squirmed and cleared his throat a little apologetically.

"Uh-huh," he said thoughtfully. "Then you aim to keep movin' right along?"

"Shore," answered Hopalong, nodding. "We'll keep outa yore way." He reached for tobacco and papers. "We're a full day ahead of you now."

Gibson squirmed again.

"Well, hardly that," he said uneasily. "We're on th' trail an' figgerin' to keep on goin'." He pulled at another weed stem. "What I come up to see you about was to tell you that we're goin' on past you, seein' that you've throwed well off th' trail." He broke the stem and tossed it into the fire. "We throwed th' T Dot Circle cattle in with our own herd. Th' bigger th' herd, th' less men it takes to handle 'em, in proportion. We couldn't hardly do nothin' else, with them fellers havin' no cavvy."

Hopalong's face grew hard, and an angry light flared up in his eyes.

"You did, huh?" he growled, looking steadily at his visitor.

"Yeah," answered Gibson uneasily. "We figgered that if we drove all night we'd be far enough ahead of you by mornin' to open up a good gap; an' if we pushed 'em extry hard we could keep it open."

"If you do that th' cattle will be so plumb tired out, after that, that they'll drag along unless you lay over to rest 'em up," said Hopalong angrily. "What'll happen to th' gap then?"

"You might lay over tomorrow," suggested Gibson.

"Yeah, I might; but I won't," replied Hopalong. "Look here, Gibson: if it was just yore herd I might do it; but you've gone an' got hooked up with them T Dot Circle coyotes, an' I wouldn't move a finger to do a good turn for them fellers. What happened, down south there, was their own fault. You listen, an' I'll tell you why it is. I don't reckon they had anythin' to say about it."

It did not take long to tell the story, and at its conclusion the visitor slowly stood up.

"Don't see how I can blame you for th' way you feel," he admitted, with a wry smile. "It was Halliday's idear that we bunch our herds an' keep on goin'. Halliday is th' T Dot Circle boss."

"Yeah," replied Hopalong, grinning. "It was his idear that we play rear guard for him while they skinned along th' trail an' got outa their trouble. An', also, beat us to Bulltown before we could lower beef prices."

Gibson faced the speaker, his lids narrowing a little.

"But you told both of us that yore herd is sold, right now!"

"Shore I did. I told th' truth, too. We are sold, right now. You believed me, but Halliday didn't. I wouldn't mind lettin' you go past me, if yore herd was separate; but not nothin' wearin' th' T Dot Circle brand is goin' to make any dust for us to eat. You can tell Halliday to put that in his pipe an' smoke it; an' if he don't smoke, then shore as hell he can *chew* it!"

"No," said Gibson slowly and thoughtfully; "he didn't believe you, an' I did; but I shore didn't have no real reason to."

He nodded to the men around the fire and to the trail boss and stepped to his horse. By this time his herd and the T Dot Circle cattle should be almost even with the Circle 4 camp, clicking off the miles in the darkness; and by the time this outfit could get into its stride, he would be ahead of them; and once ahead of them, he would stay there, come hell or high water. He raised his hand in a parting salute and swung his horse. In a few minutes the sounds of its hoofs could no longer be heard.

In the camp he had just quitted there was swift and purposeful movement. Men were on their feet, rolling up bedding and tossing it into the wagon. Others were moving toward the night horses, ready to join the herd and start it on the way again. The cook was picking up odds and ends, making the wagon ready for the team when it came in. Hopalong was still squatting on the ground, gazing steadily at the incandescent embers of the fire. The cook hastened toward him, water bucket in hand. Hopalong stirred suddenly and checked the cook's swing.

"Let it burn," he said. "We're stayin' here."

The moving figures stopped and turned, looking

curiously at the trail boss. The cook sighed with relief and hurriedly placed the water bucket under the wagon. Bed rolls were being dragged into sight again, and this pleased him: especially when Pete hauled his own out. That meant that Pete wouldn't crowd him in the wagon. Cook knew who was going to sleep in that wagon.

"Them T Dot Circle fellers didn't have no cause to believe that I was tellin' th' truth," said the trail boss judiciously. He tried to be fair with a man. "They'd never seen me before. They're on th' trail, an' in trouble. Us trail outfits got to stick together when things bust wrong. Gibson did what he shoulda done. I got a purty good idear where them thieves drove to, seein' Red an' me was there before. Reckon we better help 'em out. Let th' herd drift as it grazes. There won't be enough of you to drive 'em on th' trail without takin' chances."

He turned and looked at Red, and that person grinned; but Johnny, an indignant expression on his face, pushed swiftly forward.

"I told that red-headed Siwash that *I* was goin' on th' next war party!" said the Kid loudly. "Red ain't goin' to hog all th' fun!"

"You ain't got no call to beef about it," rejoined the trail boss, frowning at the youngster. "I need a third man, an' th' experience will mebby do you good. You see that you beat th' cook outa th' blankets in th' mornin' an' do somethin' besides beller. There's a hoss to be well loaded with grub: me an' Red near starved to death last time."

"You mean I'm really goin' with you?" yelped Johnny, his eyes shining.

"What else do I mean? You want I should write you an invite on a piece of paper?" growled the trail boss.

"Hell!" said a low voice on the fringe of the firelight. "You couldn't do that: you don't know how to spell."

"Nor write, nuther," said another, with a chuckle.

"Shut up!" barked Johnny, flipping open his bed roll. "Shut up, so a man can sleep!"

"Meanin' you?" snapped Lanky, turning sour as the Kid turned sweet. He had nursed the hope of going to war; now all he was going to do was nurse cattle.

The trail boss looked at the seated figures, ignoring the remarks.

"You can fix up yore shifts to suit yoreselves," he said. "If Gibson gets past us, an' I reckon he's goin' past us right about now—seein' which direction he rode away from this camp—let him open up a good gap. Let th' herd drift ahead as it grazes. You'll see———"

"*I won't nurse th' cavvy, an' I won't flank th' herd,*" sang Johnny as he squirmed into the blankets.

"Throw a loop over yore mouth," growled the trail boss. "Can't you hear I'm talkin'?"

"You 'most generally are," said Pete. "Not that you say nothin'."

"Shut up!" snapped Billy, squirming suddenly in his blankets. "Don't you know I got a shift to ride?"

"*I'm plumb sick of beans, an' sow-belly, too,*" hummed Johnny and ducked barely in time to avoid the boot.

"Would you mind throwin' yore *own* boots?" growled Pete, lumbering off to retrieve the missile.

Dawn found a camp already stirring. The cook rubbed sleepy eyes and mooched about his troubles. He glared at the alarm clock and vowed that he would blow it apart when they reached Bulltown, if they ever did reach it. Johnny was loading provisions on a much surprised horse, deftly throwing pack hitches which might well be the envy of a much older man.

Breakfast out of the way, the trail boss took one final look around, stepped into the saddle, and led the way westward toward the wide baldness of the great cattle trail. He did not know where to find Halliday or any of his men, and he did not especially care to find him or them; he knew pretty well the territory where Waggoner's friends ran off their stolen animals, and that part of the country lay well west of the trail. He led the way across the great beaten welt which stretched from the warm waters of the Gulf almost up to the Canadian line, and pushed on in a direction a little west of south, heading for a certain chain of little valleys in all that great expanse of plain as a homing pigeon heads for its cote.

XVII

THEY struck the line of puddles which marked the watercourse, and found horse tracks, a welter of them. They were fresh enough to have been very recently made. A significant fact soon became noticeable: every little while a few tracks left the main sign and led off to one side or the other; and in each of these instances the tracks of one horse returned.

Hopalong glanced up from one of these divergent signs and smiled knowingly.

"Scatterin' 'em as they go," he said. "A few here an' a few there. Th' main herd is gettin' smaller all th' time, an' th' scattered animals can be rounded up and driven in whenever them fellers feel like doin' it. Looks to me like Halliday has purty near lost his cavvy, or most of it."

"But," protested Johnny, "soon's it got daylight these fellers could see by th' brands that they didn't get our cavvy. They'd know they got th' wrong herd."

"Shore; but it would be too late then," replied the trail boss; "An' hosses are hosses, just th' same. They got th' wrong bunch, but they shore did get ridin' stock. Hoss for hoss, Halliday's are worth as much as ourn."

"But these signs of scatterin'," said Red, "show that they had time to do it: they wasn't bein' hard-pressed. They didn't have no such start as that over th' T Dot Circle outfit. How you figger that out?"

"Only a couple of ways that sound sensible," answered Hopalong slowly. "They could have left a rear guard to hold th' outfit back, or they could have split th' cavvy an' made Halliday take his choice of which bunch to foller."

"Huh!" snorted Red, in strong disbelief. "If it had been us, we'd have split up, too, an' follered both bunches. Halliday has a full crew, which is more than we have. He coulda done that."

"Well, however that is, we know that these thieves had time enough to scatter 'em. Th' signs tell us that. They mebby mighta stampeded th' cattle along after th' cavvy, blottin' out every damn hoss track. Where you've got a faint or blotted sign, made on th' run, it takes trackers a lot longer to figger 'em out than it takes th' makers to blot 'em. Halliday mighta figgered, by signs like that, that th' cavvy an' th' herd had run together an' got all mixed up; that when he rounded up th' cattle he'd find his hosses." He scratched his head. "It ain't a question of what they did or how they did it: it's been done. Suppose we save up all these arguments for some time when we're all settin' around th' fire, an' do a little more ridin'?"

The divergent signs continued to be found. Every mile or so a set of them led off to one side or the other; with the single horse track returning in every case.

The main herd had been steadily shrunk, until at last it was only a handful. At each of these divergent trails Hopalong took good notice of the tracks of the returning horse; and some of these tracks had characteristics, faint or otherwise, which could be made out and memorized. By the time the main herd had shrunk to a dozen animals he knew the signatures of the horses ridden by the raiders.

They pulled up at the last divergent trail. Ahead of them lay the tracks of six horses, tracks evenly spaced, tracks made by six men riding side by side. The signs were eloquent: the stolen cavvy had been well scattered, and now the half-dozen raiders, free to ride where they pleased, were going on unhampered by loose saddle stock.

"There's only three of us," growled Hopalong thoughtfully. "It'd take us a long time to hunt out an' herd up Halliday's hosses. We could do a much better job with his outfit helpin' us. Sooner or later they'll be ridin' this way, once they get th' trail; you can't fool all them fellers. Th' thieves know that, too. All they played for was time—time to scatter th' cavvy an' get away. By now they figger they've done that. Shall we round up what hosses we can an' drive 'em back; or shall we leave that till we have help, an' keep after these coyotes an' teach 'em a lesson?"

"Hell with th' hosses!" snapped Johnny, his eyes glinting. "It was *us* they was hittin' at. An' it's too big a job for three men, combin' out an' roundin' up all these animals."

"You'd rather fight any day than work, wouldn't you, Kid?" chuckled Hopalong.

"It ain't too big a job," corrected Red; "but too long a job. Looks like we oughta try to make th' big trail safe for trail herds. There's mebby dozens of 'em headin' up it right now; an' next year we'll be comin' up it again, like as not. I say to foller these six tracks an' make some of them fellers sick at his stomach."

Hopalong nodded, his eyes on the alluring tracks.

"I've talked a lot with that trail cutter," he said. "He knows this whole country. It's his stampin' ground. I've let him talk an' listened to what he said. That means we ain't follerin' these tracks right along. Them fellers will hole up when they get to th' right place, waitin' in th' brush in case th' T Dot Circle comes a-ridin'. They can empty three, four saddles th' first fire. They'll wait a reasonable time an' then, if nobody shows up, they'll either ride on to some rendezvous, or they'll start back to drift th' stolen hosses outa th' brush an' bunch 'em into a herd again. If th' trail cutter was right, I know about where that rendezvous is. What you say we head for it, cuttin' straight acrost country, an' lettin' these tracks alone?"

Johnny fidgeted with eagerness.

"Cut straight acrost!" His gaze ran along the telltale tracks, and he thought that he, too, had memorized their identifying characteristics: he would know them again, wherever they were found.

Red nodded, but so perfunctorily that the trail boss looked at him curiously.

"What's on yore mind, Red?"

"If we cut acrost to any rendezvous, an' they head back toward th' scattered cavvy, then we won't see 'em. We'll mebby be all snug an' waitin' for 'em like three fools, an' they never show up a-tall."

Hopalong nodded and again scratched his head.

"I figger they'll show up sooner or later, with th' hosses or without 'em," he said; "but we got to consider th' time that's passin'. We got a herd up th' trail, an' we got a delivery date to worry about. For once in yore ornery life yo're right."

Johnny's eager expression changed to one of disappointment.

"Aw! Th' rest of th' boys can drift th' herd ahead," he growled. "If they throw it in with Gibson's mixed herd, they can push it right along at a good trail gait."

"Gibson's outfit went past us th' night he called on us," said Red. "They'd be steppin' right along an' openin' up a bigger trail gap every hour. That ain't no good."

"But what good does it do, settin' here an' talkin' about it?" demanded Johnny impatiently.

"Yo're doin' th' talkin'," growled Hopalong. *"We're* thinkin'."

Johnny's snort of derision was far from complimentary, but his companions ignored it.

Hopalong stirred out of his preoccupation and looked thoughtfully at Red.

"We'll circle off an' swing back every once in a while," he said. "That'll save us from follerin' th'

tracks like damn fools an' keep us from losin' 'em altogether. We've wasted considerable time: let's get
goin'."

Even with the start that Waggoner's gang had enjoyed, they were not far ahead by now, and Hopalong knew it. It had taken time to drive the loose
horses, and more time to scatter them in small
bunches, no matter how expeditiously it had been done.
The three friends rode on as swiftly as the pack horse
and the going would allow, making arcs of varying
length to the chord of the cattle thieves' trail, returning again and again for a quick look at the tracks of
the six horses; and each time they cut the trail they
found the signs no older. On the other hand, they appeared to grow fresher; and then, suddenly, they became very fresh.

"We're close to 'em—right close," said Hopalong
in a low voice. "From now on we're not ridin' so fast,
an' we're ridin' more cautious an' keepin' our eyes
skinned for trouble. We also got to spread out more.
Kid, you take that damn pack hoss an' keep west of
us."

For the second time in the last hour Johnny worked
the lever of the Sharps until the falling breechblock
let him see the dull gleam of the brass cartridge case.
Reassured as to proper preparedness, he slowly followed his companions from the trail to begin another
arc which he hoped would lead to war. He kept within
sight of Red, at some trouble, and found himself being shoved farther west, in a larger arc than any made

so far. It seemed to him to be a long time before Red
began to swing the other way. The country was still
rough and broken, with gullies, dry washes, and thick
scrub, ideal for hiding riders who tried to ride unseen.
The arc of his riding still swept back to the east, and
then Red suddenly flung up an arm and became lost to
sight as Johnny stopped to wait.

Red pushed on at a little better speed so as to join
his leader, and together they cautiously approached
the trail running along the bottom of the narrow little
valley. As they came within sight of its edge, they dismounted without a word, dropped the reins over the
heads of their horses, and crept forward, keeping
close under cover. After a few moments they peered
down into a shallow basin and studied it carefully.
There was nothing to be seen except the faint, beaten
trail leading southwestward. It was too far away for
them to be able to distinguish individual tracks on its
rough surface.

"Wait here, Red," said the trail boss, studying a
brush-covered little promontory which thrust out into
the valley and forced the trail to swing well out and
then to pass it close by.

Red nodded and watched his companion disappear
in the brush, marveling at the other's uncanny silence.
An Indian would make no more noise, but Red doubted
if any white man could do as good. Minutes passed,
and then Red gave a little start at the voice behind
him.

"No fresh tracks come down this far," said the trail

boss. "We've got ahead of 'em. We mebby won't have time to go back for th' Kid; be just as well to keep him outa this, anyhow. That gang oughta pass here purty soon."

"One or two of 'em might get past," admitted Red grimly.

"I mean oughta come in sight," corrected Hopalong. "Let's lay low an' keep still."

More minutes went past, but there were no signs of the thieving half-dozen. More time passed, and then Hopalong began to give this matter his full thought. Time enough had elapsed to bring the riders this far down the trail. Still he waited, silent and motionless, and waited in vain. He stirred, squirmed sideways, and looked at his companion.

"We passed a little rill about a mile back," he said thoughtfully. "It's th' only runnin' water we've passed in a long time, an' I noticed it particular."

"Yes," agreed Red. "I remember it."

"There ain't much decent water down in this part of th' country," continued Hopalong slowly. "Hardly none a-tall in this valley, except little pools that smell. I got th' idear that they've camped at th' outlet of that rill. Either that or they've growed wings."

"Figger yo're right," said Red. "Won't take us long to find out. What about th' Kid? You want I should go back an' get him?"

"Not yet. We'll leave our horses where they are an' work back up this rim on foot. Hadn't oughta be more'n a mile or two."

"Mile or two!" growled Red, who hated walking over rough country in his high-heeled boots as a cat hates a bath; but his growl was for his own benefit, and he followed his boss without lagging. Nearly half an hour went by, and then the leader held up a hand and stopped. Red carefully joined him, and they looked down into the little valley where the rill flowed into it to form a sizable pond in a hollow. An adobe house, squat and square, sat at the edge of the tiny stream, and on a bench against its front wall four men were loafing. A faint finger of smoke came from the rock-and-mud chimney, and located the fifth man, evidently cook *pro tem*. Where was Number Six? There should be six according to the tracks, and according to the six saddled horses which had made the tracks, and which were grazing a hundred yards below the building, with neither hobbles nor picket ropes to restrict their movements. That was the worst of such scant feed.

"They're shore takin' things easy, for a gang that has just run off a whole cavvy," whispered Hopalong. "They ain't afraid of bein' come onto unawares, an' that's unusual. That's th' one thing that mebby tells us about Number Six. We're lucky he didn't spot us; but, of course, we've come up from th' wrong direction. He's watchin' th' north trail. Betcha he's up on th' top of that little hill behind th' house. Well, that'll be a job for me—takin' care of *him*."

"An' th' Kid accused *me* of hoggin' things," growled Red with strong disgust.

"I want a *good* rifle shot layin' right here, with that

door an' them two little side winders under his sights,"
rejoined Hopalong. "You figger you could hit a head,
at this distance, shootin' from a rest?" Hopalong was
a little sarcastic.

"From a rest?" sneered his companion. "Hell! I
can make four-inch groups at this range! I got a
gun!"

"All right, then," said the trail boss, inching backward. "You stay here, holed up, while I go get th' Kid.
I want him farther south, close in to them horses.
Somebody might make a dash for 'em. We don't want
nobody loose to pester us when we're drivin' out an'
roundin' up that scattered cavvy."

"That cavvy won't be so very much scattered very
long," said Red. "Hosses like to drink, an' th' only
water there is for 'em is in them little pools along th'
trail. That rill is too far south. It won't be a terrible
job to bunch 'em up an' head 'em back."

Hearing no reply to his words, Red looked around
and found that he had been talking to himself. He
grinned and forthwith gave his attention to the scene
down in the valley. Occasionally he searched the opposite hillside but could make out no watcher on its
slope. However, he did see a man or two on the bench
lift his head and look up in that direction.

Johnny had done what he could do to expedite his
entry into the action, and this had consisted of driving
the pack horse off and leaving it side line hobbled in a
deep little hollow surrounded with brush. Then he returned to his place and awaited Red's arrival, steadily

growing more impatient; but he was consoled by the thought that the action could not have begun, since he had heard no shots. Then he heard a well-known voice calling his name, and he swung quickly around.

"Here, Hoppy. Over here," he replied, and then for the first time heard sounds of human progress through the brush. He grinned as the trail boss pushed out into sight. "What's th' matter? Lose 'em?"

"Found 'em," grunted Hopalong. "Found 'em at home, settin' on a bench as calm as if they never stole a hoss. Come on, Kid: want you to get close to their hosses an' stay close. No shootin' unless you have to. They got a lookout holed up on th' hill behind th' house, an' he's th' only dangerous man in th' crowd. We got to get him outa th' way. That's my job. Yore job is to stampede their hosses an' run 'em off. Head 'em up toward th' house so they'll foller th' trail back th' way they come. After you get 'em started, Red'll keep 'em goin' till they're around th' bend an' out of them fellers' sight. While he's doin' that, you cut back this way, hit th' valley above th' bend, an' keep them hosses goin' till you get 'em back where th' cavvy was scattered. Red an' I'll meet you there. But don't you make a move with th' hosses till after I take care of that lookout. When Red starts shootin', that's *yore* signal to start things."

Johnny nodded his understanding and was about to start for his new position when his companion checked him.

"Where's th' pack hoss, Kid?"

"Over yonder," answered Johnny, waving a hand.

"Show me," ordered the trail boss. "Me or Red will have to pick him up—you won't have time for that."

Johnny led the way to the little hollow and then, returning to his horse, mounted and rode southward, keeping well off ridges and high ground. He was glad that he had been told about the lookout.

Hopalong slipped back to Red, making his approach known before showing himself.

"Looks like we're wastin' a lot of time," growled the red-headed sentry. "This fight coulda been half over by now."

"I shore wish you'd quit tryin' to think!" retorted the trail boss. "You allus make a mess of it. Now you listen to me."

"All right," sighed Red, with a vast and very apparent resignation.

"Not a move outa you till after I get through on that hill over yonder," ordered the trail boss. "An' I won't be all through till you hear me fire three shots as close together as I can put 'em. Then, an' *not before,* you open up on that bench. You had a lot to say about four-inch groups—I don't believe there's a gun in th' country can make groups like that at this distance. That don't matter. I don't care whether you hit 'em or miss 'em, as long as it's close shootin'. All I want is to have 'em drove inside that house and kept there till I say to let 'em out. You savvy?"

"They'll be close, Hoppy: they'll be right close because there ain't no use gettin' fancy an' shootin' at heads when I can pick a target six, eight times bigger. I'm figgerin' to hold on th' place where th' middle shirt button oughta be. Anyhow, they'll be close enough."

"All right," said the trail boss, and then he carefully explained what Johnny was to do and how Red was to help him do it. They discussed other necessary angles for a few moments, and then, everything made clear, Hopalong slipped away to take care of the job he had given himself. It was a job he did not particularly fancy, but one which had to be done; and the reason it was there and had to be done was that cattle thieves themselves put it in front of a man and then forced him to do it. The rights, property, and lives of honest men on an open trail were things to be safeguarded. And so, with the determination to make and keep that trail safe, Hopalong faded into the brush and put his whole mind to the task in front of him.

XVIII

Hopalong proceeded on a roundabout course, keeping under the cover of the brush and every available hollow and ravine, moving steadily southward toward the jutting promontory which shut off the lower end of the main valley from the view of anyone at the house. He passed Johnny on the south and smiled at how well the Kid had concealed himself and his horse from anyone at the house. The Kid would make a good man—in fact, he was a good man already.

Then Hopalong found the ground rising and made his cautious way up the increasing slope of the hill until he reached its crest. Here he flattened and waited while he scrutinized the country about him. Through an occasional small opening in the brush he could see the rear wall of the house, and he was glad that it had no windows. The 'dobe was a veritable jail. He moved on again, just below the top of the hill and on the farther side. From time to time he crept up to the crest and looked over it, searching the slope below him. It was on perhaps the sixth or seventh of these little side excursions that he saw what he was looking for: a man lying prone on a small shelf, snuggled down behind a boulder, hat on the ground beside him and his rifle resting across the rock. Here was the reason for the apparent carelessness of the men below; the reason which that carelessness had preached to an observing man.

The trail boss could have killed the lookout from where he was, with one shot from a Colt. The power and accuracy of a big-calibered Colt are vastly underestimated by those who are not familiar with such a weapon. One shot would do it; but Hopalong was not a cold-blooded murderer. With all his hatred for cattle thieves, when face to face with such a deed he could not do it. He had taken life, and would take more lives before he died, but he would always accept the risk of an even break, of a fair chance, and depend solely upon his own expertness.

Hopalong moved with cautious care, working over the crest and down the north slope, his eyes on the quiet watcher below him. Not a leaf rustled, not a twig snapped. Naturally enough, the thoughts of the man below were concerned with the territory in front of him and not with that behind him. He regarded his job as more or less a matter of form, a necessary safeguard, and his thoughts were turning more and more to what the cook was doing in the kitchen of the house below. He simply was standing his trick on guard.

Hopalong deliberately shook a dead branch, its dry leaves rustling noisily. The warning thus given was a general one, and not a particular one, such as a shout would be. It simply gave notice that something was moving in the brush, and it served to make the lookout squirm around and look up toward the sound. While it did not tell him that an armed enemy was close to him, it did save him from that momentary shock of surprise which might slow his offensive action for a second or more. It put him squarely on an even footing with his danger.

Then a twig snapped to his left, and he faced the new sound with one hand on his belt gun. As he touched it he saw a stranger step out into full view, also with hand on gun. The two men acted as one. The two shots sounded almost as one. The man above felt a sudden sting on an ear, and a clipped branch fell behind him; the man below folded up like a hinge and dropped against the boulder.

Hopalong watched him for perhaps two seconds and then raised the still smoking gun and fired three quick shots into the air. He slipped back into cover, and as he did so he heard the heavy roar of Red's rifle, sudden shouting from below, and Red's crashing second shot.

The trail boss stood up and calmly and openly worked his way up the hill, serene in his confidence of Red's marksmanship. Hurrying along the top of the ridge, he came to a place whence he could look down upon the six saddle horses, and smiled again.

Johnny was after them, slapping with his quirt, shouting like a wild Indian and firing his Colt. The frightened animals bunched, milled for an instant, and then stampeded for the trail, with Johnny in close pursuit. The Kid followed them almost too far, as evidenced by the puff of dust in front of his horse and the angry song of a ricochet. Johnny swung his horse into a swift, short arc and raced off in a safe direction. He rode roundabout for the thrusting promontory and disappeared behind it. The stampeded horses kept on past the house, Red's heavy bullets raising little puffs of dust at their heels. They knew the trail, and they kept to what they knew. In a few moments they swept out of sight around a bend in the upper end of the valley and were lost to sight.

Red had waited with placid patience until those two close shots had sounded on the hill across the valley. He slipped the butt of the rifle against his shoulder, steadied the weapon, and bent his head. This smacked too much of murder. Four men, loafing on a bench until the hillside shots aroused them; then quick risings and short runs to the corner of the building. At the triple signal Red's finger gently, steadily pressed against the trigger. The bullet struck the end of the house, and the exploding adobe filled the first rustler's eyes and nose with dust, making him sneeze as he frantically ducked back. There was a concerted rush for the safety offered by the open doorway, and as the last man dashed into the house he closed the plank door upon the passage of a slug which tore a heel from his boot.

Red sent the third shot through an open window and sighed gustily from relief: he had taken a chance, two of them, with such close shooting; but he had gotten away with it, murdered no one, and his conscience was clear. After this warning, and such close shooting, his conscience would not be at all concerned: he would, if he could, hit any head which showed itself, and he rather thought he could.

He was conscious of sudden activity south of the house and risked a quick glance: Johnny was stampeding the saddle horses. Suddenly Red swore: the Kid was following them too far and was getting into the sector commanded by a front window. He dropped his head to the sights and fired just in time: not in time to stop the shot, but in time to make it a wild one. He could see the chunk of adobe fly from the side of the window, where his bullet had struck, and he could imagine what had happened to the face and eyes of the man it hit. There was no second shot at the Kid, and the horses swept on, now even with the building, now past it. They showed faint indications of milling, and Red began to drop bullets where they would do the most good. Gravel began to explode behind hoofs, and a shot grooved the hip of the last horse, whereupon the indications of milling were lost in the sudden surge of the frightened animals. They raced past him and around the bend. His gaze went back to the building as a bullet hummed high to his right. There was a pale, vague spot framed by a window, and his answering shot dropped it from sight. He had the feeling of being "on," that every good rifleman knows, and he counted it as a hit. Changing his position by a few yards, he again lay down to cover the house, to keep its door closed and its occupants inside it. Occasionally he fired at a window, with due regard for his supply

of cartridges, and during one of these lulls he heard
a well-known voice.

"Yeah, Hoppy," answered Red. "They're penned
up tight as hell, an' right glad of it."

"All right; keep 'em penned," said the trail boss,
fading back into the brush. "I'm gettin' our hosses an'
th' pack hoss. I'll leave yours where we dismounted,
back yonder. I'll go on with th' others, an' then Johnny
an' me will keep busy with th' scattered cavvy till
'most dark. You figger you can hold 'em in th' house
that long?"

"I don't see where you got no call to insult a man!"
retorted Red with spirit. "You get busy with th' hosses
an' let me mind my own business for myself. Two of
them coyotes are half blind, another's head is mostly
missin', an' they're all on foot. Clear outa here: yo're
only wastin' time."

"All right," chuckled the trail boss. "You want to
get away from here before it gets too dark for you to
find yore hoss, or makes you waste too much time gettin' down to us. An' if you'll figger *that* out to be an
insult, I'll be much obliged."

"You go to hell!" snapped Red and gave his attention to the house.

Johnny was busy, very busy. The rustlers' six horses
had stopped running and were placidly grazing, as if
nothing unusual had occurred. Red's prediction regarding the scattered animals of the cavvy was partly ful-
filled, and becoming more so with each passing minute.
Driven hard and watered insufficiently, the T Dot Cir-

cle animals were coming out of the brush to drink at
the pools. They were tired and had had their fill of
running, which perhaps explains why Johnny found
them so tractable.

The Kid was doing very well by himself when Hopalong rode into sight with the pack horse and gave him
a hand; and they had hardly gone to work in earnest
before Hopalong's restless gaze descried moving
dust over a slight rise in the valley's floor. It was to
the north of him, but, even so, he shouted a warning
to Johnny and took to cover.

Horses' heads and soiled hats appeared above the
rise, and then a compact body of horsemen popped
into sight. They drew rein for an instant at the scene
before them and then pushed forward with rifles at
the ready as Hopalong rode out of the brush and into
their sight. His left hand was raised, palm out, and
the sheriff's answering gesture caused the trail boss to
sit a little less erect in the saddle. The sheriff said
something to the riders behind him, and they stopped.
The peace officer pushed on at a walk, alert as a cat
in a strange house, his keen eyes on the lone horseman
down the trail. Then, suddenly, he recognized the Circle 4 trail boss, and a wide grin slid over his face.

"Where'd you git 'em all?" asked the sheriff, looking at the cavvy.

"Right around here," answered Hopalong, waving
his hand in a gesture which took in considerable of the
surrounding brush. "There's more of 'em back in th'
brush, I reckon; don't know how many head Halliday

had. Now that him an' his boys are here, they can get busy drivin' th' rest out. I'm glad to get 'em off my hands." He looked curiously at the officer. "How come yo're with Halliday?"

"Just sorta bumped into him, this side th' big trail," answered the officer. "He had just begun to git things figgered out. I knowed about where to ride, an' we all come a-kitin'. You all alone, down here?"

"No. Two of my boys come with me. Johnny's in th' brush, somewhere close by. Red's layin' on his belly, couple miles south of here, keepin' five hoss thieves penned up in a 'dobe shack down below him. I had to shoot th' other feller."

"I know that 'dobe," said the sheriff. He turned and motioned to the men behind him. "You reckon they're still in it?"

"You ask Red that, if you want to get insulted!"

Halliday pulled up beside the two men, his outfit close behind him.

"Howdy," he grunted, his face wearing a suspicious frown.

"Howdy," replied Hopalong, trying not to smile.

"What th' hell's goin' on down here?" demanded the T Dot Circle boss.

"Just a couple of round-ups: hoss thieves, an' trail herd cavvy," answered Hopalong and turned to the sheriff.

"Reckon you can take care of th' hoss thieves an' let Red pull outa there. There's enough men here, without me an' my friends, to take care of .th' 'dobe an' these hosses, too.''

Halliday had a glimmer of light, and a look of great surprise came over his face. He pushed forward, his hand held out.

"Sorry, friend," he said frankly, like a full-grown man. "Sorry I pulled back onto th' trail after tellin' you to pass. But I never saw you before; an', you know, you *mighta* been lyin'.''

"Shore! That's about th' way it looked to me, after I'd had time to set down an' wrastle it out," replied Hopalong. He laughed. "It just happened I wasn't lyin'. Now, there's six saddled hosses in th' bunch that don't belong to you. Mebby th' sheriff will give 'em to you when he gets through: th' saddles, anyhow.''

"If he gives 'em to anybody, he'll give 'em to you," said Halliday, his eyes on a commotion in the brush. His eyelids narrowed as a horseman pushed out into sight. "Who's that?''

Hopalong looked around.

"Johnny, one of my riders." He raised his voice. "Hey, Kid! Show th' sheriff where Red's holed up, an' tell Red to get a move on. We've lost too damn much time now, with a delivery date gettin' closer every day, an' only half a crew with th' herd.''

He turned to the sheriff, who had started to ride forward at the head of three men.

"I reckon you can handle them thieves without us," he said loudly.

"Reckon mebby we can, if yore man ain't let 'em get

out," replied the sheriff and went on to join the impatient Kid.

"What'd you say, Halliday?" asked Hopalong, turning to the T Dot Circle boss.

"I was sayin' that mebby them thieves won't need their hosses," grimly repeated Halliday. He was looking at two trees on the farther hill, the limbs of which seemed to be high enough and strong enough for the purpose he had in mind.

Hopalong followed the look and laughed gently.

"Mebby they won't," he said; "but I'm bettin' th' sheriff gets them fellers to jail, an' no worse off than they are when he captures 'em."

Later he learned that his bet would have won.

XIX

THE small fire glowed on the slope of the hollow, casting huge, faint shadows against the rising ground and picking out small details of the near-by wagon. Overhead the hard brilliance of countless stars studded the clear, dark sky. There was not a sound to break the silence, not even the gentle whisper of a wind. Then a sapwood stem exploded with a sharp *pop,* abruptly disturbing the glowing coals of the fire.

Pete Wilson stirred, lazily recrossed his legs, and sought an easier position on the hard ground.

"Wonder how soon they'll be comin' back?" he inquired speculatively. "We've done lost five days a'ready."

Skinny Thompson looked across the glowing coals at the speaker and let his gaze flick around the radiant arc of the fire.

"Don't know," he grunted, shifting in turn and taking advantage of the movement to drag a tobacco sack from a pocket. "They won't waste no time." He finished rolling the cigarette and looked up again. "Anyhow, we ain't lost no five days: we've been lettin' 'em move ahead as they grazed."

The cook rested a hand on his blanket roll. He had

discovered that prairie rattlesnakes were not only diminutive, but also scarce along this section of the trail. He no longer slept in the wagon. There were several bolt heads in the bottom of the wagon box that a man could not avoid. He reached out a foot, pushed a stick farther into the fire, and ventured an opinion.

"Hoppy said it was about two days' ride each way. He works fast. I wouldn't be surprised if they rid in 'most any minute."

"Mebby," grunted Pete. Instinctively he glanced in the direction of his thoughts, looking southward down the trail. "Some of them herds will be catchin' up with us," he growled.

Skinny smiled.

"I've been lookin' down that way for dust signs near all day," he confessed.

Pete's thoughts leaped to his absent friends and to what they had set out to do.

"It was a damn-fool idear," he growled. "We shoulda let them fellers get back their hosses by themselves. They had it comin' to 'em, didn't they?"

"Hoppy done right. Trail outfits oughta stick together," said the cook smugly.

"Hell!" said Pete, looking the cook in the eye. "That sounds right good. So does turnin' th' other cheek sound good; but try it, an' you'll mebby get it blowed plumb off yore face. Them smart Alecks got what they deserved!"

"Ain't you near outa wind?" asked Skinny, pulling off his boots. He reached behind him for his blanket roll. "Shut up; we got a trick to ride." He unbuckled his gun belt and placed it close to his hand. "Time passes fast at night, 'cept when yo're out with th' herd; an' we're three men short."

"Huh!" sneered Pete. "An' *you* talkin' about bein' outa wind!"

"Figger yo're *both* right," grunted the cook, pulling a blanket over him and sighing with relief.

Dawn and a cloudless sky. A faint thread of smoke streamed upward, straight as a plumb line. Two men wiped their mouths on a sleeve and strode toward their horses, already impounded in the little rope corral. In a few moments they were riding northward, toward the grazing herd. The cook stuck his finger into the dishwater, snapped it suddenly, and swore gently under his breath. Some day he would lose that finger. He went to the wagon, tossed a few more sticks of wood toward the fire, and reached for a dipper of flour. He had bread to bake. The outfit much preferred biscuits, and that was the reason why he was making bread. The last guard with the cattle rode rapidly nearer, and the cook glanced around at the sounds of the nearing horses. He grinned frankly: it was double turns with the herd now, since Hopalong and his two companions had ridden from camp.

"I near shot that damn bummer!" Pete was saying. "Everythin' was sweet as blackstrap till he started in to raise hell. Once I thought that bunch never would lay down ag'in. Pokin' round an' buttin' sleepin' steers off their beds!"

"He wanted a nice warm spot to lay down on," said Skinny, grinning.

"Warm spot? Hell, th' ground ain't cold these nights!"

"Thought we didn't have no bummers?" said the cook. "Wasn't it you that told me that?"

"You ever hear of range strays gettin' into a herd?" growled Pete.

"Yeah, lots of times; but only when th' riders ain't no good," said the cook.

"Oh, that so?" demanded Pete, shortly.

Skinny glanced at the tailboard of the wagon and turned hopeful eyes to the cook.

"Biscuits?" he asked, grinning.

"Nope," grunted the cook. "Bread."

Pete slanted a glance in the cook's direction.

"Huh!" he snorted. "You been makin' bread ever since we started out; but we ain't had no *bread* yet."

"Ain't, huh?" retorted the cook, bridling a little. "Where *you* been all this time?"

"Oh, I been along, lettin' range strays join up with th' herd," said Pete. "Just th' same we ain't had no *bread*."

Skinny pushed his big hat up on one side of his head and cogitated judiciously.

"No, we ain't: Pete's right," he said, flatly, sadly, and positively.

"Hell you ain't!" retorted the cook, the veins of his neck swelling.

"No, we ain't; but we shore have been eatin' some

right good stuffin' for hoss-hair sofas. How you make it hang together like you do? All hell couldn't bite through it with one chaw."

" 'Tain't sawdust," volunteered Skinny. " 'Tain't 'dobe, neither. What th' hell is it?"

"Some of these here days——" began the cook, and stopped suddenly, his eyes on the back trail. "There they come—all three of 'em!"

"How many you s'pose would be comin': four, five?" asked Pete, turning to look southwestward.

"No! But only one or two might be comin' back!" snapped the cook, knowing that the little expedition had been one of war.

"That's right," admitted Pete. "Them that didn't come back mighta got to thinkin' about that stuff you call bread."

"Most generally when they go off with Hoppy they all come back ag'in," said Skinny placidly. "Hoppy's got a head on him."

"Yeah, an' so have you," said the cook. "You have to have a head or you couldn't wear no hat. Talk about stuffin' in hoss-hair sofies! Damn if you don't make me laugh!"

"You ever laugh till you cried?" softly asked Skinny, inching forward.

The cook knew the length of that reach and the knobs of bone at the end of it. He backed away, instantly solicitous about his bread. Skinny turned, grinned at Pete, and waited expectantly for the distant riders to come up.

The three horsemen came on steadily, and one of them suddenly raised a hand above his head, raised it as high as it would go. The gesture was not casual, not just a greeting: it was exultant, prideful.

Skinny's lean face was immobile from concentration, his steady gaze on that upraised hand, and suddenly he sighed.

"They did th' job," he said flatly. "Th' Kid'll be a damn nuisance from now on—he's all swelled up like a poisoned coyote. Lookit him!"

"Yeah," agreed Pete slowly. "Just like a poisoned coyote. Well, yearlin's are allus bumptious."

The cook looked up from his work, a gleam in his eye.

"Yeah," he said with placid satisfaction, "they are." He reached for more flour. "But," he added gratuitously, "there warn't no bummer in this man's herd while *he* was here." He smacked his lips and waited, and the wait was very brief.

"Oh, so you got it all figgered out, ain't you?" growled Pete, glowering at him.

"Shore have," said the cook, stripping dough from his fingers. He was enjoying himself.

"Have, huh?" inquired Pete, his voice rising.

"On yore own say-so," retorted the cook, and then he laughed outright.

Pete scratched his head, cogitated briefly, and found that he had nothing further to say.

The three riders came down the slope and stopped

near the fire, Johnny's grin proving the tensile strength of epidermis.

"We got 'em!" he exulted. "Got 'em! Me an' Hoppy an' Red got 'em! We got everythin'!"

"Too bad you didn't get th' colic, too!" grunted Skinny in disgust.

"You shore got a swelled head," said Pete.

"Yah!" jeered Johnny. "We got th' cavvy an' th' hoss thieves, too!"

"What did you do with 'em?" asked Skinny, his fingers itching.

"Huh!" snorted the Kid. "Turned 'em over to their owners: gave 'em back to th' T Dot Circle."

"I didn't ask you about th' damn hosses!" retorted Skinny, edging a little closer. "Hell with th' hosses! What happened to th' thieves?"

Johnny freed one foot from a stirrup, the foot on Skinny's side of the horse, and held it ready. Skinny stopped edging, and Hopalong spoke.

"Left th' rest of 'em for th' sheriff to smoke out," said the trail boss. "Skinny, you wrangle us in some fresh hosses. We got to get th' herd movin': there's dust climbin' high, back down on th' trail. Them herds will be steppin' on our tail, first thing we know. Cook, you cut out yore work hosses after you throw us some grub, an' get this wagon rollin' soon———"

"But I'm makin' bread!" interrupted the culinary artist and scowled quickly at Pete and Skinny.

"Bread?" sarcastically asked the trail boss. "Hell

with yore bread! Thow it away an' try yore hand with some biscuits for a change. *Bread?* My Gawd!"

Hopalong stood up in his stirrups and swung his big hat above his head, swung it once, twice, thrice, in a well-known signal. The riders with the herd, their eyes on the camp, came to life with a snap, their long-range curiosity driven from them. The grazing animals nearest the camp suddenly left off feeding and pushed toward the animals just ahead of them, picked these up and kept on going. Slowly and steadily the herd compacted, the natural leaders moving up into their accustomed places, the falterers filtering back to later become the drag. Movement was general, and in almost no time the entire herd was moving toward the great cattle highway like the trail-broken veterans they were. The low, spreading dust cloud concentrated and began to climb into the air, a gray-white fog, dense here and opening there; and through the swirling openings could be seen dark and sometimes shapeless objects plodding doggedly onward. The Circle 4 was throwing back upon the trail again.

Riders streaked from camp to join the herd, each man taking up his regular position. As yet there was no drag, since all the animals were fresh and rested. Hoofs thudded, horns clicked; and behind them a swearing cook loaded his wagon, hitched up his work horses, and rolled down the slope on his way to the next camp. He, personally, did not care for biscuits, which seemed to him to be reason enough for the making of bread; and besides, the outfit's capacity for biscuits seemed to be unlimited, and it seemed as if some of their stomachs had no bottoms.

"But if they're goin' to Canady, then I'm a-goin', too,
Me an' my roll with th' whole damn' crew!"

sang Johnny in the soaring dust, his voice carrying above the noise of the hoofs and the horns.

"All swelled up like a poisoned coyote," growled Pete, and deftly drove back an erring steer. He looked over the moving animals, hoping to catch sight of the pestiferous bummer; but the bummer was well hidden by the dust and, likely as not, well in the middle of the herd. Having a guilty conscience, no doubt, and a canny instinct, the bummer was keeping well hidden.

XX

THEY struck the trail and swung into it, rolling along at a good traveling gait, kicking up a dust made deeper by the thousands of hoofs which already had cut and churned it; but while they were shrouded with dust, there was no dust to be seen either behind them or before them; they were in the middle of a long trail space.

Noon came and passed, and still the herd went plodding on, the drag beginning to grow a little now; but the main herd was holding the pace it had set when starting out. Past mid-afternoon they struck the first water, a shallow, sluggish creek whose banks were littered with dead and trampled brush and grass. Into it went the herd, loitered there while its thirsty units nosed the water, drank and let it flow around their legs. Then out again and up the gentle slope from the northern edge, up the slope and over the crest and on again. Along here the feed was poor, cropped close and trampled down by many bedded herds. Mindful of the difficulty of starting a herd from water, and wishing for better grass, Hopalong kept the cattle moving for another hour.

The trail boss finally gave the word, and the herd

swung in a wide circle from the beaten welt and moved to the right, toward the east, heading for the bed ground. Again he signaled, and the flankers fell back while the pointers crossed the front of the herd, checking it; and the tired animals slowed, stopped, and spread out, industriously searching for grass. The dusty and hungry riders sighed with relief and hopefully looked toward the little wagon camp; for the cook, as usual, had rolled past them on the drive, stopped when the herd turned off, started his fire, and even now was ready to place the coffee pot on the glowing coals.

"We picked up some time today," said Hopalong with satisfaction, as he joined Red and rode in toward camp. "An' we'll have to pick up plenty more. That delivery date's gettin' closer every day." He did not believe it necessary to explain that the delivery date they all knew so well was a full week ahead of the real date, the date mentioned in the contract.

Red nodded and let his gaze flick up the trail, another thought coming into his mind.

"Well, I reckon we can push 'em if we have to," he said, thinking of trail space. "We ain't seen no dust in front of us to worry about; an' we haven't seen none behind us since we joined up with th' herd. Anyhow, them follerin' herds ain't as close to us now as they was this mornin'. We got plenty of room, front an' back."

"Mebby," grunted Hopalong, estimating the distance as well as he could between themselves and the big, mixed herd ahead. "But we've cut down some on Gibson's lead. They'll be driftin' easy till Halliday's crew joins 'em with th' cavvy."

"Yeah," rejoined Red. "They wouldn't drive 'em very hard with th' outfit they got."

"They'll have to cut them two herds apart, soon as they can," said Hopalong, smiling: "an' that's when we'll go past 'em. There'll be a mighty big gap ahead of them that we'll fit into right snug an' make good time from then on. We got things about where we want 'em."

The cook grinned at their approach and looked meaningly at three pans of biscuits resting on the tailboard of the wagon.

"There's yore biscuits," he said, waving a hand at the pans. "Turn to an' make hawgs of yoreselves."

"When did you bake 'em?" asked Hopalong.

"Stopped around noon long enough to do that," answered the cook. "They're cold, but they're good hawg stuffin': I reckon you can eat 'em."

"We'll do our best," grunted Red, dismounting and heading for the tin cup and the water bucket. He drank deeply, dragged a sleeve across his lips, and rolled a cigarette. Then he went back to his horse, stripped the saddle off, rubbed the sweaty back with the saddle blanket, and spread the blanket out to air and dry. Hopalong was doing the same with his horse, and the two men stepped back to watch the animals roll enthusiastically before they fell to grazing. Simultaneously the two men turned and moved toward the fire.

"Well," said the cook, smiling at the trail boss, "we shore high-tailed it today. Made a good drive."

"Shore did," said Hopalong, his gaze on the distant cavvy being driven in by Skinny. "An' we high-tail it ag'in tomorrow, too: we got some lost time to make up." He flashed a glance at the brown-topped biscuits. "We'll keep you movin' so damn fast you won't have no time to bake bread, 'less you do it while we sleep."

"Work while you-all sleep?" said the cook with indignation. "Like hell! I can make hawg stuffin', if that's what you-all want."

"Time you found that out," retorted Red, heading for the washbasin. "How'd you like to get up in th' night an' ride shifts with th' herd?" He washed his face, slicked his hair, and then, getting his saddle blanket from where he had draped it over a bush, shook it out and hung it on a wagon wheel, to match Hopalong's blanket on the other wheel. Then he joined the trail boss and helped to rig the flimsy rope corral for the cavvy. They cut out and impounded the night horses and watched Skinny drift the riding stock off again, to check them not far from the wagon, where they were held to wait for the other tired horses of the rest of the outfit. When the two men turned back to camp they saw Pete and Johnny riding in toward the wagon. Not long thereafter the cook raised his hand, grabbed the coffee pot, and yelled; and the short line quickly got into motion past the tailboard.

Pete stole a biscuit from Johnny's plate and grinned as he dragged it through the smear of sorghum on his own plate; and then, looking up, checked what he was about to say and stared southwestward, in the direction of the trail they had just left.

"Here comes a pair of pilgrims. Ridin' th' grub line, I reckon," he said, his gaze on the nearing horsemen. "You got any biscuits left, cook?"

"Yeah, I have," growled the cook, glaring at the newcomers. "Damn these visitin' empty-bellies! You notice how you never see any of 'em around 'cept at meal time?"

"That only shows that they use their heads," grunted Johnny, grinning. He glanced at the slowly riding newcomers.

Hopalong put his plate down beside him on the ground and looked at Red.

"You see anythin' familiar about that right-hand rider?" he asked.

"By ——!" said Red, slowly. "I shore do: it's th' sheriff."

"Yeah, shore is," replied the trail boss. "With *one* prisoner. Them fellers musta fought it out after we left."

"It shore looks that way," admitted Red. "There was three, mebby four when we left, far's I know. You got one, an' I'm right shore of another. Huh!"

The two riders were near enough by now to distinguish details, and the low sun flicked intermittent glints from a narrow band of steel on the left-hand

rider's wrists. A closer look, as his horse swerved sideways, showed that his legs were tied together under
the animal's belly. He was riding a little in the lead,
and the bandage around his head, partly covered by
his big hat, showed a spot of red. Hopalong stood up
and took a few steps toward the newcomers and slowly
raised his hand in answer to the sheriff's gestured
greeting.

The two riders pulled up near the edge of the camp,
and the sheriff slowly swung from his saddle, his
leathery face devoid of expression.

"Howdy, Cassidy," he said. "Glad we're in time to
eat without makin' no trouble for th' cook." He turned
to his prisoner, untied the ropes from the man's feet,
and then stepped back to let him dismount. The sheriff
pointed a finger at a spot on the ground, not far from
the fire.

"You set down right there," ordered the peace
officer in a friendly voice, "while I get you some grub."

"I can't eat with these damn cuffs on," growled the
horse thief sullenly as he slowly obeyed.

"I ain't asked you to try it, yet," retorted the peace
officer, striding toward the wagon. He filled a tin plate
with food and a tin cup with coffee, carried them to the
prisoner and placed them on the ground at his side.

"There: that's yore fodder," said the sheriff. "You
wait till I get mine an' then we'll eat." Again he strode
off toward the wagon and in a moment was back with
his own plate and cup. Removing the prisoner's hand-
cuffs, the sheriff dropped them into a pocket and seated

himself a few feet away; far enough away so that a
sudden reach would miss the gun in his holster.

Red watched the two visitors stowing away their
supper, and after a moment he spoke, looking at the
busy sheriff.

"So they fought it out with you, huh?" he asked, as
an explanation of the one man taken prisoner.

"Yep: they did," grunted the peace officer, gulping
down a mouthful of food.

"Put up much of a fight?" persisted Red, his glance
flicking at the sullen captive, who was hardly more
than a boy.

"Hot an' short," answered the sheriff. "One of 'em
was dead when we started in, an' two others had their
eyes so full of 'dobe they couldn't hardly see. We
thought this feller was dead, too; but he was only
creased." He stuffed in another mouthful with keen
relish.

"If I hadn't been, I'd-a fought it out," growled the
prisoner with a show of anger.

"You done well enough, I reckon, as it was," replied
the sheriff.

"If I only knowed who it was that drove us inside
that damn 'dobe in th' first place——" mumbled the
prisoner and left the sentence unfinished. He reached
for the coffee cup.

Red's gaze was direct and unwavering.

"It might come in handy for you to know that, some
day, in case you get away," said Red slowly. "Seein'
that I know what you look like, it's mebby only fair

to let you know what that feller looks like. *I'm* th'
hombre that drove you all inside an' blew half th'
head off one of yore friends. Take a good look at me,
so you'll know me ag'in."

"I'll know you, you —— ——," growled the horse
thief and fell to eating again.

Hopalong looked thoughtfully at Red and then at
the prisoner and cleared his throat. He did not intend
to let Red bear the brunt of any future trouble which
might grow out of this incident.

"Red, here, did only what he was told to do," he
said. *"I* ran th' whole thing, from start to finish. You
better take a good look at *me*."

"An' I stampeded th' hosses!" said Johnny, eagerly
claiming some responsibility.

"Hell you did!" sneered the prisoner. "Any damn
fool could do that. Th' feller that I'd really like to see
is th' coyote that killed my brother."

"Where was he?" asked Hopalong quietly. "In th'
house?"

"Up on th' ridge behind th' house, keepin' watch
for us."

"Sorry," said the trail boss, shaking his head.
"Sorry he was yore brother. I gave him an even break,
an' he lost."

"Nobody could give Tom an even play an' beat him
to it!" snapped the prisoner angrily.

"I gave him one, an' he lost out," repeated Hopalong evenly.

"Well," snarled the prisoner, "I'll shore know *you*

if I ever see you ag'in—an' I'll know you for a liar!"

"Have it yore own way," replied Hopalong without anger, "if it'll make you feel any better. I'm sorry he was kin of yourn."

"Sorry?" sneered the prisoner. "Like hell you are!"

"Time to talk about somethin' else," said the sheriff. "We've done played out this here subject. After all, if you don't want to lose kin an' get into trouble, let other folks' hosses alone. Jake, you sleep on yore right side?"

"Yes," growled the prisoner sullenly. "Why?"

"Want you to rest as comfortable as you can when we turn in. I'll cuff you to a wagon wheel so you'll lay on yore easy side."

Hopalong looked at the placid peace officer.

"You takin' him in to Bulltown?" he asked curiously.

"No. They only got a plank jail there, an' I ain't figgerin' on shootin' up any of my friends to keep 'em from lynchin' a damn hoss thief. He's goin' wide around Bulltown an' then straight on to th' county seat, where th' bars are set in stone walls, an' th' doors are faced with iron."

Hopalong looked at Pete and Johnny and gestured toward the distant herd, whereupon the two men reluctantly got to their feet and started for their night horses. After a moment they rode off to relieve Lanky and Billy, who soon rode in. As the two hungry riders dismounted at the camp, they were just in time to see the sheriff snap the cuffs on his prisoner's wrists and sit down again. Both of the newcomers stared for a moment, and then, turning toward the tailboard, got their plates and loaded them generously. They ate in silence, and silence seemed to be the fashion. It was finally broken by the handcuffed man.

"Who's got th' makin's?" he asked, looking around the little circle of faces.

Hopalong handed him tobacco and papers and absent-mindedly watched the shackled captive roll a cigarette without spilling a flake of tobacco. As the prisoner glanced up, the trail boss struck a match and held it for him,

"Thanks," grunted the other and inhaled deeply.

The trail boss glanced at the quiet sheriff.

"Halliday round up his cavvy yet, you reckon?"

"Figger so. They all went right to work in th' brush as soon as th' fight was over. Some of them hosses was right well scattered."

"They've got a mixed herd to cut out an' separate when they get back to it," said Red, thinking of trail progress. "Take 'em some time, too."

The atmosphere of restraint eased up a little, and the talking became general and less forced, the prisoner taking part in it at times; and then, when darkness settled down, Hopalong and Red got to their feet and moved to the wagon to get their blankets. As they returned, the sheriff glanced at his prisoner.

"Well, Jake," he said, somewhat apologetically, "reckon it's time for us to roll up. I'll make yore bed near th' front wheel of th' wagon, an' cuff one hand to it. We'll get an early start in th' mornin' an' strike straight for town. There ain't no use for us to foller th' trail."

"No, there ain't. Much obliged," said Jake, glad to know that he was going to escape the hostile eyes of the outfits strung along the cattle highway.

The night passed uneventfully, but dawn brought a sky with a different color, and air with a different feel. Breakfast was soon out of the way, and the sheriff and his prisoner, once again in the saddle, nodded farewell and left the camp. Skinny turned from watching their departure, glanced at the sky and looked at his boss.

"Reckon th' weather's been too good to last," he said.

"Reckon so. Looks like it's makin' bad weather for trail herds," admitted Hopalong, studying the sky. "We'll high-tail it as long as we can without gettin' too close to anythin' ahead. Th' tireder these animals are tonight, th' better I'll like it."

Skinny nodded, mounted his horse, and drove off the cavvy.

The trail boss turned to the busy cook.

"Make a noon camp," he ordered. "If we keep on goin' past you, pull out ag'in; but while yo're camped, get somethin' cooked an' see that you've got plenty of coffee all ready to heat up in case th' storm breaks."

"She'll shore bust, an' she'll be a hellbender," said the cook, with the traditional trail cook's pessimism.

"If I was as cheerful as you I'd shore blow my head off," retorted Hopalong.

"Why not do it anyway?" growled the cook, and then he grinned. "Wonder how that feller feels with them steel cuffs on his wrists."

"Why didn't you ask him?" retorted the trail boss. "You usually ask fool questions."

Hopalong turned on his heel, swung into the saddle, and rode off after the moving herd. For the third time since breakfast he turned in the saddle and looked back along the trail, searching for the dust sign against the southern horizon which would tell him of a nearing herd. There was no such sign. Then another thought came to him to add to his worries: Big Muddy Creek was not so many miles ahead now, and if a heavy rain fell its boggy bed and bottoms would be a bottomless mire to hold up everything on the south of it. Nothing on four legs could cross that slough after a hard fall of rain, and it would take days to drive up around its head, by which time it would be passable at the regular crossing. The herds to the south of him would have plenty of time to overtake him. He swore gently under his breath and sent the horse on at a faster gait. Damn any man who did not have sense enough to keep from trailing cattle: there were so many easier jobs in the world.

Noon came, and as the herd topped a rise the riders could see the cook's wagon off to the right. The cook had timed it nicely. He was watching the moving cattle, and he knew they would not stop, for the storm was still far off. He was so certain of it that he had the team hitched to the wagon, ready to roll on again; and he was right, for he caught the hat-waved signal of the trail boss and almost instantly was on his way again. Having cooked supper while he waited, he now held to a pace even with that of the cattle, to be close at hand if the storm broke before dark.

The gray day had not lightened, but, if anything, had grown grayer. Gusty currents of wind swept here and there, bending the grass and brush, tearing rifts in the soaring dust clouds and sending yellow-white streamers aloft in fantastic shapes. Here was occurring one of the things which made trails endure, which made them lay nakedly across the prairies years after they had been abandoned: the wind scouring of the loose dust which lifted the light particles of earth and carried them away, leaving the hard-beaten soil exposed and below the level of the surrounding ground. Here in turn poured the infrequent heavy rains, scouring anew and cutting ever deeper, to carve a mark across the plains to endure for generations. And as the wind increased, it flung up a wall of dust which stretched as far as the eye could see and tinted the daylight with its faint color.

Well down the back trail there now appeared a small dust cloud, and the trail boss slowed his horse to investigate it. It was rolling so swiftly forward that it could not be made by cattle traveling at ordinary trail speed; and it was too small, despite the efforts of the wind, to be caused by a herd of trail size.

The answer popped into Hopalong's mind, and he pushed on to rejoin the herd. It must be Halliday and his outfit, driving up their recovered cavvy. They had taken longer than he thought they would. They were coming up rapidly, as rapidly as they could, urged on by the threat of the impending storm. They swung wide as they approached the Circle 4 herd and went past on the leeward side with every animal at a run. Halliday, silhouetted against the dense dust curtain behind him, raised his arm in salutation and then gave his attention to the job in hand. A twisting cross current swept the dust over him, and he was instantly lost to sight.

The cook's wagon stopped shortly after mid-afternoon as the herd was swung to the right and driven off the trail. The wind was dying out, only fitful gusts toying wtih the lessening dust as the first riders left the cattle and rode in to the wagon. Two of them went off at a tangent to give Skinny a hand with the cavvy, and soon the saddle stock was held near the wagon for the selection and cutting out of the night horses. Skinny waved his hand, and his helpers swung away toward camp.

The trail boss met them as they rode in, and frowned in the face of their broad smiles.

"What's so funny?" he asked them, his face lined by worry.

"All this worryin' about th' storm," said Billy, the smile growing. "It's headin' off th' other way."

"Is it?" snapped Hopalong. "*I* know how much it's

headin' off th' other way. We can't hobble th' whole
damn cavvy, an' if we could we'd only cripple near
every hoss in it; but we've got to have double mounts
tonight an' have 'em handy. You an' Lanky stuff yore
faces, dig out some tie ropes, an' limber up yore rope
arms. Soon as we cut out our night hosses, you fellers
rope, throw an' hog-tie an extra hoss all round. Throw
'em an' tie 'em close to th' wagon, south of it, where
they mebby won't get trompled flat, an' where we can
find 'em in th' dark. You savvy?"

"Nobody ever heard of any such fool thing as that,"
protested Billy in surprise, although Billy had roped,
thrown, and hog-tied many head of cattle in the chaparral country of the south.

"I'll mebby do a lot of fool things before I die, so
I might just as well start now an' get my hand in," retorted the trail boss; "but, shore as hell, we're all goin' to have a change of hosses tonight if we need 'em."

"That's a new play to me," said Lanky, scratching
his head; "but damn if it don't sound good! Come on,
Billy: fill up that big belly of yourn. Hoppy, I don't
know if yo're real smart or just plumb loco; but I'll
find out, I reckon."

"If I was plumb loco you couldn't tell me from anybody else in this left-handed outfit," retorted the trail
boss, with the trace of a smile. "We'll either need
them saddle hosses or we won't. If we need 'em, they'll
be there."

"But, hell," said Billy, "there ain't no storm comin'! Lookit how th' wind's died down! There's hardly a breath stirrin'."

"I've seen it die down before, on th' prairies," said Hopalong, heading for the tailboard, with Lanky at his heels.

"Yeah," said Lanky reflectively. "Yeah, so've *I!*" He looked over his shoulder at the reluctant Billy and jerked his head impatiently. "Come on, you fathead: hell will pop before mornin'!"

"So'll yore gran'father!" snorted Billy, but he joined the little line-up.

Cook looked at the sky and the earth and the cavvy and then at the trail boss.

"An' yore mother an' father was proud when you was borned!" he said in great disgust. "Storm? *Hell!*"

XXI

THE night horses cut out and impounded in the little rope corral, Billy and Lanky went to work with ropes and tie strings, and soon seven good, extra saddle horses were lying on their sides just south of the wagon, its bulk interposing between them and any wild-eyed cattle coming down from the direction of the herd. This done, the two riders went off to join the men with the cattle, following their boss, to relieve and send in the riders with the herd. These four ate hurriedly and in silence, and as they were about through they saw a well-known figure riding toward them in the failing light, and his appearance brought smiles to strained faces. The grinning trail cutter, back from a ride up the line, swung down near the tailboard, his astonished gaze on the prostrate horses. After studying them for a moment he looked curiously at the seated figures around the fire, helped himself to eating utensils and food, and dropped down beside the nearest man.

"Idear of th' boss', them hosses," explained Skinny, with a broad grin. "He figgers we'll need fresh saddle hosses tonight, an' he wants 'em to stay put."

"I reckon they will," said the trail cutter, uneasily looking at the threatening sky.

"He shoulda hobbled 'em," said the cook, looking wise.

"Anythin' on four laigs will shore go crazy to-night," said the trail cutter; "so crazy that they'd cripple themselves with hobbles."

"Huh," said the cook, scratching his head. He chanced to be looking at Pete, and a slow grin spread across his face.

"We got a bummer in th' herd," said the cook to the man whose job it was to trim range cattle out of passing trail herds. "Range stray, an' a pet of Pete's."

"They shore will get in," said the trail cutter, stuffing his capable mouth. "If it wasn't for that I wouldn't have my job."

"Kinda funny thing, that is, strayin' in with a herd, like that," said the cook.

"Plumb nat'ral. Cattle are gre-garious," explained the trail cutter, trying not to look self-conscious. It was his pet word, and he liked to spring it on the unwary.

"Oh," said the cook, his eyebrows going up. "Huh," he muttered reflectively. "An'—an' what's good for that?"

The trail cutter flashed him a sidewise glance and kept his expression unchanged.

"Why, cuttin'," he said and stuffed his mouth again.

"Uh-huh," said the cook, thinking in terms of surgery. "Cuttin' what?"

"Strays," answered the trail cutter, reaching for another biscuit.

The cook pondered this statement and scratched his head again. He felt that it called for some kind of comment and tried to play safe.

"Well," he said, "cattle ain't got no brains, but shore as hell they get notions, just th' same."

"Like you," said Red, getting up to saddle his night horse.

"Oh, that so?" snapped the cook. "Too bad there ain't somethin' gre-garious th' matter with you!"

The trail cutter nearly strangled on a swallow of coffee and instantly became the focal point of the cook's suspicious eyes; but his gaze shifted as he heard the sounds of a running horse.

Hopalong swept up to the fire and on to the wagon, dismounting and crawling under the canvas. When he emerged he had his slicker, and he quickly fastened it to his saddle.

"Be a good idear if you boys carried yore own," he said, getting into the saddle again. Then he faced the cook. "You remember what I said about ready grub an' plenty of hot coffee?"

"Yeah, I do. I'll keep a good fire goin' an' th' pot handy to it."

"When it gets dark, which will be right soon," continued the trail boss, "you light a lantern an' hang it where we can see it from th' bed ground."

"Shucks! I'll keep th' fire goin'. Won't that be light enough?" asked the cook in surprise.

"You mebby won't have a fire very long after this storm busts!" retorted the trail boss as a wink of light

flashed along the northern horizon. He called to Red
and Lanky, telling them to help Skinny drive off the
cavvy and to locate it, if possible, out of the way of
a stampeded herd, and then for all three to lend a
hand with the cattle. The cavvy would have to get
along by itself. He whirled and rode swiftly out
toward the herd as the others saddled their night
horses.

The trail cutter slid his eating utensils into the
wreck pan and strode toward his horse, thankful that
he had not ridden it hard that day.

"Joinin' up with you boys," he said. "Hell shore is
goin' to bust before mornin', an' you'll need every
rider you can get."

"Good for you," said Lanky. "Here comes Johnny
an' Pete to feed an' go back." Another faint wink of
light against the northern horizon caught his eye.
"Looks like she's on her way, all right."

The trail cutter, wise in the ways of the weather
in his own land, pondered for a moment.

"Yeah," he said; "but I don't figger she'll bust till
after midnight."

Lanky swore with deep feeling.

"They 'most allus hop us in th' dark," he complained. "Be bad enough in daylight, when a feller
could see what he's doin'; but they allus wait till
night."

"You hop in here with th' cavvy!" bellowed Red, as
lightning again flashed above the horizon, this wink

brighter than the last. Lanky jumped at the summons, and the trail cutter loped off toward the herd.

Twilight developed early and faded quickly into dark. Not a breath of wind stirred the grass. The animals grazed restlessly, loath to lie down, here and there a low bawling voicing their uneasiness. The encircling riders, not able to see anything at a distance, rode by instinct and by the monotonous singing of the man ahead.

The trail cutter slowed to a walk and let his ears guide him and after a while heard the plaintive song of the nearest rider. He called out in a singsong voice and, after a moment, fell in line behind the trail boss. The lantern shone brightly at the chuck wagon, and he made use of its interrupted beams, when on the far side of the herd, to locate himself more definitely in regard to the cattle. Occasionally the hat and shoulders of some rider were silhouetted against the sector of lantern light. The lightning was flashing higher in the sky, and now the faint mutter of thunder could be heard. On and on he rode, around and around; and the lightning flashes now gave light enough to see the herd, every animal standing on its feet, every head turned to the north.

Still the air was dead, and the trail cutter found that it required an effort to breathe. A vivid flash zigzagged earthward, and the roll of the thunder was sharper. He had a glimpse of other riders ahead of him, and the glimpses became more frequent and the thunder increased in sharpness and volume. All at once the air seemed to be sucked from his lungs, and then a gust of wind struck him and forced him to lean against it. He buttoned the slicker and turned up its collar, and as his hands fell down again the rain and hail smashed against the weatherproof with a sound like shot against wood. The rain and hail were so thick that the lightning flashes seemed to make hardly more than a ghostly opalescence, and the herd was blotted from sight. A voice, roaring above the sound of the storm, spoke in his ear, and he found the rider almost knee to knee with him.

"Come on! Get away from here! We're right in front of 'em!"

He followed the running horse across the south side of the herd, realizing the deadly danger of his position, realizing the impotence of one man or a score of men to stand in the path of the avalanche of flesh that a stampede would release, and it would release it almost like an arrow from a bow. The place to turn a stampede was on the corners of the front lines, to force the cattle inward, with a cross direction; to turn them in, to start a circling movement of the animals themselves, to get them milling; to force them to run and to get nowhere, to let them run themselves down. As he followed that racing horseman he had no complaint to make about darkness: flash followed flash so quickly that the ghastly light was almost constant. He wondered why the herd had stood so long, and as the thought passed through his mind he saw greenish glows on the tips of two thousand horns, heard one soul-racking crash and saw the green-white ball explode in the middle of the herd. Above the roar of the rain and hail, above the crashing of the thunder rose the instant drumming of four thousand hard hoofs, the clicking of horns against horns; and a close-packed mass of maddened steers, steam rising from their heated bodies, moved almost like a section of the earth itself past him and thundered into the explosive night.

He found himself in company with three other horsemen, riding as if the devil were after him, along the flank of the stampede, pressing slowly sideways in vain efforts to turn the cattle, and time after time forced backward and saved only by the agile sure-footedness of his horse. During one desperate retreat he chanced to face north and received the impression that the sky was clearing; but here there was no let-up. The hail had ceased, but the rain was pouring down in sheets, whipped and driven into his face until at times he could not see, and even had to turn his head to breathe.

A rider crowded against him, and a flash of lightning revealed his identity and also showed that the whole outfit was concentrating on this side of the herd in an effort to turn the frightened animals toward the east and away from the main trail.

"They ain't spreadin' out much!" shouted Hopalong in his ear. "If we can turn 'em before they scatter, we won't lose none to speak of. Th' tighter they're packed th' more they're in each other's way."

"Yes," shouted the trail cutter, and an almost un-related thought, since the cattle were already stam-peding, popped into his mind: the mind does tricks like that. "Any chronic stampeders among 'em?" he yelled, using a second pet word, and again he pressed in against the mass of running animals.

"No!" shouted Hopalong after a perceptible pause while he wrangled with the word. "They ain't got th' habit yet!"

Another thought popped into the trail cutter's mind, this one pertinent: when the run had started, the riders had been more or less evenly spaced around the cat-tle; but now, after what seemed to have been a very brief interval of time, every man of them was in one spot, at the side of their boss, adding their individual efforts to the power of the whole. Perhaps this ex-plained why a seven-man crew had thought itself suffi-cient to handle a trail herd which usually was a job for an outfit four men larger, and none too large, at that. He laughed in his throat and drove in again, the trail boss on one side and Red on the other. By God, they'd make this bunch of locoed beef swap ends! Yes, an' make 'em like it!

The riding was dangerous and desperate in an attempt to force a quick mill. Stampedes have been stopped in a mile or less, others have run for a score of miles and more, the animals scattering so widely that recovery of the entire herd became impossible. These animals were not chronic stampeders and had no clique of chronic stampeders. They had been well trail-broken, they had been driven hard all day and were well watered and fed. Their fright was natural and excusable. There came a sudden shout of exultation: it sounded like Johnny, a youth not yet out of his teens, and it was pitched high in excitement.

"They're turnin'! Come on, fellers: all together! Turn 'em! Turn 'em!"

The answering surge was instant. The weight of the outfit was thrown against the yielding point, and it yielded more. The outer steers began to press inward at an angle, toward the center of the front line; others joined in the crisscross, and before long the sweeping circle was forming, the inner animals forced to join it by the wall of running flesh in front of them. They were still running without an appreciable lessening in speed, but they were beginning to run without forward direction, to describe a great circle, and soon the whole herd was racing around like a lively eddy in a stream. There were no physical traps on this part of the plain, no steep-banked washes to cripple horses and throw their riders, no thick clumps of scrub timber. The lightning still flashed but was growing more distant, and the pelting rain was easing up a little. The riders were now on the flanks of the milling herd, keeping it spinning; and here and there a voice could be heard raised in song. Gradually the running animals lost speed and compacted; and as the noise of their running died down, the sound of the singing voices increased.

The trail boss dropped out of the line of flankers

and looked around for sight of the cook's lantern, but it could not be seen. His sense of direction, like that of any plainsman, was well developed; but after the mad ride through the dark and all the excitement he frankly admitted to himself that he did not know just where the wagon lay. Time in itself has no meaning, no measure; they might have run for an hour or for half that time. The sky was still too heavily clouded to see the stars: one glimpse of the pole star would be enough for practical orientation; but the glimpse was denied him. Even the wind might have changed direction. He rode forward again to join the flankers and passed the word along: hold the herd where it was until the sky cleared or until daylight came, when they would find the wagon and get fresh horses. He laughed a little: they had fresh horses, all right; seven of them, if they could be found.

The cattle were still moving, but at a much slower pace, and the encircling riders still pressed in, to compact them further and still further hamper them. All right, keep them moving and tire them as much as possible: the night was not yet over, and the storm might swing back. At last the animals dropped to a walk, still milling, and the riders gradually ceased pressing them and rode on a greater circle to remove the feeling of restraint. Then the general movement ceased as animal after animal finally stopped. They would not lie down, of course, on the wet and sodden earth. A bit of song floated toward him, a bit of song after such a race with death:

"I've rid all night long in a pourin' rain,
An' I'll shore be damned if I'll do it again——"

and was ended abruptly by a laugh as the singer realized that he was doing what he had just sung that he would not do.

"Better cross yore fingers, Kid," called a voice, "or mebby you'll be ridin' ag'in before you know it!"

"That you, Kid?" asked the trail boss, heading toward the indistinct blot at his right.

"Yeah, shore is," answered Johnny. "Man, oh, man: I coulda lit a cigarette with one of them flashes! Huh. Well, we've shore stopped 'em, but th' rain don't show no signs of stoppin'. Who's that?"

"Me," said the trail cutter, moving up. "Reckon they've had all th' runnin' they want, huh? Let's find th' wagon an' get some of that hot coffee I been hearin' about; but I don't know how th' hell he'll make it hot!"

"Me neither," confessed the trail boss. "We're shore lucky, gettin' 'em stopped so soon. I figger th' wagon oughta be about over—— *What's that?*"

The three riders listened intently, holding their breath to aid their hearing.

"Thunder, I reckon," muttered Johnny. "Sorta steady an' a long way off, but it don't sound very much like it——"

"*No!*" shouted the trail boss, suddenly. "It's a stampede! They're comin' down this way, th' T Dot Circle an' th' 3 TL!" He raised his voice in a shout of warning. "Look out, fellers! Here comes that mixed herd, all alather!"

"But they was ten miles north of you when I rode past yesterday," expostulated the trail cutter.

"Well, they ain't ten miles now!" retorted the trail boss and again shouted a warning.

Here was possible death, to strike them or to miss them, and they helpless to get out of the way. If the avalanche passed on either side they were safe; if it struck them, no man was safe. Coming such a distance, the mixed herd would not be compact but would spread out over a sizable front. If it passed on either side, their own herd might stampede again; if it struck them, their own herd would almost certainly stampede again; but if it did so, it might take a moment to acquire momentum, and the animals already had used up some of their energy in the first run. The safest place, although a desperate choice, was in front of their own herd.

"Over *here!*" shouted the trail boss at the top of his voice. "Over *here,* with *us! Pronto!*"

Shouted replies answered him, and quick-drumming hoofs tore through the dark, guided by the faint light of the distant lightning flashes. The riders pulled up, forming a close group, ready to ride at top speed, while the distant rumble of madly running cattle came steadily nearer.

"There they come!" cried Lanky, standing up in the stirrups and looking over the backs of his own herd. "Looks like all th' cattle in th' world!"

"There's hosses!" yelled Johnny, pointing. "A whole cavvy! Them fellers shore have had bad luck with their saddle stock *this* trip!"

"Ready to go, fellers, if our herd breaks," ordered Hopalong, "an' shore as hell it will!"

Red's comment was profane and had something to do with their being able to handle their own herd, but not all the so-and-so herds on the main trail.

The front line of the stampeding cattle struck the herd, piled into it, split and flowed around it, pressing from the rear and enveloping it on both sides; and then the whole bunch, unable to withstand this added strain and terror, was off again like a runner from a mark, a solid mass of flesh thundering through the dark. And before the maddened, threatening cattle rode eight men, tight-lipped, silent, each giving his whole attention to his horse; each man's life balanced against the stumble of his horse, the loosening of a cinch. The wind increased suddenly, and the rain poured down again in sheets, and against the increasing roll of the thunder was the steady roar of thousands of hoofs.

In the press of it, in the face of deadly danger, a vague shape twisted around in a saddle, searching for a face he could not see.

"I told you to cross yore fingers, Kid: you sung that song too damn soon!"

Somebody laughed.

XXII

Stars blazed in the dark heavens, unobscured by even a single cloud. What vague movements there were in the blanketing darkness were unhurried, casual: six thousand cattle and three cavvies of saddle stock were somewhere resting or grazing in the dark. They had had their fill of running.

"Hello!" called a voice, and a flash of fire spurted in the night, the sound of the flat report dying out swiftly.

To the right there came a second flash, a second flat report. South of these two came a third, and another winked far off to the left. The four men rode slowly toward a common center, an occasional gun flash showing them the way. There was an instant wink of faint light well to the west of them, so far away that the report barely could be heard; and south of that came another, with no report at all.

Hopalong Cassidy picked out the blot moving ahead of him and called:

"Hello!"

"Hello," came the reply, and the two blots moved toward each other.

"There's six of us accounted for," said the trail boss, stopping his tired horse. "Who're you?"

"Red," said the other, also stopping. "Talk about a mess of cattle!"

"Yeah. All mixed up to hell an' gone," agreed the trail boss. He raised his gun and fired into the air again, and the answering flashes were much nearer. He glanced up at the pole star, cogitated for a moment, and continued:

"While th' boys are comin' together I'll be on my way back to th' wagon. There's seven fresh hosses hogtied up there, an' we can use 'em. I'll drive 'em back with me."

"I shore could eat somethin'," said Red.

"Yeah, reckon we all could," replied the trail boss. "I'll bring cook back with me, too. While I'm gone, you an' th' rest of th' boys see if you can find his work hosses. If you can, he can take 'em back with him an' bring th' wagon down here. It oughta be here, anyhow, where we'll be workin'."

"Hi!" shouted a voice faintly, and the speaker headed for the shouted reply. To the south another gun flash spurted, asking direction, and Red's Colt replied to it. As Red lowered the weapon he found that the trail boss had been swallowed up in the night.

"One hell of a night," said the newcomer with great disgust. "Wish I had some hot coffee."

"Hello, Kid," said Red. "You an' me'll stay here to wait for th' others. Hoppy's gone up to find th' wagon."

"Shore hope he don't miss it. My belly's so loose it rattles."

Red glanced up at the North star and smiled in the darkness: by its light roaming humans had been shown the true way for thousands of years.

"He'll find it," he said.

"I crossed th' trail back yonder," said Johnny. "You reckon I oughta go after Hoppy an' tell him? He'll be lookin' for it."

"He'll find it," repeated Red. "Here comes another: wonder who he is."

"Anybody missin'?" shouted the rider in question as he pushed up in the dark.

"Only four now," answered Red: "an' two of them are headin' this way. I saw their gunfire. How're you, Pete?"

"Wetter'n th' Gulf, an' hungry as hell. Who's that with you?"

"Me," answered the Kid. "How come we busted apart like we did? I reckoned we was all bunched together."

"Bunch of cattle split me an' Lanky off from you," answered Pete.

"Reckon that's what happened to all of us," said Red, his voice tense and worried. Two of his friends might be lying dead or wounded somewhere out on the sodden plain. Again he drew his gun and fired into the air and smiled a little at three answering flashes from widely different points. "There's three of 'em: only one still missin'."

"No!" shouted Johnny as his alert eyes caught a faint wink of light far to the east behind his companions' backs. "There's another!" He drew his own gun and fired above his head. "How'n hell did he ever get away over there?"

"Wandered off to pick him some posies!" snapped Red, his grouch returning with this promise that all his friends were safe.

"Anybody got some dry tobacco an' papers?" asked Pete hopefully.

Gentle, unhurried movements replied to his question, but they replied to it in vain: there was neither dry tobacco nor papers in the crowd.

"No grub, no coffee, no smokes," grumbled Pete. "Damn if I'll ever go up th' trail ag'in. A man's a fool to."

"That shore goes for me!" snapped Johnny.

Red laughed knowingly, his eyes on a faint movement between him and where the trail should be. He raised his voice.

"Over here," he directed. "We're holdin' a meetin'. Pete an' th' Kid have just sworn off trail-drivin'."

"Hello, Red," said the indistinct rider, coming steadily nearer. "That so? Sworn off ag'in, huh?" He laughed gently. "Hey! Who's got th' makin's of a smoke? Mine's soggy."

"If you'd take care of yore makin's you wouldn't be beggin' a smoke," retorted Johnny with more spirit than good sense.

"All right, Kid; you win: now I'll beg some of yourn."

Red laughed again.

"He's preachin', Skinny; not practisin': his tobacco is mostly water. Well, there's five of us showed up, an' two more on their way."

"Five?" asked Skinny, counting faces. "Where's th' other?"

"Off to get them hog-tied hosses," answered Johnny. "It's Hoppy. Mebby he wasn't as crazy as some fools figgered, throwin' an' tiein' them hosses."

"Reckon not," grunted Pete. "Here comes somebody else. Hey! There's eight of us, an' not seven: you forgettin' that trail cutter?"

"Damn if you ain't right," growled Red. "He's shore one of us by this time. Wonder where he is." He again pulled out his gun and fired it into the air. Three flashes replied to him, one of them close up, another several times as far away, and the third could barely be seen far to the south.

"That makes eight!" exulted Johnny.

"Who's got a match that'll light?" asked a voice out of the darkness.

"Hello, Lanky!" cried the Kid. "You got dry makin's?"

"Yeah; but I can't light it. Who-all's there? . . . Yeah? That's good. Reckon that must be Billy, then, back there behind me. Where's that match?"

Again there were little, gentle movements, and again they were futile. There was not a dry match in the crowd. Lanky regarded this as an outrage and said so with his well-known frankness:

"Fine bunch of growed-up men! Not a dry match among you! You-all make me sick!"

"All right: get sick, an' stay sick!" snapped Red. "Why'n hell ain't you usin' yore own matches, then?"

"Mine are all wet! That's why!" flared Lanky and flushed at the instant burst of laughter. "Aw, that's all right; but I *did keep* my makin's dry!"

"Lot of good that did you!"

"Hi!" called a voice.

"That you, Billy?"

"Yeah. Anybody got some dry smokin'?"

"Shore: I have," answered Lanky; "but we ain't got no dry matches."

"H-a-a-w! That's good. I got dry matches. Everybody here?"

"Yeah; all of us," answered Pete. "Reckon th' trail cutter's on his way, too. Hey, Lanky: how long's it take you to roll a cigarette?"

"Long as I want!" retorted Lanky. "Seein' that I own th' makin's!"

"I only got one match," said Billy. "I been savin' it."

"What else would you do with it?" snapped Red.

There came a flash from the south, much nearer this time, and Pete's gun answered it. He chuckled deep in his throat.

"Hope that *is* th' trail cutter: he's one damn white feller," he said and then looked around. "Gimme that match, Billy."

"Wait a minute!" snapped Red. "I want some of that match!"

"You can light yourn from mine, can't you?" demanded Pete.

"Shore he can!" said Skinny. "Come on, Billy: light her up."

"Nobody uses this match till I get my cigarette rolled!" retorted Billy. "Where's them papers an' that tobacco?"

In due course of time every man held a cigarette, waiting for Billy to strike a match. This he did thoughtlessly, along the tightly stretched cloth of his trousers; and his trousers still being very wet, the head of the match dissolved in its dragging progress, and he stared through the growing light at the naked head of the stick; and then ducked barely in time. The ensuing language was as sulphurous as the match had been, but was suddenly cut short by Lanky's command.

"Hell with *that!*" he barked. "We got work to do. We got to round-up these damn cattle an' get th' cavvies cut out an' herded by themselves. Th' hosses first, so them other outfits can shift their saddles when they has to. Come on: get a move on!"

"An' Billy figgers he's a human bein'," snorted Pete in great disgust, wheeling his tired horse to go to work. He looked southward and grinned. "Yep: he's safe. There's th' trail cutter."

Hands rose in the air in swift gestures of greeting to the oncoming rider, and then the little group whirled about, spread out, and started in on the day's work;

a day's work which was to be hard and long: the rounding up of six thousand head of cattle and more than eleven score riding horses; the rounding up and the cutting out necessary to sort and hold the cattle into three trail herds, and the horses into three cavvies. Cold, wet, hungry, they went to work with jibes and laughter.

Up the trail, at the Circle 4 wagon, a comparatively warm and dry cook crawled out from under the wagon cover as dawn broke, looked around the soggy and puddled plain, regarded the seven thrown riding horses just south of the tailboard, and shook his head. He reached up behind him, took down the lantern, blew it out, and placed it inside the wagon box. Going back under the cover, he reappeared with an armful of dry firewood and climbed down to the ground with it. After a few moments of pocketknife labor he had a little pile of shavings, and shortly after that he was judiciously placing his precious firewood on the curling, licking flames.

"Shore was one hell of a mess," he muttered as he took the coffee pot, still full to the brim, and placed it near the briskly burning fire. Then he returned to the wagon, hauled out a pot of beans and a pan of biscuits, and rolled himself a smoke. His tobacco was dry and so were his matches. As he lit the cigarette he looked more closely down the trail and nodded.

The horseman turned off toward the wagon, riding at a steady lope, caring nothing about the fatigue of the horse.

Cook watched the rider with interest and again nodded.

"Th' boss," he said and turned to place the coffee pot on the fire. "He'll shore be ready for some of *that*," he said. "An' so'll I. Wonder how th' other boys are. Gawd, but it was terrible!"

The horseman pulled up at the fire and spoke briefly. The cook threw his saddle out of the wagon, took the coffee pot from the fire, and helped to untie the prostrate horses. In a few minutes he was riding beside his boss, the little herd of riding stock trotting before them.

"Anybody get hurted?" asked the cook, his eyes on his companion.

"Don't know. They hadn't all been heard from before I left."

"Gawd, what a night!"

"Musta been, all snug under that canvas cover," retorted the trail boss. "Didn't even get yore tobacco wet, did you?"

The cook squirmed, sat around in the saddle, and looked straight ahead. He felt that he had nothing further to say about the storm.

"Didn't get yore tobacco wet, did you?" persisted the trail boss.

"No, reckon not," muttered the cook.

"All right, then: gimme th' makin's an' a dry match. I'll have a smoke for breakfast."

They were riding diagonally up the slope of a steep rise, the trail boss gratefully drawing smoke into his lungs; and as they rode even with the top of the rise and looked over it, he muttered something under his breath as he stared at a distant bunch of saddled horses and a close group of men. The men all had their hats off. He turned a worried face to the staring cook.

"Keep these hosses goin' as they are. I'm headin' over there to see if I can give a hand. I don't believe it can be one of our—our boys, but———"

The cook watched him go, driving the tired horse at its best speed, and sorrowfully shook his head; but he had his orders, and he kept the little horse herd on its way.

As Hopalong drew near the group one of the men slowly turned and looked at him. It was Gibson, trail boss of the 3 TL, and his face was set and grim. To one side of Gibson lay a saddled horse, one leg twisted grotesquely sideways. The bullet hole in the white spot on the forehead had stained it red. The horse was out of its misery. The story was plain to read, and in his mind's eye Hopalong could see the rider pitching head-long from the saddle and under the smashing hoofs of scores of maddened cattle while the livid lightning flashed and the rain poured down. He took off his hat and clamped an arm over it, and he felt his throat constrict a little. His own men had not been all accounted for.

"Who is it, Gibson?" he asked, anxiously, his face hard and set.

"Luke: Luke Potter. It ain't a nice sight, Cassidy."

"No. Never is," replied Hopalong, looking through

the gap which Gibson had made in the close-packed circle of hatless men. He saw a trampled mass of mud-and blood-covered clothing, a thing which had been a face. It was not a nice sight. He drew a deep breath and relaxed.

"My wagon must be all of a dozen miles up th' trail," said Gibson slowly, thoughtfully. "Yourn oughta be quite a lot closer. Can we use yore shovel, Cassidy?"

"Shore. I'll go get it," said Hopalong quickly.

"No. You've got plenty on yore hands. I'll send one of th' boys," said Gibson, turning toward the little circle. "George! Go up th' trail to th' Circle 4 wagon. They got a shovel. Make time."

"You know where it is?" asked Hopalong.

"Reckon so," answered George. "I saw its lantern as I went past last night." He took two quick steps, landed in his saddle, and urged his tired horse up the slope. In a moment he was out of sight.

"All yore boys show up yet?" asked Gibson.

"Don't know. I left before they all had time to," answered Hopalong. "You want I should stay here an' give you a hand?"

Gibson shook his head slowly.

"No. We'll take care of Luke," he said. "He was a damn good man: gentle with hosses, square with his friends, an' a first-class hand with cattle. Funny thing: he didn't want to go on this drive."

"Yes," said Hopalong. He glanced again at the little circle. "Leave th' shovel here, standin' up so th' cook can find it," he said. "He'll be comin' back with th' work hosses to hitch onto th' wagon an' haul it down where we'll be workin'. You an' yore boys feed at our wagon till you have plenty of time to go after yore own. We'll round up an' cut out enough hosses for you-all to use, an' we'll all be workin' together on th' same job. Well, I can't do nothin' for Luke: see you later, Gibson."

"Shore," replied the 3 TL trail boss, tears forming in his eyes. "Gawd! I don't know how I'm goin' to tell my daughter."

"Tough," said Hopalong, slowly. "Son-in-law?"

"Yes. An' a damn good one!"

Hopalong pressed the bony shoulder in a grip which hurt, turned without another word, walked to his horse, and rode away. One more good man to mark that cattle trail. He shook his head, blew out his breath, and sent the horse into a gallop: he had no son-in-law, but every man in his outfit was a mighty good friend of his —and the sooner he knew all about them, the better he would feel. The roan buckled down to it and sent the wind whistling past its rider's head. Cook and the fresh horses came swiftly nearer, and as the trail boss flashed past he waved his hand toward the south and kept on going.

"My Gawd, what a night!" said the cook.

XXIII

THE plain looked like round-up time, and in a way
it was. The three wagons, perhaps a mile apart, could
be located by their cheery fires. The mass of cattle and
horses had been herded together and cut out according to their respective road brands. Further than that,
each herd and cavvy had been counted, and the tallies
were surprisingly good in consideration of what had
happened. The 3 TL had lost less than two dozen
head, the T Dot Circle less than that; while the Circle
4 was more fortunate than either of the others, owing,
perhaps, to the quick checking of its first stampede.
Under the stars three herds rested on their bed
grounds, ready for the trail again.

Hopalong put down his tin plate and felt for tobacco
and papers. He had been silent and preoccupied ever
since he had ridden in for a late supper; and this despite the outcome of the storm and stampede of two
nights before. Big Muddy Creek and its bottomless
morass held his thoughts: that quagmire would most
certainly hold them up for several days. Even at its
best it was treacherous. He looked around the little,
seated circle and smiled at the contentment on each
face.

Lanky grinned at him.

"Well, we'll soon be on our way ag'in," he said.

"Yeah," grunted Hopalong with little enthusiasm. "How many herds do you reckon are behind us?"

Lanky shook his head.

"No tellin'," he said; "but they all got that storm, too. They ain't movin' along any faster than we are. We're just as far ahead of 'em now as we was two days ago."

"Yeah," said the trail boss slowly; "but Big Muddy Creek will hold us up so long that they'll all catch up with us, an' then there'll be another jam of cattle. Seems like our hard luck is all comin' to us at this end of th' drive."

"Big Muddy shore is mean," said Red, recrossing his legs. He shook his head.

"Wonder who was drivin' them range stockers, up ahead?" said Skinny. "They was lucky, th' hull nine of 'em. They had time to get acrost Big Muddy before th' storm. It musta been purty well dried out then."

Sounds of walking horses came nearer, and in a few moments two riders pushed up into the light of the little fire and smiled down upon the seated outfit. The two callers were Gibson and Halliday.

"Light down an' set," invited Hopalong, getting to his feet.

"Reckon we ain't stoppin' long enough for that," replied Halliday. "We just rid over to tell you to throw back onto th' trail first. You boys been damn white, an' you got a delivery date. Wish we had. Me an'

Gibson'll hold back tomorrow, an' give you all th' start you want. Besides, I got a boy in th' wagon with a busted laig, an' it won't do him no harm to get a couple more days' rest. We'll foller Gibson day after tomorrow. I'm sendin' a rider back down th' trail to see how close th' next herd is. Well, take it all in all, you fellows an' us was right lucky: I been goin' up th' trail for several years, an' I never saw a worse night."

"That's right kind of you boys, lettin' us get away first," said Hopalong. "We'll shore try to get outa yore way; but I'm afraid Big Muddy'll bunch us all up ag'in, an' mebby pile up some of them follerin' herds to make things all th' meaner. Big Muddy just won't have no bottom at all after that rain."

"I ain't so shore about that," said Halliday, with a grin. "John Slaughter sent up three herds late last year. He went along with th' first one hisself. John lives down in my part of th' country, an' I see him once in a while. He told me that when they reached Big Muddy it was so damn soft an' mean that they reckoned it would mebby hold them up till after th' first frost. John, he's a damn smart cattleman, from every angle: an' he had three whole outfits with him, thirty-three men, leavin' out th' cooks. He scouted up Big Muddy till he found heavy brush. It was growin' near a narrow place in th' creek. What did he do but put them three outfits cuttin' brush an' layin' it acrost th' creek. When they had brush enough to show above th' water, they heaped on th' dirt. When that sunk down, they cut an' piled on more brush, an' piled on more dirt. John said it took 'em four whole days to bridge that mire, but bridge it they did. 'Tain't wide, but it's wide enough to git wagons over. Then they planted posts an' made a brush fence, runnin' out from th' south end of that bridge like a V, an' they pushed their cattle acrost in small bunches, an' never had no trouble at all after th' first bunch got over. Some of that bridge still oughta be there. Me an' Gibson'll throw our shovels into yore wagon, if you reckon you'll need 'em. If you take 'em, leave 'em stickin' up at this end of th' bridge for us to find. I hate to part with any of my boys, after what happened two nights back; but it ain't fair to pile all that bridge fixin' onto you: if you want a couple of my boys, you say so."

Hopalong's expression had grown less serious as Halliday talked, and now he was smiling and shaking his head. Perhaps this end of the trail would be kinder from now on.

"You lend us th' shovels," he said, with a grin. "My boys ain't never worked up a sweat or done a honest day's work with their backs in it. If there's enough of that bridge left for us to find, we'll make it good enough to get cattle acrost it."

"Won't be no trouble findin' it, not with that V-shaped fence pointin' it out," said Halliday, with a laugh. "It's up above th' old crossin'. Seems to me like it would be a good idear for every trail outfit to stop there long enough to throw a little more dirt onto it. You fix it up good enough to cross yore wagon, an' little bunches of cattle, an' me an' Gibson'll make it wider. By Gawd, that's *one* trail trouble we can cure!"

Hopalong nodded and looked at Skinny.

"You foller these boys back to their camps, Skinny, an' get them shovels," he said and again looked at the visitors. "Light down an' have some coffee."

"No, reckon not," replied Halliday, picking up the reins. "After that storm th' other night, I find I'm fidgety unless I'm close to my herd. Well, good-night an' good luck, boys."

"Good luck," came the answer in a chorus.

Hopalong stepped over to Halliday's silent companion, clapped his left hand on Gibson's leg and held out the other. They shook hands silently, gripping hard. In another moment the two visitors were riding back to their respective camps.

Hopalong looked after them for perhaps a minute and then turned to smile at his seated friends as Skinny got up to go to his horse and ride off to get the shovels.

"Well, come hell or high water—we've shore had th' hell, an' that bridge of Slaughter's will mebby clean up th' high water for us—we're on our way ag'in at th' first crack of dawn: *an' we're goin' through!*"

He was right, for at the first crack of dawn there sounded again the old, familiar *clack, shuffle, clack* of thousands of hoofs and horns: but this time the dust did not blanket the herd, because there was no dust.

*"But if they're goin' to Canady, then I'm a-goin' too:
    Me an' my roll with th' whole damn' crew!"*

Pete looked across the heaving backs of the plodding cattle and frowned at the singer.

"All swelled up like a poisoned coyote," he growled and then resumed his scrutiny of the herd, looking for the pestiferous bummer. A gladsome thought suddenly popped into his mind: perhaps the damned bummer had been one of the animals killed in the stampede. He grinned happily and faced forward again.

XXIV

THE Circle 4 herd was stepping along on its way, and the gap between it and the last herd up the trail, the nearest herd in front of them, was wide enough to suit even the most pessimistic trail driver. Behind it were two known herds, respectively one and two days distant. The delivery point was coming steadily nearer, where the responsibilities of the drive crew would come to an end; and, so far as the riders knew, the way was open and clear to the shipping pens at the end of track. True enough, Big Muddy Creek was drawing closer with every passing mile, but Big Muddy at last had joined the ranks of the unimportant, thanks to John Slaughter and his three trail crews.

Hopalong looked back along the herd and smiled with satisfaction. These thousand steers were trail veterans now, and they were moving like trail veterans, plodding steadily onward. They were not grazing on the move: they would be grazed later, when thrown off the trail at the end of the day's drive. Right now they were opening up a promised trail gap, a gap promised to the bosses of the two following herds. Hopalong swung around in the saddle and spoke to his companion, an amused but wistful smile on his lean, tanned face.

"You know, Red," he said with a chuckle, "we've all, at one time or another, swore that we was on our last trail drive; but th' way these critters are movin', damn if I wouldn't like to drive 'em clean up to th' Blackfoot Agency!"

"Ye-ah," replied Red, thoughtfully rubbing the stubble on his face. "Yeah: or even acrost th' line an' into Canady!" Then he shook his head slowly. "Not much chance to drive no animals like these to no Injun agency: they don't feed Injuns on beef like this."

"No," admitted Hopalong, an ironic smile spreading over his face. "No," he repeated, as various details of agency cattle and agency deliveries paraded through his mind. Other details, too, presented themselves and made him grimace. "But cattle like these are sometimes *paid* for, for Injun deliveries."

"Shore," replied Red, nodding and grinning; "an' mebby weighed an' counted twice, to boot."

"Injuns like their beef on th' hoof," commented Hopalong. "You ever see Injuns handle agency beef when it's turned over to 'em?" he asked, the mental picture making him spit to clear the taste from his mouth.

"No, I ain't; but I've shore heard all about it."

They rode on in silence for a few moments, and then the trail boss straightened up in the saddle and came back to matters of the immediate present.

"Reckon I'll be on my way up to take a look at Big Muddy," he said. "Th' wagon ought to reach there about th' time I do. If Slaughter's bridge needs fixin',

then me an' th' cook will have a good start at it before
th' herd gets there. You water 'em at th' next creek an'
then keep on comin', 'less I ride back to stop you. I
don't want no thirsty cattle near that damn mud hole.
If they ever get into that there'll be hell to pay, with
th' devil keepin' cases. We'll take it in our stride. If
it ain't ready to cross over by th' time th' herd gets
near it, we'll bed down well this side of it, an' water
'em at th' next creek tomorrow."

"Mebby I better hold 'em on th' next creek till I
hear from you," said Red thoughtfully. "It's only a
two-hour drive from there on to Big Muddy, if I remember right. I figger th' two creeks come together
not very far to th' east."

"Reckon that's th' better play," agreed Hopalong
and rode forward at a brisk pace.

Red nodded and watched his boss and friend ride
away. He glanced across the herd at Lanky Smith, over
on left point, and then looked back along his own flank
and grinned cheerfully at Johnny Nelson, the rider
nearest to him. The herd kept on, shoulders and hips
rising and falling, heads and tails swaying gently, the
clacking of their hoofs on the hard, rain-swept ground
interspersed with the occasional clicking of horns on
horns. The sun was shining, the air was clear of dust,
and the day was cool. When Red faced about again, he
was humming a plaintive melody with disgraceful
words, well pleased with himself and with the job in
hand. When they left the next creek they would shape
the herd into a thinner and longer line, so it would

feed easier, bunch after bunch, onto Slaughter's bridge.

Hopalong saw the top of the dirty wagon cover trying its best to shine in the sun. Its variegated patches were very noticeable and accounted for the final use of various trouser legs, the seats to which had been worn out. In those days in the southern cattle country no one threw away anything which could be used. The grip of poverty was still on the land, although it was slowly lessening, thanks to the movement of its four-legged wealth, a movement greatly due to Joe McCoy.

The wagon came into sight from the top down and revealed the cook draped lazily on the board seat. The horses were still in harness, drowsing on each side of the pole. Three shovels lay on the ground near the front wheel, one of them bright from recent use. Beyond the wagon was the sheen of water, with slough grass and rushes rising above it. Crossing it was a dirty, yellow-brown streak, here and there pushing up above the surface. Almost in the middle of the streak was a wide break, but there were no ripples to indicate that a current was flowing through it. Just this side of the water's edge were two lines of poles and piles of dried brush, starting out from each edge of the rusty streak and diverging into a huge V. This was John Slaughter's guiding fence, to funnel cattle onto his causeway.

Hopalong pulled up at the wagon, his gaze flicking from the lazy cook to the harnessed horses and back again.

"Been here long?" he asked.

The cook stirred, tossed away the bedraggled butt of a cigarette, and shook his head, seemingly with an effort.

"Half-hour, mebby," he answered, yawning widely.

"You looked at th' bridge?"

"No-o," grunted the cook and reached for tobacco sack and papers.

Hopalong's face reddened under its coats of tan, but he said nothing: a cook was a cook, one of nature's little jokes on trail bosses. He glanced down at the shovels and gently raised his eyebrows.

"You throw them shovels out of th' wagon all by yoreself?" he asked in mild surprise.

"Huh?" said the cook. "Oh, shore," he answered, looking curious.

The trail boss pressed his knees against his mount and rode on to the apex of the pointing V and stopped at the end of the causeway. The horse stretched its neck for more leather, obtained it, and sucked noisily at the water, letting most of it spill out again. The animal plowed it several times with his velvety nose and then raised his head with a toss. Then he obeyed the knee pressure and stepped onto the causeway. At the edge of the break he stopped abruptly. Hopalong was about to put him into it when he remembered the soft, sticky treachery which had made this sluggish creek famous and infamous along the cattle trail.

He swung the roan around and rode slowly back to the bank. The hoofs of the horse did not cut in deeply,

even where water lay across the causeway: Slaughter
had done a good job. Hopalong rode on to the wagon,
where he stopped and dismounted. The cook, watching
him languidly, leaned the other shoulder blade against
a wagon bow and recrossed his legs.

"You got any choice of shovels?" the trail boss
asked the cook as he pulled off his boots.

"Huh?" ejaculated the cook, his wandering
thoughts cut short.

"Any one of them shovels a pet of yourn?"

"Hell, no! Why?"

"Then pull off yore boots an' socks, if you got any
on; roll up yore pants, grab one of th' shovels, an' get
ready to spit on yore hands," said the trail boss gently.
"That storm plumb washed out near a dozen feet of
John's bridge. Th' break ain't deep, but it looks damn
oozy. We can have it all filled up by th' time th' herd
gets here."

"Me an' you?" asked the cook with a rising voice.
He was no longer languid.

"Me an' you, an' anybody else you can find around.
We got an extry shovel."

"Hell, there ain't nobody near here but us!" retorted
the cook, staring at the shovels; "but th' boys will be
here in a few hours," he suggested hopefully. "Th'
hull outfit."

"If I wasn't dead shore they'd get here, an' th' cattle with 'em, I wouldn't bother to fix th' bridge," explained Hopalong.

The cook studied the calm face of his boss and then

looked at the shovels, and from the shovels to the wide slough, and then down at his boots. His gaze lifted from his boots to his boss, and what he saw far back in the cold, steady eyes of that person was almost like an impact. He sighed deeply and raised one foot, bending slowly to meet it. Under his breath he said things which appear in print only in modern novels. Feet bare at last, and trousers rolled up, he climbed down from the wagon seat, slowly picked up a shovel, and reluctantly followed his boss.

Armfuls of Slaughter's dry-brush fence, weighted down by shovelfuls of earth, layer upon layer, finally filled in the treacherous gap. The trail boss, shovel in hand, crossed over the fill and went on to the opposite bank. There were wide, shallow places where he had to wade. The surface of the causeway, however, was firm enough. He stepped out on the farther bank, grinned happily, and then recrossed the bridge.

"She'll do," he said.

The cook heaved a sigh of relief and turned toward the wagon, dragging the shovel behind him. The two men, tired and covered with perspiration, gratefully dropped the shovels and let their feet and legs dry in the sun. The cook was looking southward, his thoughts on the nearing herd. He felt that it would not go on far after the slough was crossed, and he wanted to go about preparing camp and have his fire ready to light. He also wanted to get away from the slough: there was no telling what might happen in the next few hours.

"Reckon me an' you better get this wagon acrost before th' herd gets here?" he asked as casually as he could.

The trail boss looked at him.

"No," answered Hopalong, slowly shaking his head. "I want th' boys here with their ropes before we try that," he said—and then explained himself: "In case th' wagon slides off."

The cook paused for a moment and then drew on the second sock and reached for the second boot. He saw Hopalong's gaze fixed on the bare heel sticking out of the sock and shook his head.

"Ain't had no time to darn 'em," he said and then answered the words of his boss. "Yeah," he said, grunting as he forced the foot home. "I'll get out my saddle an' be all ready."

Hopalong glanced at him out of the corner of his eye.

"Where you aim to put it?" he asked curiously.

"Put what?"

"Yore saddle."

"Why, on a hoss. Where'n hell you s'pose?"

"Well, I figgered mebby you was goin' to cinch it onto th' wagon seat," replied the trail boss, "because that's where you'll be settin'."

"But she may slide off, you said!" exclaimed the startled cook.

"There's considerable less chance of her doin' that if there's a good man drivin'," replied the boss. "Considerable," he repeated.

"But, hell! I can't swim!"

"You won't have to," explained Hopalong, beginning to enjoy himself. "If she slides, just jump an' stick up yore arm. When it comes up somebody'll drop their rope over it an' haul you out."

"By —— ——, *I* hired out to *cook!*" said the culinary artist of the Circle 4 trail herd.

"You also hired out to drive this wagon all th' way to Bulltown—an' back ag'in, if I want you to," retorted Hopalong. "Every foot of th' way."

"Well, I've done it so far, ain't I?"

"Except that time you got dead drunk, an' I had to drive you *an'* th' wagon to camp from Waggoner's."

The cook frowned at this unkind reminder of a jocund moment with the fruitful corn, turned his head and looked at the watery expanse of the slough. It now looked dark and mysterious. Then he turned about and slowly straightened.

"My back's near busted," he complained.

"Yeah? Well, just think of th' rest yore busiest end has had."

The cook's attention was now on the watery gaps in the causeway, a causeway in which he now took a keener interest.

"But you said you found her good an' solid all th' way," he said.

"Solid enough," replied the trail boss, "but kinda narrer in a couple of places; an', of course, they had to be where she's under water. In case you can't see where to drive, I'll go over first an' drop a shovel on th' other

bank for you to aim at. Kinda front sight, like. Two of
th' boys'll ride ahead of th' team, with their ropes
hitched onto th' wagon. When you start, aim at th'
shovel, travel fast, an' keep a-goin'. We'll empty th'
wagon first, though: ain't no use riskin' gettin' our
grub an' stuff all wet. If th' herd balks, you go over
first."

"No, there ain't no use of gettin' th' stuff wet,"
agreed the cook slowly and again looked out over the
placid water.

"I got to go back to th' herd an' keep it comin',"
said Hopalong, glancing southward. "By th' time it
gets here, that water'll be settled an' mebby give you
a chance to see th' footin'."

"Yeah, mebby," growled the cook without enthusiasm. He was pondering over treacherous bogs, quick-
sands, and various river bottoms he had known, and
suddenly he looked at his companion. Drop a rope over
his arm, huh, and yank him out! "I once saw a cow
pulled out of a quicksand, an' shore as hell she left
one front laig plumb behind!"

"Yeah," agreed Hopalong, nodding; "but this hole
ain't quicksand. It's just—just mud. An' you ain't a
cow. Anyhow, you won't hit bottom, I reckon; but if
yo're scared of losin' a front laig," he said, keeping his
face straight only by an effort, "I'll tell th' boys to
keep their ropes coiled."

"Hell!" barked the cook. "I'd ruther lose a laig or
arm than git drownded!"

Hopalong nodded gravely.

"So would I," he agreed and then glanced up at the sun to get the time of day. "After we get you acrost, you make camp about two miles up th' trail and east of it. Th' herd may go over as slick as bull butter, or it may take us till tomorrow night to get it acrost; but if th' cattle are balky, th' wagon goes over as soon as th' boys get here, right side up or bottom side up; an' you go with it, drivin' th' team."

The cook lifted his hat and rubbed the red mark made by the sweatband.

"Anybody that goes with a trail herd is just a plain damn fool," he growled. "This shore as hell is *my* last trip, an' that's flat!"

Hopalong controlled his facial muscles and stared gloomily at the placid water, and then he nodded his head very slowly and sighed.

"Yes," he said thoughtfully. "Mebby it is. They generally run in threes."

The cook turned halfway around to look at the speaker.

"What you mean?" he demanded sharply.

Hopalong muttered something about the first one being buried by Gibson, got to his feet and stepped toward his horse. He swung into the saddle and gripped his knees. As the horse shot forward, its rider turned.

"Get everythin' out of th' wagon an' be all ready to go!" he shouted and faced around to meet the whistling wind.

The frowning cook stood with feet spread far apart and with arms akimbo.

"Yessir!" he exclaimed, talking to himself. "Any man that goes up th' trail with cattle is just a plain damn fool!" He looked at the creek again, scowled at the causeway, and slowly turned toward the wagon, to begin the task of emptying it.

XXV

Hopalong reached the herd as it watered at the creek next to Big Muddy on the south and found that the trail cutter again had become one of the outfit. They exchanged grins, and the trail boss pulled up for a moment.

"I'm beginnin' to figger you've forgot all about cuttin' this herd," he said. "If you reckon you'll hurt our feelin's by lookin' it over, yo're figgerin' wrong."

"I know that, Cassidy; but seein' how much I've been with it, an' how well I know it, I reckon I *could* forget cuttin' it without much harm bein' done," replied the cutter. "I'll take a good look at 'em when they string out to head over Slaughter's bridge. I saw 'em all while they was bein' cut out an' rounded up after th' stampede; an' one look will be enough. Red tells me you was up lookin' at th' bridge. Last time I was there it was all right, but I reckon that storm washed out some of it."

"Yeah, it did; but me an' th' cook fixed it up good enough," said the trail boss, and then, catching Red's eye, waved his big hat toward the north an' Big Muddy; and a few moments later the cattle reluctantly left the creek and began their forward march again.

Two hours later the chuck wagon came into sight, and then the V-shaped fence which was to funnel the herd onto the causeway.

At that moment an apparition emerged from under the canvas cover of the wagon. It was the cook, as naked as the day he was born. Piles of impedimenta were on the ground near the wagon. He seated himself on the wagon seat and reached for the reins; and then looked in surprise at Hopalong's impatient and violent gesture. His surprise increased as the gestures increased in vehemence, and he finally got it into his head that his presence was not wanted. All uncertainty was banished when the trail cutter raced toward him, shouting profane instructions.

"Get back outa sight, you —— —— fool!" yelled the cutter. "One good look at a thing like you, an' there's no tellin' how long it'll take to get th' herd acrost! They got their fool minds on walkin' right along, an' we don't want nothin' to get their minds off that. Get back outa sight!"

"But th' wagon was to cross over first!" protested the cook, not without indignation.

"Th' wagon'll go over first, *after* we find that th' cattle *won't!* Get back outa sight!"

The cook glanced at the distant trail boss, and that person's hat was still violently signaling. The dictates of modesty were slowly observed, though not without a muttered protest, and the wagon cover soon kept its secret.

Hopalong raised his hand, and the herd was slowed

a little while a dozen of the leaders were gently urged forward at a little better speed, the rest of the herd following slowly. The proper psychology of the thing was to let the herd take the bridge in its stride, if it would; to take it as a matter of course and without stopping; without giving it time to discover that anything the least bit unusual was before it. If it stopped, the chances of it readily crossing would be less.

While the leading cattle moved forward, Skinny and two other riders swiftly drove the cavvy in before them and started to feed it onto the bridge. The horses crossed readily enough, and this phase of the operation was timed so nicely that the last bunch of them was hardly on the causeway before the selected steers reached it. These steers were the natural leaders of the herd and had been the leaders since the first few days of the drive. They were well trail-broken and dependable as steers can be and would be likely to cross over more readily than any of the others; and if they crossed, the herd would follow.

It was an anxious moment. If the steers balked, it would mean balking by the whole herd, and hours might be lost. Hopalong flashed a quick glance at the wagon, found it innocent of added attractions, and then gave his whole attention to the subtle and gentle urging onward of this little group of steers. The animals stepped onto the bridge, hesitated, looked to the right and to the left, and broke into a nervous run, heading straight for the farther side. That was the big moment, and almost before the remainder of the herd knew what it was all about, it was sent forward at a brisk pace and in a thin stream across Slaughter's bridge, breaking into a lumbering run as it passed the middle. Two animals were forced off into the creek, but were allowed to swim around until the last of the herd was safely over; and then two riders pushed in after them and herded them away from the treacherous banks and back toward the firmer footing of the causeway. In a few moments both cattle and horses had clambered up the side of the bridge and were moving across it to solid ground. Big Muddy was no longer a threat.

Hopalong sighed and looked at the trail cutter, who had been too busy in scrutinizing the passing animals to notice much of anything else.

"Well!" said the trail boss, exhaling gustily. His relief was manifest.

"You bet! Slick as a greasy fryin' pan," replied the trail cutter, now taking time to smile. "No strays in yore herd, yo're out of my territory, yo're acrost Big Muddy, an' there's nothin' ahead of you but th' saloons of Bulltown: th' saloons, th' gamblin' joints, th' ladies south of th' tracks, an' a hard-drinkin', gunfightin' bunch of bad hombres. I'm leavin' you here an' wishin' you luck."

"You figger I'll need lots of luck, huh?"

"W-e-l-l, you'll need some. It depends a lot on how well you hold yore liquor; an' how close you can keep yore boys to camp. There's a hull lot of folks in Bulltown that make their livin' off'n strangers; an' most of 'em make a purty fair livin'. Th' gamblers do right well."

"Steve Hardy still marshal?" asked Hopalong.

"No. He was shot from behind a wagon. Scatter gun blowed him all apart. Th' gamblers run th' town. It's their turn now. Three Spot Bolton is marshal. He carries a short-barreled gun stuck behind his belt buckle. He's left-handed, an' th' buttons of his coat are on th' other side." The trail cutter pushed up his hat and then held out his hand. "Well, Cassidy, I'm right glad I've met you. That goes for yore whole outfit. Hope I see you ag'in next year."

"Why don't you spend th' night at th' wagon?" asked the trail boss. "Th' day's purty far gone now. Hate to say good-bye to you yet awhile." He smiled. "Them two herds behind us won't be up here till to-morrow or th' next day. Drop yore saddle off at th' wagon tonight."

"All right; reckon I will."

"That's good talk. Man, did you see 'em cross that bridge?"

"I shore did," chuckled the trail cutter, "outa th' corner of my eye. An' I shore saw one of them range-stockin' herds raise merry hell right here. They wasn't handled right, an' they was wild, anyhow; an' by th' time th' riders got through chousin' 'em, they balked strong, an' it took two hull days to get 'em acrost; an' then blame' near a hundred of 'em was crowded off th' bridge. She was shore excitin'."

"Well, we was lucky," responded Hopalong and

looked at the wagon. "Now we got to get cook acrost."

"I cut most of my herds up here or just below," said the trail cutter, glancing from the wagon to the causeway, "an' I know that bridge. There's two bad spots for wagons. One side of th' bridge is softer than th' other. It's th' east side, an' both bad places is right where she's narrowest. You got to come fast an' keep a-comin'."

"That's about how I figgered it," replied the trail boss. "Cook's half scared to death. That's why th' damn fool undressed. He figgers he'll mebby have to be drug out."

"An' mebby he figgers right," said the trail cutter. "I know this bridge. If it'll make you feel any better, I'll drive yore wagon over."

"That's right nice of you," replied Hopalong. "If I'd found cook usin' one of them shovels when I rode up, a few hours back, I might say yes to that—or drive it myself; but now he's shore goin' through with th' job. He hired out to drive that wagon, an' he's goin' to do it if I'm man enough to make him."

They rode slowly back over the causeway, Hopalong turning in the saddle for another look at the herd. It was moving on toward the bed ground up the trail, placidly plodding along. The drag rider, suddenly remembering his instructions, swung around and rode rapidly back toward the bridge, to throw his rope on the wagon, alongside his boss, and help yank the vehicle across the tricky causeway.

"Here comes Billy," said Hopalong, facing around

again. "He'll put his rope onto her, alongside mine, an' we'll show th' cook th' way."

"I know this bridge," repeated the trail cutter. "Billy can go back to th' drag, or you can have him foller along behind th' wagon with his rope hand ready in case of accident. Me an' you'll jerk her over."

Hopalong nodded his acquiescence and drew up at the wagon, where he laughed aloud.

Modesty blushed as the cook emerged from under the tarpaulin. He was bony, he was freckled, and he badly needed a bath. His face was strained with an expression of grave anxiety, and he looked at his boss accusingly.

"You still figger she oughta be drove over?" he demanded. "Seems to me that a couple of good riders at th' bits of this team would do a hell of a lot better job."

"It mebby does look that way to you," replied Hopalong. "You get yoreself set on that seat an' pick up th' reins," he ordered as Billy rode up. "Billy, you foller along behind in case she slips off an' cook has to jump," he said, winking at the grinning rider. "He says he'd rather lose an arm than get drownded; but I don't reckon you'll have to pull as hard as that."

"Hell," said Billy, gravely; "he'll be usin' his arms to keep him afloat, an' I won't be able to rope 'em. I'll drop th' rope over his head: it ain't so likely to slip off, that way, an' let him go down ag'in."

"There ain't nothin' th' matter with you, Billy," retorted the cook, "except you ain't got no brains!"

"All right, cook," ordered the boss. "Climb onto that seat an' start her rollin'."

The trail cutter and the boss made their ropes fast to the running gear as the team started, and rode out ahead, their ropes drawing taut. When they reached the bridge they were moving fast, the wagon bounding and rattling along behind them. Billy grinned, sat where he was, and calmly rolled a cigarette. Any rescuing that might be needed could wait until after he had enjoyed his smoke. Anyhow, he had noticed that the cook had lashed the wagon box to the running gear, and he figured that the box would keep both the gear and the cook afloat for a few minutes. He was worrying more about the harnessed horses than he was about the cook, if the truth were known. Harnessed horses can drown each other.

Billy saw the wagon strike the first submerged place and send the spray flying. It tipped sharply toward the east, but quickly righted itself under the pull of four horses and rolled over the next stretch of exposed bridge on all four wheels. Then it splashed into the second low place, careened wildly as the rear wheels slid sideways, sent a sheet of water into the air, seemed to hang on a hair, and then, rolling along with the right rear wheel off the bank, was yanked back squarely onto the causeway and rolled along without further mishap. A few moments later its wheels were grinding on the gravelly soil of the farther bank, and another cook had been spared to aid the cause of dyspepsia. Billy grinned, pressed his knees against his horse, and rode calmly over the causeway. He reached the wagon as it came to a stop and pulled up beside it.

The naked cook dropped the reins and stepped to the ground as the two leading horsemen loosed their ropes and began to coil them.

"Gawd!" he said, and wiped the sweat from his face. "For a minute back there I felt a hull lot better for knowin' that Billy was right behind me an' ready with his rope!"

Billy took a long drag on the cigarette and tossed the butt away.

"I was behind you, all right," he said without being explicit; "an' I was all ready to be a hero about th' third time yore head come up; but you tricked me. Well, now, let's get back an' start gettin' that stuff over. Don't see why it was ever took outa th' wagon in th' first place. Just makes that much more work."

The cook glanced across the creek at the little pile which represented all the clothing he had on earth.

"That's what I said," he remarked. "Bring me my clothes first trip, will you, Billy?"

The wagon repacked, Hopalong sent it on its way and watched it roll along parallel with the trail and to the right of it, on its way to make the night's camp. The trail boss felt so good over the way Big Muddy had been crossed that he was going to call it a day and graze the herd early. He had kept his word with the two following trail outfits, was within striking distance of town, and the delivery date was no longer a matter to worry about. The drive was practically ended.

Billy took up his position with the drag, and Hopalong and the trail cutter pushed forward to gain the
right point. As the two overtook Johnny, the trail boss
looked at his youthful friend and laughed outright.
Johnny had been one of the two riders who had gone
into the creek after the luckless steers.

"Kid," said Hopalong with a laugh, "you an' Pete
better go on to camp an' get into dry clothes. You'll
have more time now than you will later."

"I'm wearin' th' only clothes I got, except shirts,
an' so is Pete."

"You better go on, dry yore pants an' boots as good
as you can. I'll take over yore trick."

"How long before we throw off th' trail?" asked
Johnny.

"About an hour. We're stoppin' early. Might as well
let th' cattle feed up th' last few days."

"That'll be time enough to get dry," replied Johnny.
"Anyhow, my boots won't be dry till mornin'. I ain't
no wetter now than I was th' night of th' storm, an'
neither is Pete."

"Well, all right; it's yore funeral; but as soon as
th' herd stops, you an' Pete go in to th' fire."

"All right," replied Johnny. He moved the toes of
both feet and felt the water squish up between them.
He grinned and held out a hand. "Gimme th' makin's
an' a match," he said, and the grin grew as tobacco
and papers were passed over to him. He leaned over,
struck the match on Hopalong's saddle, blew out a
lungful of smoke, and waved his hand.

The trail boss and his companion pushed on and joined Red up at the point. The herd stepped right along, minute after minute. It seemed less than an hour when the wagon came into sight, well off to the east of the trail, and the smoke of the cook's fire seemed to beckon them. The herd was headed off the highway and drifted on toward the bed ground.

The cook was busy when Hopalong and the trail cutter rode in to the wagon, and the latter rode on to the fire to see if he could lend a hand. The fire was half a dozen paces from the wagon, but the trail cutter rode the distance in preference to walking it. The cook looked up and glimpsed two riders coming swiftly from the herd.

"What *they* ridin' in for so early? They know damn well they won't get nothin' to eat till we all eat!"

"They're comin' in to dry their clothes," explained the trail cutter. "What can I do to help you?"

"You can get outa my way," replied the cook and grinned.

Johnny and Pete dismounted at the wagon, stripped off their wet saddles, briskly rubbed the backs of their horses, and then strode toward the fire. They were laughing and chaffing each other, and they kept it up while they got out of their wet clothes. The trail boss, digging around in the wagon, emerged with the war bags belonging to the wet pair and dropped them on the ground near the fire.

"Huh!" laughed the cook, eyeing his two friends.

"My Gawd, Pete: you got muscles on you like a steam en-jine."

"Never knowed steam en-jines had muscles," replied Pete. "What do you know about steam en-jines? You never saw one."

"Well, no: I didn't; but I saw pitchures of 'em. Saw 'em in *Harper's Magazine*." The cook's face brightened suddenly. "But I'm shore goin' to see some, right soon."

Johnny slid into a dry shirt and then, picking up his gun belt, drew the weapon out of the wet holster, pushed out the cartridges, and placed them on his hat to keep the greasy bullets from picking up sand. As he straightened up to go to the wagon, he found that Hopalong had anticipated his needs, and he took the screwdriver and rag from Hopalong's hand and went to work on the gun.

Talking was general. Pete took the rag and screwdriver in turn and began cleaning his own gun as Johnny went over to shift the position of his clothing before the fire. The Kid had the gun in his hand, the base pin and cylinder still lying on the hat beside the cartridges, and as he returned from the fire he playfully stuck the harmless weapon against Hopalong's stomach and ordered the boss to put up his hands.

Hopalong grinned and obeyed and then, yielding to a sudden coltishness, he swung his left hand down and out, across his stomach and out past his side. It knocked the gun aside and closed over the weapon. The hammer clicked, but too late to have done him any harm if the gun had been loaded.

Johnny laughed, but there was a strange, thoughtful look in his eyes.

"Yo're quick as hell, Hoppy," he said. "You beat me to it. I'd-a missed you by a foot. See if you can do it ag'in."

"What's th' use?" laughed Hopalong, making a playful pass at the Kid's head. "You wouldn't be so slow, next time. I'd know better than to try that ag'in you." He was moving toward his horse as he spoke, and he kept on going.

"I was just as quick as I know how to be," called Johnny. "You beat my trigger finger, fair an' square."

Hopalong waved a hand behind him, swung into the saddle, and rode off toward the herd.

"Seems like you mighta shifted my clothes, too, while you was there," growled Pete, " 'stead of fool-in' with that damn gun."

"All right, Pete: I'll shift 'em anyhow," replied the Kid, and he turned and walked slowly back to the fire, shaking his head as he went. He shifted Pete's clothes without thinking about them and slowly and thought-fully returned to his hat.

"Lord, but he's quick!" he muttered.

"You just findin' that out?" asked Pete. "Hey, cook: where's th' oil?"

"Right where *you* can put *yore* hand on it," retorted the cook.

XXVI

THE sun beat down, and the heat was punishing. Here the trail was wider, with wider, trampled margins; and in places its course was lost, as the course of a brook is lost in ponds and lakes of its own making: herd after herd had lost momentum along this homestretch of the beef highway, to be drifted off and grazed while their trail bosses rode hopefully on to town, there to busy themselves with inquiries about buyers, about empty cars on the siding at the shipping pens, and about many and sundry other matters; while south of them or west of them on the range their crews waited impatiently for time off in which to taste the liberty and license to be found in the town. But all through the trampled side trails, all divergencies, past miles of ruined grazing, and grazing herds far from the beaten welts across the prairie, the main line trail pushed ever on, heading almost like an arrow for the Platte and the vast regions beyond; for while Bulltown was a shipping point, *the* shipping point for a while, it was not for all herds the end of trail. Only for those animals bound for the stockyards of the Middle West was it the end of the cattle highway; but other thousands of cattle were pushed on past this tur-

bulent cattle center, bound north, and then north-
northeast, northwest and west to stock that great em-
pire of grass and to put back the wealth taken out by
every previous era. Instead of being drained, now the
West was being stocked.

Hopalong Cassidy loped along the great trail, his
herd far behind him, for he was now alone, with neither cattle, outfit, nor chuck wagon under his watchful
eye. Behind him, at this moment two full days' drive
away, plodded his Circle 4's under a competent outfit
and a canny second boss. Before him, still miles away,
lay Bulltown with its memories of buffalo slaughter,
with its cattle pens, its railroad, its rough and turbulent population; Bulltown, for him and the Circle 4's
the end of the trail. He, too, had business to attend to:
somewhere in town was the buyer of his herd, ready to
count, to receive, and to pay if the cattle came up to
the specifications mentioned in the agreement. Bulltown, with its shantyville south of the tracks and its
famed Boot Hill north of them.

He followed up the little creek, its narrowing valley almost devoid of grass. It had been trampled and
pounded by thousands upon thousands of hoofs. Some
trail drivers felt that they had left the South behind
them when Red River had been crossed; but the mouth
of this little creek and the river it poured into left no
uncertainty in that regard. Once across this prairie
river, this boundary line of the old Spanish territory,
one was truly in the North.

The trail climbed the slope, angling up it, and forsook the little creek as if impatient to get over the little watershed and reach that pounded flattening of the low cut-banks of the river, where the narrow belt of cottonwood trees and willows revealed a gap which was noticeable for as far as the eye could see it. One might regard this flattened place as a funnel through which poured the cattle from thousands of square miles of southern range, cattle pointed here and funneled from the South into the North.

At the top of the watershed Hopalong drew up and stopped, sitting quietly in the saddle while he scanned the country under his eyes. Cattle. Grazing cattle, herd after herd of them, loosely herded but herds no less, occupied those areas where the grass sufficed. It would not suffice them long, nor would it need to, because the end of trail for them was the shipping pens. Back of these and beyond them and north of them and east of them there were others, herds which neither waited for cars on the siding nor for canny buyers, herds summer grazing.

Hopalong pressed his knees against the horse, but checked the animal almost instantly, his gaze flashing back to something north of him. It was something tenuous and faint, something so faint that only its background had revealed it to a plainsman's eye; something so far away that, by watching it, it did not seem to move; but glance away and back again, and its position had shifted by a hair. Had he been closer, up on the edge of the right of way, that faint plume would have dusted him with ashes; and the roar and the clangor, the hiss of steam and the clicking of pounded rail joints would have sent his horse into a frenzy of terror. At last the cook would see a locomotive instead of the picture of one. For perhaps a full minute he watched that faint smudge and then, sighing for no known reason, rode on again.

The river was low, and this was in the days before the irrigation ditches of the next state on the west had robbed the stream of water and turned it into a mere trickle. That country got rid of its storm waters quickly, for swiftly they poured down slopes where nothing interposed to check them, and quickly they rolled away.

The gap in the cottonwood fringe came nearer. The roan trotted down the gentle incline to the river's edge and paused to flick the water with its nose. Across the river lay another gentle incline where the trail left the stream, this one soft and wet from the water which had dripped from bovine bellies and rolled down bovine legs. Hopalong noticed this difference between the two slopes and smiled: nothing seemed to be southbound in this part of the country, except perhaps the stagecoach into the Nations, and small groups of cowmen riding homeward. To the right and the left of the gap were the low cut-banks, backed by the eternal cottonwoods and willow brush of prairie streams.

He sent the horse into the river, raised his feet and the stirrups with them, and rode up the farther bank dry-shod. The little incline led to ground which, although several feet higher than the level of the stream, and free from springs, was wet and deeply puddled by hoofs which had cut in to a depth of several inches. He rode on again.

Ahead of him at some distance was a horizontal line, without a dip or break in it, and it stretched from far on his right to still farther on his left. Such a thing in nature as a long, straight line was strange to his experience; and suddenly he knew it for what it was and marveled at the progress in the westward pushing of this railroad. It had not been there last season. Well, when it got to Raton Pass it would not push on so swiftly! He rode up to it, and as he crossed over it to gain the old wagon trail on the other side he looked westward along the rails and could not see the end of them. The heat waves made them shimmy and writhe, contorting them out of parallel.

He rode eastward along the deeply rutted and multiple-rutted dusty highway, which once had led to a foreign land. Here it was very wide, a series of roads, each new pair of tracks made when the ruts of the older had grown too deep. Along these tracks heavily laden mules had plodded, great wagons had creaked and strained as they clacked and rattled behind the straining ox teams. Here along this beaten baldness had ridden and trudged an army of conquest, call it what else you will; over this hammered highway had rolled the intermittent stagecoaches to and from the land of adobe; and later the great bull teams of the professional freighters had kept the dust aloft. Here Kiowa, Comanche, Pawnee, and other red tribes had

killed their buffalo and one another. He glanced at
the twin rails just south of him and frowned.

He was now riding with the sun at his back, and its
rays were hot enough to make him shift his necker-
chief. He passed the wreck of a great freight wagon,
thriftily stripped of iron: time was when its timbers
would not have been left, but would have been eagerly
gleaned for campfires. Again he glanced at the rails,
and his frown had grown. A rusty scraper, worn out
and abandoned, lay bottom up just beyond the wagon,
setting the air above it aquiver with reflected heat.
What it was, he did not know or greatly care to know.
He hoped it would be many years before the railroads
ruined his part of the country, and he became busy
with his thoughts; but the roan loped on, not cheating.

The plume of smoke he had seen from the crest of
the little watershed between Mulberry Creek and the
river was now streaming upward, not now so faint and
tenuous, from in front of a curious structure of vertical posts and horizontal boards. This affair was
divided into sections, and each section had a runway
slanting upward on the side nearest the track, and to a
height even with the floor of a cattle car. In the fence
on the opposite side were gates opening into each section; and along the tops of the dividing fences between the pens were narrow footwalks, the width of a
wide board. A man in high-heeled boots would not feel
any too secure when prodding cattle from such a pre-
carious footing. Each section was as wide as the length
of an empty car, and the door of each car on the sid-

ing was even with its own runway. It might even be that this train of empty cattle cars was the one which would carry the Circle 4 cattle on to the stockyards.

The plume of smoke broke suddenly into jerky, coughing movement, jetting upward furiously, and the bell-stacked engine forsook its cars and drew away with a fussy clanking, its bell ringing clangorously. Hopalong came out of his reverie as the saddle suddenly smashed upward under him, and for several moments he had his hands so full of terrified horse that he was oblivious of everything else. When the flurry was over he relaxed and looked around him and discovered that he was, indeed, in Bulltown; but during his fight with the frightened horse he had not noticed one of Bulltown's citizens who had taken a swift, deep, and furtive interest in him; and who had taken quick advantage of the pitching of the horse to slip out of sight behind a pile of boards and rubbish, only the top of his head showing above the pile.

This citizen wore a full beard and was only now enjoying the restored use of right arm and shoulder, both of which had been put out of commission by Hopalong himself many miles down the great cattle trail. This bearded gentleman was the only survivor of the outfit which had been led by the fake trail cutter south of Waggoner's, and he yearned for revenge. He yearned for it so much that for an instant he held a Colt leveled across the rubbish pile, and only the glimmering inspiration of avarice kept his finger from tightening on the trigger; this horseman was a trail boss and evidently bound for the pens. That meant, perhaps, sale and delivery of his herd; and this, in turn, meant money received: money in an amount amazing to a shiftless man. Revenge could wait and perhaps, by waiting, grow fuller, sweeter, and very profitable. The bearded gentleman crouched lower behind the rubbish pile and sheathed his gun; and, when the way was open, scurried swiftly roundabout toward the center of the town. He knew where a trail boss would go to meet a buyer; and, better still, he himself was an habitué of the bar in that hostelry.

Hopalong rode past the barn of the Fort Sill stage, a few corrals, a line of false-fronted buildings which extended along only one side of the street, and stopped in front of a two-story frame structure across the face of which was a faint legend in sun-bleached paint: TRAIL HOTEL. Tossing the reins across the tie rail, he left the roan to itself, crossed the narrow porch, and slowly entered the open door.

The clerk looked up, nodded, and spoke:

"Yes, sir?"

"Has John Babson got here yet?" mildly asked the trail boss.

"Yes, sir. You'll find him in th' bar."

Hopalong nodded and moved on again. He stepped through another open door and found himself in a long narrow room, cluttered up with a bar, tables, chairs, two cold stoves of the big-bellied type, sand boxes on the floor and chromos on the walls. One of the latter portrayed Julius Cæsar in a stagy posture, and right through the center of the Emperor's right eye was a neat round hole a little under half an inch in diameter. It gave the noble Roman a most peculiar expression, which became much more peculiar at certain hours of the day when sunlight stole in to shine through that optic. Hopalong fairly itched to balance the Emperor's eyes, but put the whim from him and gave his attention to a group of men talking and smoking at a far table. He moved on again, his gaze on the group, and stopped at the side of one chair.

"Hello, Babson," he said quietly and smiled.

The well-dressed man leaned quickly back in the chair, looking up curiously at the dusty and booted newcomer. Then he smiled suddenly and stood up, his right hand going out in greeting.

"Hello, Cassidy!" he cried. "Here I've been expecting you almost every day, and yet I didn't recognize you for a moment. How are you?"

"All right, I reckon, an' a year older," replied the trail boss, shaking hands heartily.

"Huh! So you are: so am I; but a year don't show on young fellers like you. I should have known you as you stepped through the door. Here: meet the boys," and the introductions were properly made and acknowledged.

"Have a drink," invited one of the men and waved toward a chair.

To refuse would be a discourtesy, and Hopalong knew that one round must grow until it was all square before the idiotic amenities were complied with. He did not particularly want a drink, unless it was water, but he went through with the ritual, serenely careless as to the number of drinks involved, for even then he was comforted by the knowledge that he had an amazing capacity for hard liquor. He could go farther and stay more sober than any other man in the group. The rounds followed one another in due course, and the talk was idle and got nowhere. After a little while of this, Babson slowly pushed back from the table.

"If you gentlemen will excuse us, Cassidy and I have a little matter of business to talk over which would only bore you," he said. "We won't be long."

The two men passed through the office and sought chairs on the narrow board porch, and as the chairs creaked with their weight, a bearded gentleman walked swiftly through the rear door of the barroom and entered the office. He nodded to the idle clerk, bought a cigar, picked up a *Harper's Monthly,* and sauntered toward the front door; but just before he got that far he became so deeply engrossed in the pages of the magazine that he stopped suddenly, leaned lazily against the frame of a window, and read intently. The voices from the porch could be clearly heard.

Hopalong reached for his tobacco sack, but found a cigar pushed under his nose.

"Try this," invited the cattle buyer with a smile.

Hopalong abandoned the quest for the tobacco sack, took the cigar, turned it curiously in his fingers, and read the band. He handled it gingerly, for already the dry prairie air had sucked the moisture from it.

"Reckon he was a right smart man," he gravely observed.

"Who?" demanded the buyer.

"Henry Clay," explained Hopalong, glancing again at the band. "I've heard about him."

"Guess he was. He was so smart that us Northerners could only find one man to match him," laughed the buyer, and held out a lighted match after waiting for the stinking sulphur to sizzle and burn away. Then he touched the match to his own cigar and flipped it into the street. "Well," he said, "you're about on time."

"I figgered to be," replied the trail boss. "Trail drivin' is right oncertain, an' I left myself a little give-an'-take. Th' herd'll be here day after tomorrow. When it gets here I'm comin' in after you."

"You're coming in after me?" repeated the buyer in some surprise. "Aren't you going to stay in town until it gets here?"

"No, reckon not: as I just said, trail drivin's right oncertain, what with one thing an' another. There's plenty of two-laigged scum hangin' 'round cow towns," explained the trail boss, smiling a little. "Gosh, but this cigar stings considerable."

"Havana always stings the nose. Nobody'll bother your herd when it's so close to town."

"No?" drawled Hopalong. "Where you find th'

most humans you'll mebby find th' most thieves." He
glanced at the roan, lazily switching flies. "I just rode
in to see if you was here an' ready to receive. I didn't
aim to drive th' herd too near to town until you was.
Anyhow, I wouldn't-a done so because of th' poor
grazin'. Now I'll go back an' keep it comin'."

"Well, I'm here, and I'm ready," replied the buyer.
"The money's in the safe, and the bill of sale is in my
pocket ready for signing. I suppose the herd's up to
specifications?"

"Anythin' with Bar 20 burned onto its hide allus
is," answered Hopalong. He was looking at his companion rather curiously. "You just said th' *money's* in
th' safe: last time it was a draft, which is a lot better.
What kinda money, for Gawd's sake: hard or soft?"

"Soft," answered Babson and laughed outright.
"Man, you don't suppose I'd be carrying hard money
in that amount? At twenty dollars a head at the pens,
a thousand head would run into weight, even in gold;
in silver it would take a wagon to carry it: it would be,
let's see: well, over thirteen hundred pounds."

"Why didn't you bring a draft?" persisted Hopalong, bothered by the responsibility of carrying so
much cash and guarding it.

Babson laughed again and leaned forward in the
chair.

"You remembered my face, the first look, although
you'd only seen it once, and that a year ago," he said
earnestly; "but you've forgotten what you thought
about that piece of bank paper I gave you at that time.

Why, it took the assurance of a dozen men in this town to convince you to sign away your herd for that draft. It was just a piece of paper to you: what you wanted was money, *real* money—something you were familiar with. Remembering that little session, I thought I'd ease your mind this time."

"Oh, hell!" laughed Hopalong, his face red under its coats of tan. "I was green then. Why, I worried all th' way home about that draft, an' was almost scared to give it to Buck. It shore was a load off my mind when he took it and seemed right glad to get it." He stood up and held out his hand. "Well, I'll drift back to th' boys." He stopped suddenly as a loud crash sounded from the railroad siding, and his eyes flashed to the nervous roan. "What th' hell's that?"

"Engineer tryin' to smash up my string of empties, I guess," said Babson with a laugh. "Anyhow, I believe they're mine: station agent said they were due today. If they are, then that's one worry off my mind. Usually I have a hell of a time getting cars at this time of the year. They usually roll in anywhere from three days to a week late." He stood up and shook hands with his companion. "Sorry you can't stay over with us. There'll be a nice game of draw running almost all night."

Hopalong shook his head ruefully, for if there was one thing he loved it was straight draw poker with a good crowd.

"I'm right sorry to miss it," he said, grinning. "Only chance I'll have to play, mebby. I don't figger to hang around this town very long after I've got shut of th' herd."

"Hell, man! You aren't planning to go back the same day you deliver!"

"Well, mebby not," admitted Hopalong, well knowing what a riot such a decision would cause in his little cow camp. "Reckon th' boys deserve to have a fling; but I'd shore feel safer if they were back on th' trail ag'in bound for home." He smiled ruefully. "An' me with 'em," he added, "with all that real money in my pockets."

"Shucks," grunted the buyer. "I guess you can take care of it."

Hopalong's face hardened, and a look came into the pale blue eyes that was not pleasant to see.

"I shore aim to try damn hard."

"Oh, yes!" hastily said the buyer. "You understand, of course, that you are to load the cattle on the cars?"

"Shore," answered Hopalong with a smile. "We'd do that anyhow." He laughed gently. "Just to make shore we'd got rid of 'em!"

"Have any trouble on the way up?" asked Babson.

"Oh, two-bits' worth, here an' there," answered the trail boss; "but we kept comin' right along. Well, I'll say so-long now an' make dust. You'll see me day after tomorrow."

"Have a drink before you go?"

"No, reckon not. Much obliged, just th' same. See you later."

Inside the hotel office the bearded man yawned, turned, and held out the magazine toward the clerk.

"Read that," he said, with a frown. "An' gimme another cigar. They're still writin' us up, back East, as bein' wild an' woolly. This here feller writes about Abilene. Hell, Abilene's been dead for three years. What th' hell does them Easterners know about us?"

"Not a whole lot, but th' fools don't know it," replied the clerk, glancing at the open page. "But they're mebby right about Abilene, at that," he admitted with true small-town prejudice.

"Abilene? Gawd, yes!" fervently exclaimed the bearded man; "but take this town, now: it's so law-abidin' it makes a feller feel too damn virtuous. Why, we ain't had a killin' since—well, since last night, *anyhow,* far's I know." He ran his fingers through his beard. "You take th' buffalo days, now: *them* was real days!"

"Reckon so!" exclaimed the clerk. "When th' wind was right, you could smell them hides on th' freight platform clean acrost th' town!"

A shadow darkened the doorway, and a clean-shaven man, dressed in the gambler's conventional frock coat, stepped into the room.

"Hello, Bolton," said the clerk with oily amiability.

"Hello, Marshal," said the bearded man.

The town marshal looked levelly at the last speaker.

"Spud Murphy's lost his hoss," he said almost accusingly. *"You* ain't seen it, have you?"

"*Me?* Gawd, no!" hastily exclaimed the bearded man.

The marshal slowly shifted his gaze to the face of the clerk.

"Who's in th' back room?"

The clerk hastily told him.

The marshal grunted something, turned on his heel, and moved toward the front door. He almost bumped into the cattle buyer.

"Excuse me, Bolton."

"My fault," grunted the marshal. He grinned. "If you got a saddle hoss, you better take it to bed with you. There's been eight stole since last night."

"Well, that's an improvement!" laughed the buyer. "That's two better than the night before."

"Reckon that's because hosses are gettin' scarce," chuckled the marshal, and then stiffened as three quick shots sounded outside. He flung open his coat and stepped swiftly through the door.

"Town's comin' to life a little earlier than usual," observed the clerk.

"But what th' hell did Bolton look at *me* for when he asked about Murphy's hoss?" demanded the bearded man with a trace of indignation.

"You voted for Steve Jordan, didn't you?" asked the clerk.

XXVII

THE herd poured down the long slope leading to the river, crossed the famous ford, and streamed across the flat pasture on the other side. Hopalong was sitting his motionless horse squarely on the railroad track, watching in both directions: he hoped no train would come clanking and roaring past while the herd was in sight of the right of way. Remembering how the roan had acted in town two days before, he much preferred that these range animals should not be faced with such a test.

Over the track without pause and on again, the herd angled off toward the northeast, east to gain mileage toward town and north to take them out of sight of the track. Through herds pointed slightly to the west, bound for the Sawlog and the great trail along it; but Bulltown and its pens lay to the right. As soon as the drag had crossed the rails the trail boss swung his horse around and passed the herd, joining Red at right point.

"You figger we'll get shut of 'em today?" asked Red with restrained eagerness, the excitement of the town already stimulating him. After three months of take-it-as-it-comes along the trail, the town would look good.

"It all depends on a few things," answered the trail boss, himself feeling a mild excitement; but it was not because of Bulltown and its varied attractions, but rather because of a big job almost finished.

"Yeah?" demanded Red with ill-concealed suspicion. "I reckon you figger to hold us all in camp for three, four days, huh?"

"No," growled his companion. "Babson's got to count this herd an' look it over; he's got to have his cars at th' loadin' chutes. There's other things, too."

"Thought you said th' cars was there?" demanded Red quickly.

"I said *cars* was there: he himself didn't know that they was his. Babson's company ain't th' only outfit buyin' beef!"

"Reckon not," growled Red and went back on the offensive. "Well, what are th' other things, then?"

"After he's accepted them they'll have to be drove into th' big pen, an' then into th' little loadin' pens, an' not more'n twenty to a pen. Th' big pen'll hold 'em all; but they ain't enough little pens to take 'em all at one bite. You know that! You was there last year. Even at th' best we'll be all day, an' mebby part of th' next day gettin' 'em into th' cars. You been growlin', right along, this trip: but before th' last critter is loaded on that train you'll mebby have some real reason to growl!"

"Any growlin' I done I shore learned from you!"

"An' that goes for about everythin' you know, too!" snapped Hopalong.

"Then I wouldn't have to know very much, would I?" retorted Red.

"Don't you get all lathered up: you don't know very much!"

"I shoulda picked out a smarter boss, huh?"

"If you had, he'd-a fired you damn quick."

"That so?" demanded Red.

"You know damn well it is."

"Huh!"

On across the high, rolling prairies, over a thin coverlet of grass like no grass found off the prairies; grass curled down and scanty, but with an amazing nutrition; grass which had fed countless millions of buffalo for countless years; grass which, with their passing, would also pass. A man keenly observant of the ways of nature would have said, even then, that the grass was already passing. The freighters of an era whose dust had scarcely settled had said the same. Interfere with a natural balance, and no one can say where the repercussions will end.

They checked the herd in a gentle prairie depression between two rolling slopes. Cook stopped the wagon on the northern side of the south slope; stopped the wagon, unharnessed the horses, tossed his saddle from the wagon box, and in a few moments was all dressed for town: he had slicked his hair and greased his boots. Now he threw the saddle on the back of the nigh work horse and was cinching up. He would ride out to the cavvy, get himself a real horse, and be on his joyful way. The loose end of the cinch strap tucked in place, he for some reason of his own led the saddled animal away from camp, keeping the wagon between it and the herd. Once over the crest of the rise, he mounted and rode toward Skinny and the cavvy, careful to keep below the skyline of the ridge.

Skinny saw the grinning cook riding toward him from the other side of the horse herd, and the wrangler scratched his head at this mystery: why should the cook come so roundabout? Why should he come to the cavvy at all? Skinny grinned, believing that he knew the answer.

" 'Lo, Skinny," said the cook, with repressed excitement and unusual friendliness.

" 'Lo, cook. What you want?"

"Two things: a good hoss an' th' lend of some money."

"Well, take yore pick of th' hosses," said the wrangler, generously waving his hand at the cavvy. "There's Hoppy's bay, now: he'd only whale hell out of you if you took that. There's Red's pet roan, an' a damn good hidin' goes with that. That big sway-back is in Pete's string, an' you know all about Pete. Take yore pick, cook: but pick damn careful!"

"Show me one of Billy's," said the cook, his anxious eyes on the distant herd. "Hurry up, Skinny: I ain't got all day!"

"You figger you can lick Billy, huh?" asked the wrangler with a grin. "I figger different. Bet you two to one you can't."

"Hurry up: show me one of his; an' lend me five, ten dollars," urged the cook, squirming in the saddle.

"I've already showed you two, three good hosses, an' I ain't showin' you no more," replied Skinny, ironing out his grin. "An' I can't lend you no money because I ain't got nothin' smaller than a two-bit piece."

"Huh?" asked the nervous cook, surprised. He turned this remarkable statement over in his mind, and he did not like the sound of it.

"You heard me," retorted Skinny.

"Why, you —— —— fool! What good is two bits?"

"Listen, cook," said Skinny earnestly and in a low voice. "I'm another man of this outfit that you can't lick. Two bits is just twenty-five cents more than I would lend you if I had a hull barrel of gold; an' you make any more mouthy passes about me bein' a —— —— fool, or any other kind, an' you won't have no interest a-tall in *no* hoss *a*-tall! If you want money, get it off of Hoppy: you got three months' wages comin' to you, like all th' rest of us. Who's goin' to do our cookin' for us while yo're on yore bender? An' who th' hell ever told you that a trail cook could go to town before a rider?"

"Aw, I'm comin' right back! Lend me th' two bits."

"I never offered you no two bits, an' yo're not comin' right back because yo're not goin'. You go back to that wagon, strip off that saddle, an' start makin' up some biscuits: *biscuits*, an' not no bread! You hear me?"

"Th' hell I ain't goin' to town!"

"That's shore th' hell of it, because you ain't. Now, I ain't got no money; but I've got a good saddle, a fair belt, an' a good gun; a pocketknife, half a sack of tobacco, some rawhide strings, an' two extry shirts: I'll bet you th' hull caboodle of 'em ag'in a month's pay that you don't go to town first."

"Aw, Skinny, *we* was allus good friends!"

"Well, yo're shore gettin' fixed up to bust up th' friendship, then. G'wan back to th' wagon—before Hoppy ketches you sneakin' off!"

"Aw, for two pins I'd——"

"Listen!" interrupted Skinny in a voice which was no longer low or pleasant. "If you had two pins you'd be a rich man; an' if you did, I'd make you eat 'em! You go back to that wagon an' *stay* there!" He looked around and back again, and a grim smile slid across his face. "Take a good look: we're havin' a visitor!"

The cook looked and saw the trail boss heading for the cavvy on the roan. The animal's fanning legs made a fog of dust behind it. In a few moments the boss pulled up beside the two men, his level gaze on the startled cook.

"You'll go to town when I tell you to, an' not before," he said coldly.

"Hell, I ain't goin' to town!" protested the cook truthfully.

"No?" inquired the trail boss, looking slowly and meaningly at the saddle under the cook and at the freshly greased boots.

"Naw," replied the cook. "I was just fixin' up to go with Skinny when he went. I ain't goin' to town now, am I, Skinny?"

"Shore you ain't," answered Skinny, quite certain that his answer was true, "an' when you do go, you can go with me; but we won't neither one of us go till we get paid off. Wouldn't hardly be any use to, if we didn't have no money."

"Naw," said the cook, with a forced laugh. "All right, Skinny: I'll feed you-all on biscuits till you can't eat no more." He looked at Hopalong. "Goin' back to camp?"

The trail boss glanced from the cook to Skinny and then back to the cook.

"No," he answered shortly.

"All right," said the cook, turning his horse. He looked at Skinny. "Remember now: you promised."

"Huh!" said Skinny. "I shore will remember."

Hopalong watched the cook ride away, whistling as he went, and then turned to the wrangler.

"What th' hell was *he* doin' out here?" he demanded suspiciously.

"Don't ask me no questions an' I won't tell you no lies. You goin' to town?"

"Yes. I want to get this herd off my hands. Then we can *all* go."

"I'm shore ready for that," laughed Skinny. He had a sudden thought and he voiced it: "When you pay me off, hold back half of it: I ain't goin' back home busted flat, like I did last year. Man, how th' money just pops outa yore pockets in that town!"

Hopalong laughed, nodded, and started toward town.

The string of empty cattle cars was still on the siding, and they were the ones Hopalong had seen two days before: he knew that because he remembered that the last two figures of the number painted on the end car were a two and a zero—and the number twenty always brought Bar 20 to his mind. The same clerk was behind the desk, and he nodded as he recognized the newcomer.

"Mr. Babson ain't up yet," he said.

"Hell!" said Hopalong. "It's halfway to noon!"

"Halfway to noon," repeated the clerk and grinned. "That's a new one on me." Just then the ticking clock struck eight.

"It's light at four," explained Hopalong, also grinning. "Don't suppose you'd dast knock on his door?"

The clerk glanced into the barroom, where a whisking broom was busy shifting dust from one place to another.

"Mike!" he called, and the whisking stopped. "Call Number Nine," ordered the clerk as a frowsy head showed in the barroom doorway, and again turned to the trail boss. "He left a call for eight o'clock. Said he was expectin' you."

"Good!" grunted Hopalong and picked up a magazine. He was deep into the sins of Abilene when Babson came in on his way to the dining room.

"Morning, Cassidy. Had your breakfast?"

Hopalong laughed.

"All right, all right!" said Babson. "Be with you as soon as I've had mine. Won't be long."

"There ain't no great hurry," replied the trail boss.

Babson wheeled and disappeared, and Hopalong again picked up the magazine, found his place, and went on reading. A slight disturbance outside made him raise his head quickly, and he saw that a man was tying a saddled horse to the rail alongside the roan.

"Mr. Babson's horse," volunteered the clerk. "That's quite a piece in there about Abilene, ain't it?"

"Reckon so," grunted Hopalong, tossing the magazine aside. "Gimme a handful of cigars for my boys before I forget it."

Babson reappeared, his hat on his head and a quill toothpick in his mouth, and a few moments later was riding down the street at the side of the trail boss, bound for the herd.

"Them yore cars?" asked Hopalong a little anxiously.

"Yes. I'll be getting a bill for the use of that siding. Hope to move them off it before long."

"Good! They'll be loaded before dark, I reckon. You got yore train outfit all ready to go?"

"Yes," answered Babson.

The herd was in trail formation when the two riders reached it, and, at a signal from the trail boss, was put into motion. Babson sat in the saddle facing him, with a respectable distance between them; and the cattle were fed through this gap. Babson used his fingers, turning one down at every even hundred. He counted cattle with practised ease, and he did more than that: he appraised every animal as he counted it, which more often than not required a trained and agile mind. As the last animal passed through the little gap, Babson looked over at the trail boss and announced his figures.

"That's what I make 'em," said Hopalong. "I s'pose you'll want to look 'em over good."

"I've done that. They're all right, Cassidy. They're even better than I expected. Nice herd. You coming back to town with me?"

"No," answered Hopalong, shaking his head. "You'll see me when th' last steer is on th' cars, an' th' cars are ready to go." He looked at the herd, which had not stopped, but had kept on going as straight for town as it could move. He smiled knowingly: every man in the outfit knew that the cattle would be accepted, and was pushing on toward the end of the drive. His gaze shifted to the grazing cavvy and then around to Babson as the buyer chuckled.

"Cassidy," said the buyer, "I like you. That's why I took the trouble to find a buyer for your horse herd. I believe I got you a better price than you could have gotten. All you fellows are anxious to sell and go home. I had lots of time, and perhaps I stretched the truth. If you want to sell them, drop in and see Frank Coggswell, east of the station. Tell him they're mine."

"Why, that's right kind of you, Babson! I'd ruther sell 'em than drive 'em home ag'in, if th' price is right." The trail boss scratched his head thoughtfully. "Looks like you've done earned yoreself a commission."

"I figure to get that out of you at draw poker tonight," laughed Babson. He turned his horse toward town. "See you later."

"You shore will," laughed Hopalong, watching the buyer ride off. The rattling of the wagon obtruded, and he looked around.

"Whereat am I goin'?" yelled the cook, whose orders from Lanky had not been very specific. He waited impatiently while Hopalong told him, frowned a little at certain instructions concerning his own behavior, and rattled on again. Before he had gone a hundred yards he yielded to the tingle of his elation and burst into song: he wasn't going into town, but he'd be right handy to it.

Hopalong smiled and stirred. He looked thoughtfully at the dark mass moving slowly but steadily through the long dust cloud and pushed forward to join the herd. He hoped every last steer would have its feet off the ground before dark; but he was not unmindful of the hard work and trying difficulties ahead. Loading longhorn range cattle into cars was something to worry about. They just would rear and plunge, they just would get their legs through the openings between the slats of the cars; they would get their heads down and their horns under some other animal's legs; and then they would raise their heads. Anything over the horns came up with them. For a man to go into the cars with them was plain suicide. Everything had to be done with poles, and the prodding started in the little loading pens, the prodders balanced on the narrow planks. Hopalong's smile had faded, but when he reached the herd it was back in place again. Suddenly he laughed aloud: there was one thing spared them: they would not have to go along with this shipment—Babson had provided a crew for that!

XXVIII

THE little fire gleamed in the darkness and shone on the faces of the three unlucky members of the Circle 4 trail outfit. The grouchy cook was sullenly regarding his two companions, bitter thoughts in his mind. Over the rolling prairie swells, scarcely a mile away, lay Bulltown and its noisy, turbulent night life. Close enough to the camp for it to be vaguely seen was the cavvy, close-herded tonight and kept near the camp on strict orders of the boss. The cavvy, for weeks valuable more for what service it rendered than for dollars and cents, was now valuable only for the latter. On previous trips they had driven the horse herd home with them; this year it would be sold, and they would ride home at a better pace and with sweeter tempers.

"But there ain't no sense to th' three of us stayin' here!" growled the cook, continuing his argument. "Hell, nobody would pester th' camp or th' cavvy. We're in civilization, ain't we?"

Skinny laughed knowingly. He had drawn one of the shorter matches and thereby lost the chance of being among the first to visit town.

"That's just when you want to pin up yore pockets

and keep yore eyes skinned," he replied. "Th' closer you are to town, th' closer you are to a lot of thieves. Them hosses are worth money: more money up here than back home."

"Aw, it's just my damn luck!" growled the cook. "I allus get th' worst of it."

Skinny laughed again, this time derisively.

"Huh! Here you been settin' 'round camp all day, with nothin' to do but work up one of yore reg'lar grouches, while we was puttin' them damn steers into th' little pens, an' then into th' damn cars! For a while I figgered them cars didn't have no end to 'em. It was just one damn car after another. I fell off th' boards once, skinned my back, an' near got horned: an' Billy fell off twice. An' you set there yowlin' an' growlin' about gettin' th' worst of it!"

Billy chuckled.

"I don't know how fast I was goin' when I was fallin'," he said; "but I shore made right good time climbin' up ag'in. Climbed so fast th' last time that I skun my laig to hell an' gone. Cattle are scared of a man when he's on a hoss; but when he's on foot they're likely to get big idears. If you reckon them horns look big out on th' open range, when yo're straddlin' a hoss, you just want to fall into a pen with twenty pair of them horns, an' look up at 'em from th' flat of yore back!"

"Well, that's yore own fault!" snapped the cook. "That's what you get for comin' up th' trail. You joined on from yore own free will. *Me,* I'm all through trailin' cattle!"

"Yeah, just like all th' rest of us," chuckled Billy, yawning. " 'Long about spring you'll be gettin' yore war bag packed up an' go pokin' all over th' country lookin' for a trail outfit to join up with." He turned to Skinny. "I betcha Hoppy feels good with th' herd off'n his hands an' all that money in his pocket. You reckon he's been paid yet?"

"Don't know," answered Skinny, rubbing the stubble on his chin. "I'm goin' to get shaved in style tomorrow an' get my hair cut. It'll cost me ten, twelve bits, but it'll shore be worth it. Yeah," he said in reply to Billy's remark, "he'll shore feel good about gettin' shut of th' herd, but I'll betcha he'll be near sick worryin' about that money. Real money it is, twenty thousan' dollars of it, an' not no fool paper from some bank."

"Gawd!" exploded the cook, his eyes popping. "Twenty thousan' dollars! Gawd! *Twenty thousan' dollars!* He's shore got to let me have a good look at that!"

"Mebby he will," chuckled Skinny, but his own private opinion was to the contrary. "Then, after you see all that money, an' get a good look at a real enjine, an' not no picture of one, you'll have somethin' to talk about for th' rest of yore ornery life."

"He don't need steam en-jines or real money for that," grunted Billy, who was due to take over the first trick with the cavvy and to take it over soon.

"Hell you say!" snapped the indignant cook. Then he grinned and scratched his head. "Say, them fellers that drive them en-jines must be damn good hands, keepin' a big thing like that plumb on them little rails. An' I've heard they travel forty miles an hour! Don't reckon mebby it's so bad on th' straightaway, but how th' hell they keep 'em on th' track on th' turns is more'n I can understand."

"I'm glad there's one thing you can't understand, an' glad I know what it is," grunted Skinny, slowly and painfully getting to his feet. "I've had one hell of a day, an' I'm near dead. I'm turnin' in, an' I aim to sleep right off th' handle. You figger you can understand what I mean by that?"

A little group of tired riders stopped in front of the hotel and slowly, almost laboriously, swung down from the saddles and made the horses fast to the tie rail. They were sweat-covered, grimy with dust and dust paste. They had just come from the pens, where but a few minutes before they had put the last Circle 4 steer in the last car of the second section of the train, closed the sliding door, and gladly and gratefully turned the whole business over to the crew which Babson had hired to nurse the cattle in transit.

Hopalong led them into the office, spoke shortly to the clerk, and then herded his companions before him into the washroom. A few minutes later they filed out again, looking and feeling much better for their ablutions, and went into the dining room. As the last man stepped into the room, the doors closed behind him. They had just made it.

Babson sauntered into the office, dropped into a chair, and talked idly with the clerk until the opening door of the dining room revealed the trail boss and his friends.

"Well," said the buyer, standing up. As he spoke there sounded the forced-draft puffing of a locomotive, the squeal of flanges biting against the rails of the little curve leading to the main line track. *"That* sounds like you've seen the last of your cattle, Cassidy; or perhaps I should have said *my* cattle." He reached into his pocket and drew out a folded paper.

"Glad to get shut of 'em," said Hopalong, grinning widely; but the grin died out: he was about to become the custodian of twenty thousand dollars in real money which belonged to the best friend a man ever had; and he was still a long way from Buck Peters and the end of his responsibility, still a long way from home.

"I'll bet you are," laughed Babson, handing over the paper. "Read that, and then sign it if it's all right. The figures were copied from your own inspection papers."

It was a simple bill of sale transferring ownership of certain numbers of cattle in certain brands, under the Circle 4 road brand. Hopalong read it, took the pen the clerk handed him, scrawled his name, and gave the bill of sale back to Babson.

"Now comes the interesting part of the ceremony,"

chuckled the buyer, looking at the clerk. "Hope you haven't lost the key to that safe, Charley."

Charley saw the trail boss nod swiftly to his companions, and smiled at the quick but seemingly unhurried movements of the men. Johnny Nelson stepped into the open front door and leaned against the casing, his right hand casually and lazily resting on the walnut handles of his gun; Lanky Smith was gravely observing the barroom from its wide doorway, and it seemed that his hand, too, was tired and needed support. Red leaned back against the desk, staring reflectively at the closed doors leading into the dining room; while Pete was all wrapped up in an ecstatic contemplation of a hideous chromo which hung on the wall and snugly against the casing of the side window. His hand, too, was on walnut.

The clerk turned, bent down for a moment, and the door of the safe swung silently open. He stood up, turned to the desk, and shoved a packet of crisp green bills across the counter. There was no awe either in his face or gesture.

"If you'll count that, Mr. Babson, I'll take back our receipt for it," he said in a matter-of-fact voice.

Hopalong glanced swiftly about the room, lifted his hand from the gun butt, and pressed solidly against the edge of the desk. Babson removed the string from the packet and then slowly, one by one, placed the notes in front of the trail boss, counting aloud. The lips of both Hopalong and the clerk were moving with the buyer's, and when the last note dropped in front of him the trail boss nodded briskly and swiftly made a small, tight roll of the money. Deep down into a front trouser pocket it went, where it made no noticeable bulge. He commented upon this.

"Right small bundle for so much money," he said.

"Yes: big bills," replied Babson, sliding the hotel's receipt over the counter toward the clerk. "You can change them right here if you want smaller ones." He glanced at the clerk and nodded. "Thanks, Charley."

" 'Twarn't nothin'," replied Charley and yawned.

Hopalong glanced at the man behind the counter and decided that the clerk's lack of interest in handling so large a sum was honest, and he felt surprised.

"I'd-a figgered that you'd feel a lot better for gettin' rid of it," he said, smiling a little.

"From now on to th' end of this year's drive," said the clerk with a laugh, "that little roll of yourn won't stack up no bigger than a tick would to a cow." He grew expansive. "Bulltown is young, an' it's only a few buildin's an' a railroad sidin' out on th' prairies: last year there was about four hundred thousan' head of cattle shipped from them pens; this year there'll be more'n that. I wouldn't be surprised if ten or twelve million dollars of cattle money changed hands in this town before snow flies." He laughed again and waved his hand toward the barroom and Lanky Smith, who still stood guard despite the fact that the money was now out of sight. "I've seen poker games back there where thirty thousan' dollars was won an' lost at a sittin'; I've seen cattlemen lose trail herds at one session of poker: whole herds—two, three thousan' head. An' *Abilene* gets its name in th' magazines!"

Babson nodded and laughed gently. He knew the cow towns. He had known Ellsworth, Abilene, and Newton. His glance found the magazine in question.

"Yes," he said thoughtfully. "But Mud Creek had something that you haven't got here: it had Wild Bill Hickok. You ever see him?"

"Hickok!" sneered the clerk, loyal to his own town and its denizens. It was such loyalty which caused the county-seat wars of Kansas. "Why, we got fellers in this town that'd make Hickok step on his own tail gettin' out of their way!"

"God bestows great gifts sometimes," said the buyer quietly. "To Jenny Lind He gave a voice to thrill the world. To others, other things. To Hickok He gave speed of hand." Babson was regarding the clerk curiously. He smiled placatingly, glanced around, and motioned toward the barroom and Lanky Smith.

"But there's no use of arguing where proof cannot be had," he said. "What do you say if we leave Hickok stepping on his own tail and adjourn to the bar? A successful business transaction should be sealed as well as signed. I'm buying."

The watchful group looked toward their leader, who nodded: etiquette must be observed, come hell or high water; and he knew how to behave in town or anywhere else. He waved Babson ahead of him into the long room, his friends trailing along after him. They lined up, made known their wants, and were served just as a bearded gentleman pushed quietly away from the second window he had favored in the last ten minutes. Bulge or no bulge, he knew the secret of that pocket. Between the boards of the high fence which ran past the office window there were useful cracks, and a man needed to use only one eye to see what he had seen.

Hopalong struck a match, touched it to the cigar he had taken, and blinked pleasantly. In turn he bought a round—and shoved the second cigar into a pocket. Knowing that none of his men had money, he gave them some—and straightway accumulated more cigars. The room seemed quiet and orderly. There was a game of poker going on, and several patrons were quietly reading. He decided that Bulltown's reputation was grossly exaggerated and spoke of this to the buyer.

"An unaccountable lull," replied Babson. He laughed and glanced toward the ceiling. "Evidently the town's still asleep. I remember the first night I spent here, last year. I had a room right above us. The next night I slept over the dining room. It was a miracle I wasn't killed. There's a tip for you, Cassidy: if ever you spend a night in town, sleep over a dining room or a kitchen. But the boys are quieter on this side of the tracks. You'll find hell popping, right now, on the other side."

Hopalong grunted something and seemed to be restless. He felt that he would feel much better back in camp, where Buck's twenty thousand would not make his pocket feel so damned swelled out. He felt that every man who glanced his way could see the outlines of the roll, small as he knew it to be. If it were his own money he wouldn't worry about it. Again he shifted his feet.

Babson read the signs and smiled knowingly.

"You've had a hard day and must want to get some sleep," he said; "but it's only a short distance down to Frank Coggswell's. What do you say about going down there now and seeing him about selling him youɪ horse herd? I believe he's waiting for you."

"He's waitin' for *me?*" demanded the trail boss in surprise. He had forgotten all about Coggswell and the damned cavvy.

"I told him I'd bring you around as soon as you were through at the pens and had supper."

"Gosh! He's been waitin' some time, then."

"He won't mind that: he lives in a room behind his office. You can get this done now and have the cavvy off your hands early in the morning."

"Well, all right," replied Hopalong, smiling uncertainly. He looked at his friends, eager for a night's entertainment in town after a long, hard grind on the trail. Digging down into a pocket, not *the* pocket, he pulled out a handful of gold coins and passed them around. "Here's twenty dollars apiece on yore pay," he said. "I'll look in here on my way back, but you don't have to wait: go where you please—but if yo're smart you'll put yore hosses in some stable. Hosses get stolen in this damn town."

Johnny gently juggled the two yellow coins on his open palm and looked eagerly at his friend and boss.

"Figger I'll go along with you, Hoppy," he said, nervously important.

Hopalong studied the keen face for an instant, reddened suddenly, and let pride have its sway.

"You stay with th' boys!" he snapped. "Come on, Babson."

"What's th' matter, bartender?" demanded Pete loudly. "Yore arm busted?" He slapped Lanky across the shoulders. "Let's wake up this —— —— town! Let's take 'er apart!"

Lanky grinned at him and then suddenly became thoughtful. He leaned close to Pete's ear and whispered a few words. Pete grunted something, nodded, and turned slowly toward the bartender.

"Take it all back, friend: yore arm's all right," he said with a smile; "but right now I'm savin' up my thirst for later on in th' evenin', when things begin to loosen up in this dead town." He swung around toward Lanky and found that person gazing thoughtfully into the office. Long-headed old horse thief, Lanky was. Then he looked at Red and Johnny, busily talking at the far end of the bar. The Kid would only mess things up and act like a swollen coyote all the way home. Pete backed cautiously away from the bar, saw that neither Red nor Johnny was paying him any attention, and slipped quietly into the office after Lanky.

Lanky was waiting for him on the little porch.

"Whereat is this Coggswell's place?" he asked.

"Don't know," answered Pete, looking up and down the track. "There's two places that's got lights in 'em —one up this way, an' one down th' other."

"Yeah," grunted Lanky. "We'll save time if we split up. I'll take th' place up this way, an' you take th' one down there. Better not let Hoppy see us, neither: he'll mebby figger we aim to pin diapers onto him, an' mebby go on th' prod. Anybody that gets *that* money will shore as hell *earn* it! Get goin', you big ox."

Coggswell was glad to see his visitors. Babson introduced him to Hopalong, and in a few minutes the cavvy, minus the two work horses for the wagon and one horse for each member of the outfit, was sold. The inevitable bottle was produced to seal the bargain, and after a few minutes' desultory conversation the trail boss turned toward the door. Babson waved a finger at him.

"What's your hurry, Cassidy?" he asked.

"Want to get back to my boys," answered Hopalong, smiling. He would feel better back in camp with all that money.

"Well, all right; but you don't mind if I stay and talk with Frank, do you?"

Hopalong laughed.

"No," he said and then looked at the horse buyer. "I'll see you in camp in th' mornin', then?"

"You shore will," answered Coggswell. "Have another drink?"

Hopalong smiled, shook his head, and again swung toward the door. He hesitated a moment on the threshold, nodded, and stepped outside. The night was clear, the stars bright. To his left the rails stretched east and west, endlessly: to his right the main part of the town was dotted with lights. He was passing the recessed doorway of an unlighted shack when a sudden movement caught him unprepared, alert as he was. A gun came out of the darkness, pressed against his stomach, and a curt voice spoke sharply:

"Up with 'em! Quick!"

Hopalong stiffened and then relaxed as he took an involuntary backward step and looked into the eyes above the red bandanna handkerchief on the face of the man who moved with him. The handkerchief bulged out as a beard pressed against it. Thoughts raced through the mind of the trail boss, a welter of thoughts: Buck's money, the loss of a trail herd; friends who trusted in him; Johnny Nelson, almost as naked as the day he was born, pulling the trigger of a harmless gun, and pulling it too late. Johnny had said that he had moved as swiftly as he could. Buck's money—twenty thousand dollars!

His hands were up, upper arms horizontal, forearms vertical. A gust of rage—deadly, unreasoning rage—swept over him. Johnny was fast, as fast as any man alive—and the Kid would not lie to him, but whether he had told the truth or not made no difference in this present moment. Buck was the best friend a man ever had. Hopalong smiled into the menacing eyes above the handkerchief, and then his left hand swept down and across his stomach as its muscles drew it in. The gun was brushed aside and exploded futilely. Hopalong's moving hand clamped onto its cylinder, locking it against a second shot, and his right hand smashed against the jaw behind the handkerchief with the strength of rage behind it.* The masked man went backward, full length on the ground, just as Pete, out of breath from running, reached the scene.

Pete bent over, grabbed the ankles of the prostrate highwayman, spread his feet, and swung halfway around as he straightened up. There was a box car on the siding, its sliding door half open. The human missile left Pete's hands and, more by accident than from conscious aim, sailed through the narrow opening and crashed against the closed door on the other side of the car. For two days the bearded gentleman was among the missing—and then provided grounds for great argument among the members of the coroner's jury. They finally brought in a verdict of death from misadventure.

Hopalong's hands now held both guns, and he was crouched against the front of the shack, blazing with anger. Pete turned and looked at him, a gun in his own right hand. Pete then bent down, picked up the highwayman's weapon, and tossed it under the box car. In

*NOTE BY AUTHOR: This was not a miracle: I, myself, have seen it done.

his mind was the picture of a campfire and drying clothing. He chuckled, but there was awe in his voice:

"Th' Kid was right, huh?"

Hopalong growled something in his throat and stood erect. He flashed a glance at the box car, ready guns balanced; and he took a step toward the track.

"You stay here!" snapped Pete, thinking of Buck's twenty thousand. "*I*'ll take a look at our friend. He was goin' head first when he went through that openin', an' I heard a hell of a crash when he stopped; but I'll take a look, to make shore."

In a few moments Pete was back again, and he waved a hand toward the hotel.

"Well?" asked the trail boss, sharply.

"Some folks shoot 'em," said Pete. "*I* just bust their necks. Come on, an' get that money to camp!"

And that is where the money went, quickly and without further excitement.

THE END